I0547068

The Last Dark Place

A Comedy
of
Redemption

Richard J. O'Brien

Red Grit
Books

This book is a work of fiction. Names, characters, places, and incidents are the product of the author's imagination or are used fictitiously. Any resemblance to actual events, locales, or persons, living or dead, is coincidental.

Copyright © 2021 by Richard J. O'Brien

Cover Design by the author

Red Grit Books supports the right to free expression and the value of copyright. The scanning, uploading, and distribution of this book without permission is a theft of the author's intellectual property.

Red Grit Books
First Red Grit Edition: August 2021

The Red Grit Books name and logo are trademarks of Red Grit Books.

The publisher is not responsible for websites (or their content) that are not owned by the publisher.

ISBN: 978-1-7377027-3-3 (paperback)

Printed in the United States

2nd Edition

A Note About This Book

A reader may wonder why an author would publish a twentieth-ish anniversary edition of an obscure novel that was self-*poo-blished* (when you pronounce the word like this, it sounds much more like serious literature) when the author was a younger man. Don't worry. I have asked myself that too. And if you believe that bit about serious literature I have an invisible painting, rendered by the author himself on an imaginary canvas, that I can sell you.

Right. Back to *The Last Dark Place*.

The truth of the matter is this: I loved writing this book. I loved the handful of dedicated readers (other than the obligatory family members who had no choice but to buy my little novel) who enjoyed what I had done. Mostly, I was quite proud of this story then, and as I revisited the manuscript recently I felt that while it was a beginning writer's novel, it was still a good story.

The genesis of this book began years ago when I was an undergraduate. It was the same semester I took a seminar on John Milton and read *Paradise Lost* (referred to as *PL* for the rest of this paragraph). My takeaway from the course was this: why wouldn't Satan eventually be allowed back into Heaven? To ensure I didn't come off like a complete moron, I wrote a final paper on Milton's use of shadow in *Paradise Lost*. I barely made the requirement for minimum page count. As I remember, though I no longer have the typed paper, my professor left comments in the margins to the tune of "stunted thinking," "not true," and "what are you trying to say?"—all the hallmarks used by the gatekeepers on undergraduate papers to weed out academic non-hackers, buffoons, and the criminally insane alike. In truth, I fell out of favor with my professor early in that seminar when I suggested that *PL* was a fantasy novel in verse form. She went apoplectic (in those days English professors poo-pooed science fiction and fantasy, though they'd think nothing of teaching Mary Shelley's *Frankenstein* or Edmund Spenser's *The Faerie Queene*), and I imagine she probably went home that night to drink a fifth of Seagram's Whiskey, but I digress.

The germ that infected me in the Milton seminar became this novel after it was written first as a long short story, some forty-eight pages long, that I handed in for a final assignment, if memory serves me, in a fiction writing workshop. My writing professor told me that there was too much going on for it to ever remain a short story. She suggested I shelve it a few years, go back to it, and find the novel that existed in it. I took her advice. Several years later, I finished writing this book.

Confession time: no novel is written in a vacuum. *The Last Dark Place* had a few other influences besides *Paradise Lost*. Other influences on my book in no particular order were *The Master and Margarita* by Mikhail Bulgakov, *Invitation to a Beheading* by Vladimir Nabokov, and *The Crying of Lot 49* by Thomas Pynchon. T.S. Eliot famously once said, "Good writers borrow, great writers steal." I am not above this art of subtle thievery (which, for the record, is different from straight up pedestrian plagiarism). All writers do it. It's like masturbation. You either admit it to doing it like all the cool kids do or your lie about it.

The time after I finish writing a novel is always the hardest. I won't plague my little missive here with comparisons to letting loose grown children into the world or anything. That's ludicrous. Books are not humans. No, the hardest part is getting a book out there. These were the days before agents and publishers trusted the internet and email.

Like other writers I'm sure I spent a small fortune in postage at my local post office. Admittedly, in the mid-1990s I was rather naïve about the whole process. When I look back I wonder if some schlub in a mailroom at Knopf or FSG even tore open the thick envelope that contained the manuscript of *The Last Dark Place* before committing it to an industrial-sized shredder just like the rest of the unsolicited manuscripts that came their way.

Ultimately, I ended up self-publishing this book. Around the same time (read: after mine came out), another novel came out with the exact same title. It was a mystery novel of some sort. The author's name escapes me. I struggled with changing my title. But it was already listed in Books In Print. I said to hell with that. I was here first.

In the years following this first novel-length work, I wrote almost a dozen others. I have had the good fortune of many of them getting picked up by indie publishers.

Recently, I saw in a literary agent's wish list for manuscripts that she wanted to read "something more than two people would read." I've come close to that in my writing life. Always a bridesmaid, etc, etc, ad nauseam. As a writer I go by one credo that has been credited to the likes of Toni Morrison, William Faulkner, and John Gardner through the years: write the books you would want to read. Toni Morrison said if you can't find a certain story then you should write it. She also admitted in an interview once, while discussing revision, that she still wanted to rewrite her first novel *The Bluest Eye*. I like to think that Professor Morrison would at least have appreciated my near-maniacal obsession with this first book of mine.

So, in your hands is an ever-so-slightly revised version of the first real novel I ever wrote. There were two other novels I had completed when I first got out of the army back in the 1980s. Thankfully, those manuscripts (typewritten) no longer exist. *The Last Dark Place* is another matter. This novel was the first one that made me feel like a real writer.

In the very early days after I completed writing this book I did manage to snag a literary agent for about a week. That relationship was never meant to be. My literary agent turned out to be a porn actress only moonlighting as a literary agent. No one knows now just how naïve I was back then to the writing game better than I do. Or maybe nearly thirty years, a mini-stroke, and a heart attack later I have the memory backward. Maybe the literary agent gave it all up to follow her dream of being a porn star. Whatever the case, that's another story for another day...

Jesus was terrified. Never in his life had he been asked if God's mercy was so great that one day he would forgive even Lucifer and welcome him back into the kingdom of heaven.

—Nikos Kazantzakis, *The Last Temptation of Christ*

Part One: Dreams, Diabolism, & Dipsomania

Prologue

Knock, Knock.

"Who's there?"

"Satan."

"Satan Who?"

"Peter," the angel of darkness said. "Let me speak to God."

"Good one," said St. Peter, "but I wouldn't quit your day job."

"Peter," said the Morning Star. "Seriously, man. It's me, Satan. I know I can't come in, but could you tell Yahweh—"

"I may be a simple fisherman, but I'm hardly anyone's errand boy."

"I've come to patch things up. Why should I be the one who must remain in exile forever?"

"Ugh," the fisherman's voice sounded from the other side, "the last time I checked you went against God. Ergo, you are the betrayer. It's because of you He sent—"

"His only son, I know," Satan said. "I was there in Bethlehem. How about the one who is God? Is he there?"

"Michael is busy now. Why don't you just go away?"

"It's not that simple."

"Boy, don't we know it," the saint replied. "How come you're sniffing around here after all this time? How do I know your army is not out there waiting for me to open this gate?"

"Don't try my patience, Peter."

1

"I'm shaking, Satan. You should see me. Cold sweats. Runny bowels. The whole nine."

"Let me talk to Metatron."

"Yes, Satan," spoke the king of angels, "I am here."

"It's been a long time, Metatron," said the dark angel.

"Spare me the small talk. What do you want?"

"I want back in. Now, I know Michael is viceroy of heaven, but I'm willing to—"

"You're serious?"

"It's a losing battle. Yahweh knew it all along. I understand that now."

"So, you've learned a thing or two," Metatron said. "How do we know this isn't a scheme? Some diabolical plan for an all-out attack?"

"One ass kicking is enough for me."

"Those were the days, eh?"

"You knew all along, too? Didn't you?"

"I'm not in a position to say I told you so, but…"

"I was a fool, old friend. Arrogant, greedy, and plain ignorant."

"Not a very good mix."

"I agree."

"Character traits that are less than virtuous."

"So, what do you say?" said Satan. "Can you persuade the Old Man to talk to me?"

"What makes you sure He'll have you back?"

"That's the thing," the Morning Star observed. "I don't know if He will. But if I don't try I'll never know. All that time in Hell and I thought why not go back and ask."

"What about the others?"

"They are willing to start at the bottom, if necessary."

"Yahweh tells me you must find a replacement."

"Pardon me?"

"You can't leave an operation that size and expect to have no one look after it."

"But who?"

"How about Moloch?"

"He's stubborn, but I know he wants back in, also. They all do. Even if they don't realize it yet."

"Yahweh understands," said Metatron. "But in the past each outcast was judged individually."

"And I remember that each one was allowed back into Heaven."

"For lesser crimes than war against the Father."

"Sorry to have bothered you," Satan told him.

"Wait. There's always hope, but I admit the Old Man has his doubts."

"Come on, Met. I'm jonesing for the Elysian Fields. I miss the show. I miss the light."

"Then find someone to fill your place."

"Where?"

"Yahweh says you must find the oldest soul in all creation," Metatron advised.

"Do you remember her name?"

"Not anymore. But Yahweh says you will recognize her."

"What if I fail?"

"You won't," the king of angels announced. "In the end Yahweh decides all."

"How silly of me to forget."

"Save it," St. Peter cautioned the devil. "Metatron's gone."

"I'll be seeing you, Peter," said the fallen one.

"Not if I see you first, Dim Star," the gatekeeper's voice trailed after the humble adversary as Satan headed back to Hell.

Chapter One

"Do you accept the Lord Jesus Christ as your personal savior?"

Jimmy Christophe looked down. He saw a black man with dreadlocks seated on an Abbott's milk crate. The man's dark-colored clothes, from light grays to deepest black, consisted of layers that had no definite beginning or end.

The question poised was a loaded one. It didn't make the student feel any better. Pain in his stomach, a discomfort that bordered on nausea, made him feel weak. And there was a fever in his head. All this on the first day of classes at Rutgers University Camden campus. The uneasiness he experienced was caused, he believed, by the breakfast his mother had prepared that morning. Hungover, he slept through his alarm clock's wake-up call. The previous night Christophe had knocked back numerous shots of Cuervo tequila and nearly a dozen mugs of beer.

Abstinence from all food might have been his best bet, but his mother insisted he eat the green pepper and cheese omelet she'd cooked along with six slices of bacon. When he drove his car to the Patco Hi-Speedline station in Haddonfield he had nearly suffocated himself when he exorcised a foul-smelling gastrointestinal demon. Now came an unsolicited theological inquiry to further delay his arrival on campus.

"Hell no," he groaned. As he climbed the steps that led to the street he quoted Patti Smith. "Jesus died for somebody's sins but not mine."

"Have you read The Secret Book of John?"

"Never heard of it."

"How about sparing me some change?" the homeless man called from below.

"I don't have any coins," Christophe's voice rang through the stairwell.

On the street he was accosted by a few more of the city's displaced. He did his best to protect himself from the gauntlet they formed along the sidewalk.

"Then how about a dollar?" he heard the voice behind him.

Christophe turned, free from the other vagrants, and saw the man emerge from the Patco station. The others parted, giving the curious pursuer his space. A sign in the Rite-Aid pharmacy window begged the question, Trouble Sleeping At Night? Ask Your Pharmacist About Somnoflex. Christophe watched the man study the sign a moment before he continued his way up 4th Street toward campus. At Cooper Street he looked back.

The dreadlock-haired man stood in front of an old brownstone church. He was taller than Christophe's six-foot frame, and well built, it appeared, for someone living half-starved on the streets. Despite his tattered clothes the man exuded a regal nature. His creamy brown complexion was smooth and clean. The abundant dreadlocks atop his head fell below his shoulders. Everything about him told Christophe the beggar was more than met the eye.

"You better believe," the man shouted. His resonant voice sounded like a song. "You better believe because God has big plans for you, brother."

Christophe belched and tasted green peppers. A nauseous rumble rocked his stomach. Weary, he crossed Cooper Street and never looked back.

"You better believe," the man shouted after him as he raised his long arms in supplication. "Believe, for his angels are coming!"

5

Chapter Two

Joy Felder awoke worried one morning. She had broken up with her boyfriend of three years that summer, and since then she'd gained weight. It was her doing, the break-up and the added pounds. Her former boyfriend, a timorous fellow, did not take the news well. Her dumping him was the proverbial straw that broke the camel's back. Almost overnight, it seemed, he'd turned into a regular sociopath. Life, he told her, was not worth living without her. And with that said, he set out to prove himself. Fortunately, the Reaper's calendar was full.

In addition to those two cataclysmic events, Joy received several strange phone calls. Some, the crude sexually suggestive ones, she suspected were the work of her emotionally devastated ex-beau. But those calls didn't last long. Her former boyfriend was sent up for armed robbery, arson, grand theft auto and attempted murder. The details of these heinous crimes need not concern us; save that his dark behavior lurked within long before he and Joy met.

It was a relief for Joy when she heard the news. But that left her with no explanation for the other phone calls. Not that they were as bad as the obscene calls her ex made. Joy was not able to comprehend the speaker's language when she answered those calls. It was the time she received them that bothered her most, during early morning hours before the sun rose. She knew that wherever the calls originated, judging from the garbled static she heard, it must have been some place far away.

The true source of her anxiety that morning, however, was not her jailed ex-boyfriend nor the crank phone calls, but her alarm clock. The clock had never sounded, and now she was late. Her emotional state worsened when she climbed out of bed. The strange telephone calls she could endure. The sight of her body in the full-length mirror beside her bed was another matter. Her hips were wider. Her apple-sized, firm breasts had ballooned into intimidating grapefruits. And her stomach was a feature she avoided at all costs. Had it not been for her period arriving the day before Joy might have believed she was pregnant. Three weeks beforehand she had a one-night stand with an old high school friend. They were both drunk, licking their wounds from respective break-ups, and in the heat of sloppy, passionate groping and undressing, they decided to forgo protection. Still, the paralyzing notion of unwanted pregnancy would have left her bedridden that day. She was thankful it didn't happen.

"You're beginning to look like a regular earth goddess," she said to the reflection in the mirror. She cupped her breasts in her hands and held them close to her chin. "Be careful with these monsters, today. They might be lethal."

Joy showered and dressed. Afterward, she haphazardly applied some make-up. Beneath a pile of dirty clothes stacked high on her rocking chair she found two blank notebooks. She shoved them into her knapsack. Once the notebooks were secured, Joy ran down the stairs, bolted through the kitchen where her mother and her father were having breakfast, and headed out the back door.

The pristine early morning soothed her anxiety. The sky overhead was a vast expanse of blue peppered with high-flying birds. Sunrays danced through the tall firs to the east of the Felder residence.

"Shit," she muttered, remembering her dog Blunt.

Back inside she discovered a near-empty fifty-pound bag of Alpo. Her father had promised earlier that week to purchase another bag; but, so as not to tarnish his paternal persona, he failed to deliver.

7

Blunt, a pug of questionable character, looked at his mistress as she set down his large red bowl. His sleep patterns mirrored Joy's lately. He often lay awake in the hall outside her room powerless to stop the unseen visitors who came to her. Blunt wondered if he looked as tired as she did.

It angered Joy that her dog barked so much. At a time when most dogs were fast asleep dreaming about mailmen, automobiles and children on Big Wheels, her dog was wide awake and barking at things that weren't there.

Blunt knew better than his mistress did. Despite Joy's misgivings his mind was as sharp and alert as ever. But certain mysteries confounded the dog, including who or what entered his mistress' bedroom without opening the door. Exhausted now from his all-night watch, he regarded his food with nominal interest.

"To hell with you," Joy whispered, rubbing Blunt's head.

Her dog responded by slipping back into a light sleep. Surreal dreams came to birth inside his mind.

Joy started for the back door. She had almost escaped when her father called her back.

"Joy," his voice sounded as his eyes remained fixed on the latest edition of The Weekly World Register. "Don't forget your medicine."

"I'm late, dad," she argued.

"Remember your allergies, dear," said Annie Felder, as she sipped her coffee.

Joy granted her parents' wishes. She opened and closed every kitchen cabinet until she found her medication. The clatter of cupboard doors filled the room.

"Honey," her father said, unmoved by her theatrics, "you don't have to wreck the joint. I spent weeks refinishing those cabinets."

"Don't talk to me like I'm a five-year-old," she responded, balancing two prescription allergy pills on her tongue.

"Your father cares about you, baby," Annie reminded her daughter. "We know you're not a five-year-old. But is it a crime for a parent to love a child?"

"Define love," Joy drew water from the faucet and glared at her mother.

8

"I won't define anything," her mother said. "You know what love is."

"Yuck!"

"You should be thankful your life is so easy. College was once a luxury poor people like us couldn't afford."

"That's right," Mick Felder chimed, his voice too much like Don Pardo's for his daughter's taste. "After high school it was straight to the workforce for the likes of your mother and me."

Joy gulped down another glass of water.

"Yeah," she gasped as she came up for air, "so I am reminded at the start of every semester."

"Let that be a lesson," he warned her.

"And what lesson would that be, dad?" she asked. Joy placed her glass in the sink.

Mick Felder turned his attention again to the weekly tabloid. Joy caught a glimpse of the cover page on her way out the door. Almost by instinct, Felder hoisted the paper up high, so his daughter could get a better view. He nodded and winked at his wife, mistaking his daughter's shock of distaste for genuine interest.

Angels Among Us, the front-page copy boasted. New Jersey Family Plagued By Celestial Visit. A small blurb beneath explained, Angels Claim Wrong Address And Apologize.

"Says here the family's from the Pine Barrens," Mick Felder announced.

"Dad," said Joy, "why do you read that crap?"

"Use some sense, Joy," he said. "They couldn't print these articles and call themselves a newspaper if there wasn't some truth to them."

"Your father's right about these things," Annie informed her.

"Don't tell me," said Felder, seeing the incredulous look on his daughter's face, "that you don't think angels ever visit earth?"

"Sure, pop," her unchecked sarcasm rattled him.

"Don't get cute," he cautioned her. "We're talking about God's messengers."

9

Joy made a face.

"You don't believe that angels exist?" he pursued the debate further.

"Dad, this ridiculous," she told him, opening the door. "I have to go."

"I want to know what you think."

"And I want to get to school on time," said Joy, "for a change. Good-bye."

"Haven't you ever considered the notion?" he called to her.

The back door slammed shut. Mick Felder caught a glimpse of his daughter's auburn hair before she was gone.

Chapter Three

Agnes Christophe was lured from a strange dream when she heard her son leaving the house. She was hungover and gripped in those first seconds of waking by an inexplicable fear. It always happened whenever she had nightmares. The latest one came after a four-month hiatus. Fortunately, the fear subsided after her son pulled out of the driveway. All that remained of the nightmare were vague images sapped of their original terror.

Agnes Christophe's life was one of leisure ever since she had been awarded her lawsuit settlement. The action was taken against a bank in Philadelphia after she slipped and fell on a wet marble floor. There were no yellow caution signs in the vicinity when the accident occurred. Of witnesses, however, there were plenty. No sooner had she fallen and screamed than they were at her side. No one dared assist her. Instead, they divulged everything they knew about various legal matters, including personal injury, they had learned via television commercials.

She hired her lawyer at the accident scene after one witness, an attorney, presented his card and pressed it into her hand. Before paramedics carted off Agnes to the emergency room the deal was done.

Her victory came with a price tag. Two, to be precise. A fractured ulna and a chipped sacrum. Every time she met her lawyer he came on to her. He was fifteen years younger than she was and a greenhorn when it came to seduction, owing to certain choices he had made so far; namely, how he'd spent his

11

formative years with his head buried in books instead of pursuing the fairer sex. Agnes provoked most men that way ever since she'd been a teenager. The spell she cast was animal magnetic. The way the lawyer fumbled over his words and averted her stare when they made small talk reminded Agnes of some long-ago innocence she had never known. Agnes had always been a fast girl, given to following her instinct, her sexual instinct, rather than adhering to the mores of her time. Her lawyer, despite his bumbling ways, did have certain charms. Agnes' injuries kept her from acting on impulse; she had to wait for her tailbone to heal before consummating what both she and her lawyer longed for. When their physical union was over the handsome young introvert was never quite the same.

The money Agnes received did not make her rich. There was enough however, after medical costs and lawyer fees, for her to live comfortably for a time.

Few things in life satisfied Agnes. She loved the nightlife, she loved to drink and be with her friends and she loved being pursued and bedded by men. What she didn't count on was missed mortgage payments and mounting credit card bills. The only thing that scared her more than losing her home was going back to work. Her lifestyle caused her to look with disdain upon the workaday rat race. So, rather than face up to her burgeoning financial woes, she went on living like some aging party girl privy to an inexhaustible trust fund.

Her grand scheme was to marry into money. She had been married once before to a man who was poor, for lack of a better word. The experience left a bitter taste in her mouth. Now, she pictured herself jetting around the world, living debt-free, following the warm seasons from hemisphere to hemisphere and spending her new rich husband's wealth without care or consequence. She longed to fulfill certain hedonistic fantasies that she felt would never come true; at least, not as long as she remained middle-class. Her plan had long been thwarted, however, by two factors. One, the kind of men whose wealth she dreamed of basking in didn't live anywhere near her hometown of Bellmawr, New Jersey. And

12

two, Agnes was not willing to relocate. Thus, her gold mine remained beyond reach.

Now Agnes repeated the same promise she would break hours later. She climbed out of bed, put on her favorite powder blue bathrobe, and went to the kitchen.

On the kitchen table she found two notes. One note was from her son. The other from a man she had picked up at The Tide. Agnes did not recall seeing either note when she first entered the room earlier that morning. The details of the previous night were vague, at best. She read the second note first, hoping to recapture what she had already forgotten.

Aggy,
I'm sorry I didn't wake you up like I promised but I had to get out of here and go to work this morning. Not to mention my wife who would figure out I was up to no good if I wasn't home before the sun came up. I wish I could leave her but it's complicated. Her father put up the money for me to start my business and I wouldn't feel right divorcing his daughter before I could pay the old man back. You know what I mean?

Agnes didn't know. She could handle the perverts, the hard-asses and the drunks. Confessors were a different matter.

It won't be long now (the note continued*). I really think serial killer trading cards are going to take off like baseball cards did. Maybe even bigger. Who knows? I mean look at our society. And to think, Nicky 'The Lover' Tatasciore opened the very first trading store. I don't want to toot my own horn here, but I've always been a cutting-edge kind of guy. I like to think if I lived back in the middle ages I would have been another Dante or Michelangelo. If you knew any of my friends they'd tell you the same thing. Anyway, I'm sorry I had to run.*

Oh please, Agnes thought.

13

Last night you were great (Nicky The Lover's note went on). *If you want to get together some time, page me at 546-1709. Whatever you do, don't call Creeps (that's my store) because that's the same number as my house. Hope we can <u>do it</u> again soon.*
So long sweetie,
Love ya Nicky.

Agnes hoped she had at least achieved orgasm during her romp the previous night, but she wasn't sure. One thing she did know was that she drank too much. No self-respecting woman, she thought, would end up with a guy like Nicky. She crushed the note into a ball and threw it away.

Mother,
Is this an all-time low for you?

Agnes admired the way her son cut right to the chase. No punches were pulled. A quality Jimmy Christophe inherited, Agnes mused, from his father.

I found Nicky's note before I left this morning (Agnes continued reading her son's note*). Knowing what a romantic you are, I didn't have the heart to throw it away. Yes, I met your conquest before he ducked out the back door. The encounter happened when I innocently woke up and went to the kitchen to retrieve a glass of milk. Nicky asked me, after nearly scaring me to death since I thought I was alone, if we kept any Froot Loops in the house. He explained that the fruity residue left behind in the milk (sugary residue?) helps him to sleep. While I'm on the subject of the troglodyte, and if you don't know what that means, picture Nicky in a caveman get-up…*

Agnes laughed. She never liked how judgmental her son was, nor did she care for how he chastised her about the men she brought home. But there were times when an outsider shed new light on a situation. Her son was good at that.

14

...and that should help, he was gracious enough to impart some words of wisdom before he snuck out into the predawn night. 'Don't worry pal,' he told me, 'someday you'll be in my shoes.' I dare not speculate what he meant by that.

In the future, if not for my sake then maybe yours, exercise some caution and make better judgments.

Have a nice day.

Your loving son,
Jimmy.

P.S. Tonight I'll be going out for drinks with Mel so please don't wait up.

It pains me to think that I went to court to have my last name changed from dad's to yours. Is Nicky The Lover the thanks I get?

Agnes balled up the note and threw it into the trashcan beneath the kitchen sink.

From time to time Agnes secretly fashioned ways to get rid of her son. Some plots she mapped out on paper. Those plans, the hand-written ones that could be construed as evidence, she destroyed once her son enrolled at Rutgers University. It wasn't so much a change of heart that made her do it as her son deciding to attend college in Camden. She feared some ill-fortune might befall him, the victim of a random mugging gone bad perhaps, and worried that the authorities might trace the wrong-doing back to her, blaming her for some stranger's handiwork. Yet, for all that, Agnes loved her son. She refused to see herself as some heartless bitch that wished her son had never been born. The fact is she rejoiced the day she gave birth. But that was back when happiness was part of the equation. Now, she longed for a new life. And to start over Agnes thought it best if her son Jimmy wasn't around to get in the way.

15

Things began looking up after Christophe's junior year in high school. He'd given the military serious consideration; but, after graduation the next year, he gave up the notion of serving his country. His best friend, Mel Talbott, talked him out of it. College, Talbott told him. That's where they belonged.

After graduation the two young men took jobs working full-time at a local gas station. Agnes' son found part-time work at a 7-11 convenience store while Talbott whiled away his evening hours at a WAWA food market. Agnes thought both boys were wasting their time. A couple of years passed. Christophe and Talbott saved their money. It was barely enough to pay for a semester at Rutgers University. But the time they put in at their jobs was ample enough for the financial aid folks at the university to coach them through the process of obtaining grants and loans.

Damn that Talbott, Agnes thought. As time went on she figured her son's interest in higher education would wane. It didn't. Agnes knew it would be at least five years before he finished his degree, and perhaps another year before he landed a job that paid enough for him to move out. Three years had passed. It was toward the end of the summer that Christophe dropped his latest bomb. Graduate school, he told his mother. Agnes' son wanted to pursue graduate English studies at either Temple University or the University of Pennsylvania. When she heard the news, Agnes thought she would have a stroke. She remembered hearing about how sons and daughters didn't move out of their parents' homes until they were almost forty years old once they had set their minds to graduate school. And even then, they didn't move far away. Owing, no doubt, to their inability to adapt to life on their own. Agnes couldn't bear the thought of it.

Agnes picked up the daily newspaper her son had left on the kitchen table that morning. The Courier-Post was the only newspaper she read. There were others, to be sure, but none of them satisfied her the way The Courier-Post did. Throughout the years the newspaper went through several changes. Agnes, despite it all, remained a loyal reader.

Agnes put on a pot of coffee, lit a cigarette and sat down. She flipped through the front section of the paper. Murder, fire, armed conflict, disease, political scandal, etc. It was all the same to her. She turned to the index and noted her favorite columns. Astrology, 10C. Weather, 2A. Celebrity Talk, 4C. People Meeting People, 23B. Next to the index, in the lower-left hand corner, an article caught her eye. Strange Lights Over Pine Barrens. She read the lead paragraph. Meteorologists, she discovered, attributed the phenomenon, now a month old, to an isolated lightning storm.

"Crazy shit," she muttered.

When she finished reading her horoscope, a forecast that recapped events already going on in her life, she got up and fixed herself a mug of coffee. The beverage tasted foul. Considering how the bitter black liquid made her stomach feel, Agnes decided to forgo breakfast.

Her head ached. She lit another cigarette after the first one burned down to the filter. Six weeks ago, she might have swallowed three or four aspirins, but she had read an article in the paper that attributed aspirin overdose and alcohol abuse to liver damage.

Agnes wanted to remember her night at The Tide. But without the aid of pain relievers she was forced to rely on another healing remedy: time. As the morning wore on, memories returned.

A sharply dressed, tall, dark-haired man entered the club after midnight. His double-breasted suit, dark gray in the subdued barroom light, accentuated the shoulders of his otherwise average build. He was the antithesis of the men Agnes found most attractive, and yet she was drawn to him. He carried himself like a soldier on parade; head cocked at a perfect angle, back straight and shoulders squared. Even though he appeared rigid, it seemed the man was completely unaware of himself. Agnes' hungry gaze followed him.

The man in the gray suit was not handsome in the classical sense. His ears were too low, and his chin was pointed. His eyebrows were the most prominent facial feature; thick and dark, they met over his long thin nose. Agnes couldn't tell where one eyebrow began and the other left off.

The night crept along. Agnes drank and kept an eye on the stranger. Her two best friends sat at the bar with her. Like

17

Agnes, her friends were divorcees. When the three were together any man who possessed a shred of sanity steered clear of them. Alone, each woman was tolerable if not charming in her own stunted way. Together, they were like Macbeth's witches on crack cocaine and steroids.

"May I buy you ladies a drink?" the dark-haired man asked as he approached from behind.

The stranger's inquiry wasn't at all suspicious or suspect. The Tide was a place where such offers were the norm.

"Just one for the three of us?" Agnes' friend Mary Reilley asked.

All three women loosed a sharp, harmonious cackle.

"That's ok, buddy," Rosemarie Parillo snapped, "we're fine."

Agnes and Mary regarded their friend. Rosemarie, a garrulous woman with great breasts and a low tolerance for alcohol, compensated for a handicap that did not allow her body to process spirits adequately by drinking on a regular basis. She registered the look on her friends' faces and mumbled a lame apology.

"You don't look like you're from around here," Agnes remarked.

The man looked at her. He raised his single voluminous eyebrow and kept it there until he was certain his gaze made the proper impression.

"I am a stranger to New Jersey," he replied.

Rosemarie repeated the phrase, emphasizing the accent evident in the man's voice.

"I don't believe I had the pleasure," he took her hand in his.

"You are a rare breed," Mary cried as she slapped Agnes' arm.

When the man raised Rosemarie's hand to his mouth and planted a firm kiss on her palm Agnes and Mary plunged into a fit of hysterical, high-pitched laughter.

"Allow me to introduce myself," he said, letting go. "I am Darius Algernon."

"Rosemarie," the blushing drunk offered. "And these two banshees are Mary and Agnes."

18

"How about that drink, fellah?" said Mary.

"Bartender," Algernon barked, "a round for the ladies, please."

Tony Fiasco the bartender was a charitable advice-giver in matters concerning life's sensitive issues; namely, women and gambling, women and drinking and women who employed devious means to ensnare men. Fiasco was thrice divorced, a recovering alcoholic and a fair-weather program participant at Gamblers Anonymous. He didn't take kindly to strange men who wandered into The Tide. Often, he passed the time by constructing elaborate scenarios in his head whereby he would figure out exactly what kind of person a stranger to the club might be. When Algernon produced a one-hundred-dollar bill to pay for the round, Fiasco decided that Algernon was a bigwig counterfeiter on his way to Atlantic City to poison the prosperous flow of Treasury greenbacks with his artwork. Fiasco changed his position, however, when Algernon told him to keep the change. Now, the bartender sensed old money. A count, he thought. Or perhaps a duke.

"Thanks buddy," Fiasco said, executing a half-bow, unaware of the proper etiquette one might exercise when royalty showed up at a working-class watering hole.

Agnes had never seen Fiasco intimidated by anyone. She suspected, judging from the huge cash roll the stranger brandished, that Algernon was more than another money-flashing good-time Charlie. The envy and respect Fiasco exuded confirmed her suspicions.

"So, Darius," she said, "what brings you to Bellmawr?"

"Vacation," he answered.

"Come again?" Rosemarie asked. "There must be some mistake."

"No, no," said Algernon, "I'm where I am supposed to be. The truth is I'm on a sabbatical."

The women exchanged confused stares.

"Sabbatical?" Mary Reilley was the first to speak. "Are you some kind of holy man?"

Algernon grinned. He looked at Agnes.

"Holy man?" he said and laughed. "Heavens, no. Is there really such a thing?"

19

"Good point," Agnes quipped.

"My current position," Algernon said, "has become-if you must know-quite loathsome. I needed some time away."

"How sad," Rosemarie's condolence was earmarked by a long and loud burp.

"Yes, it is," he agreed, ignoring her boorish outburst. "It's one thing when your job means nothing to you; but, when faced with comparing the present and the past, it's a different story when you realize your prior occupation was far more fulfilling than your current one. The only thing that kept me going this long was the illusion of freedom."

"Pining for the old days?" Mary asked.

"You're on the button."

"Why not try getting back your old job?"

"It's not that easy, I'm afraid," he confessed. "There are those who believe I made a real mess of things. From the start I wanted it all, but my boss and I didn't see eye to eye on that."

"And now you're not sure if you can deal with going back with your tail between your legs?"

"My tail," Algernon mused. "That's a good one."

"No offense," she said.

"Trust me," he focused on Mary. "There's none taken."

"What now?" Agnes asked.

"Ah, my dilemma," he told her. "My current position affords me many liberties. Yet, it is little more than a farce. Experience provides the opportunity to grow, and age allows us to look back with humility. Do you agree?"

"Sure."

"Had I kept my old job, I'd still face limitations; but the prestige, such as it was, made up for that.

"Most of my old colleagues are there, even now. I'll admit I have problems with going back in a manner pretty much the way Mary described it. However, I have learned a thing or two since I left."

"How long were you at your former job?" Agnes asked.

"As long as I can remember."

"What do you think your chances are?"

20

"At one time I was the boss' favorite," said Algernon. "Now? I don't know."

"It probably won't be like that again," she told him. "Hell, just do the best you can and roll with the punches."

"That's true," he concurred with Agnes. "I suppose I should do some more work in the humility department."

"Yeah, yeah," Mary butted in, pausing only to polish off her drink. "You were probably one of those guys who strutted around the office like your shit doesn't stink. One of those assholes who thought he was God's—"

"Favorite," Algernon offered.

"Mary, please," Rosemarie hissed over the rim of her glass.

"Darius, you'll have to forgive our friend," Agnes said.

"No," he held up his hand. "It's an honest inquiry. Mary, I can only say that I did what was asked of me. I followed orders and paid attention to detail like a good little soldier. I even walked a virtuous path. I don't mind saying I set one hell of an example. But in the end, yes, I became something of an asshole."

"So, what makes you so confident now?" Mary asked. She put down her empty glass and started on the one Algernon had paid for. "What makes you so sure they'll have you back?"

"There were others like me," Algernon began.

"Bah," Rosemarie's voice carried over the barroom din. She tossed her empty glass onto the bar. "This conversation's wearing me out."

Fiasco the bartender approached the group. His deadpan expression told them he'd like nothing more than to flag the glass-tossing culprit.

"Come on, handsome," said Rosemarie, taking Algernon's hand. "Let's dance."

Agnes and Mary put Fiasco at ease, feeding him a tale of misery. It was a licentious yarn about a relationship Rosemarie had just gotten out of after being burnt. The story, a lie, was meant to serve as an apology to the bartender. Fiasco took it in stride. Agnes and Mary agreed with him that Rosemarie got out of hand at times.

"If she's got hypoglycemia," Fiasco reasoned, "she has no business drinking in the first place."

21

"She's not hypoglycemic," Mary said.

"She's just upset," Agnes added.

"Well," Fiasco adjusted his trousers by grabbing the fabric at his crotch, "if she keeps it up I'll toss her."

"Show some leniency, Tony," Agnes said, administering the alluring stare that conquered far greater men than Tony Fiasco. "It's a delicate time for Rosemarie."

Fiasco backed off.

Agnes and Mary turned and gazed at the couple. Algernon showed agility and finesse in his dance steps. His soft-shoe work made Rosemarie's drunken efforts look clumsy and languid.

"Damn, this man can dance," Rosemarie announced when she and Algernon returned to the bar. Perspiration coated her face and neck. "How did you learn to move like that, Darius?"

Algernon looked nonplussed. Most men his age would be sucking in air hard and deep after such a display.

"When you have been around as long as I have," he confessed as he signaled Fiasco for another round, "you pick up a thing or two."

"Stop it," Rosemarie said. "You're not that old."

"It's my favorite pastime," said Algernon. "Some guys golf. Other guys fuck whores in their spare time." He ignored the shocked expressions etched on each woman's face. "Me? I like to dance. I always have. Many years ago, I used to dance with women under the full moon's lunar light. Secluded fields, wooded coves, city tenement rooftops, it didn't matter. Any place that offered an open area with level footing was fine by me. The women always found my dancing irresistible. Next to my fiddle-playing, it's a charming asset."

The women looked at each other. A cacophonous racket arose. Never had they heard such a preposterous story; but, coming from Algernon, it all seemed true.

Agnes remembered now how she stayed at The Tide until closing time. As the hour drew near the crowd thickened. Men and women, all of them drunk and a few of them desperate, flirted with such temerity that the Sodomites and Gomorrhans of old would have been jealous with envy.

22

The longest hour was the one before dawn. For many of The Tide regulars it was also the loneliest. Men and women who had known each other for years often ended up in bed together for the first time after imbibing at The Tide. Often enough, blinded by intoxication and driven by lust, couplings occurred for which there was no rhyme or reason. But going home with someone you wouldn't give the time of day to when you were sober was the status quo at The Tide. Good, old-fashioned sex between two people was better than any measure of inventive self-satisfaction.

Agnes was considering that very notion, while keeping an eye on the time, when she met up with Nicky Tattisciore. The young lover stood by the ladies' room entrance near the dance floor. Agnes suspected Tattisciore had chosen that vantagepoint for practical reasons. It was a common mating practice that men his age used when they lacked the proper social skills needed to meet a member of the opposite sex. As a rule, Agnes stayed away from such savages. The eagerness they portrayed, the predatory look in their eyes and their wanton expressions told Agnes that their bedroom tactics were no doubt hurried, sloppy and hardly satisfying for the recipient. And while the ladies room lurkers often were seen in the club beating their chests over some sexual conquest, it was common knowledge that only truly desperate women took such men home. That night, however, Agnes drank more than her share. She was so bleary-eyed that Nicky Tattisciore appeared handsome in a weird Chazz Palminteri way. That night Agnes made an exception to her rule about the savages. But given her experience on the mating front Agnes should have known better. One might think they're bedding a ferocious angel in the dark only to find they've become a baboon's love toy come morning.

Agnes invited Tattisciore back to the bar. Tattisciore was cocky, brutish and not smart by any definition of the word. She sensed that he didn't like Darius Algernon. But Agnes did. Alas, Algernon was paying more attention to Rosemarie Parillo than he was to anyone else by that point. So, Agnes boosted her morale by downing four quick shots of Southern

23

Comfort bourbon before allowing Nicky *The Lover* Tattisciore to woo her.

"Nuts," said Agnes and sipped her coffee.

Chapter Four

"Asshole!" the cry sounded inside a faded, gunmetal gray Renault station wagon.

Samuel Waterson, Sammy the Junkman as he was known to his friends, business associates and barroom acquaintances, looked down at the angry young man driving the wagon. He watched with amusement as the man's face turned red.

The Junkman's Ford pick-up truck was missing its muffler. The dilapidated vehicle roared like the trumpets of doom.

Lord yes, The Junkman thought as he stepped on the gas pedal. Young people reeked of indignation.

The pick-up truck's roar lulled Sammy Waterson into a quiet reverie. He ignored the road now, dreaming of the past. When he was a boy his family moved north from southern Alabama. It was Nashville first. Then, after a few years, they moved on to Baltimore where Sammy Waterson met his late wife Marybelle. He saw her now as a young woman. Since Marybelle, The Junkman often mused, God hadn't created a woman as beautiful. The only one that may have come close was Eve, but the Junkman wasn't that old. So, he had no way of knowing which would win that contest. Marybelle's hair was straightened, dark and short. Her eyes were pale brown, big as coat buttons and sexy in a subtle way. Sammy Waterson teased Marybelle, even after she died, that her eyes led men to mischief and much worse. His wife's laughter had been like distant church bells, soft as baptismal waters and soothing like good music that put the mind at ease. When Marybelle was

25

around, life's burdens seemed not so heavy. At night the Junkman whispered to Marybelle, a practice that began when they were first married, telling her that her legs, her breasts, her hips, her stomach and her lips caused goddesses of the old pantheon to stand in awe. It was true that the Junkman loved his wife. And with her parting he counted the days until they would be together again, young and full of life in paradise forever.

The Junkman and Marybelle married in Baltimore, moved to Camden, NJ in the 1960s and had lived there since. In his younger years the Junkman worked as a welder at the Philadelphia Naval Shipyard. Not long after he retired, making plans for Marybelle and himself in the twilight of their marriage, his wife died. Like all men who loved their wives and who lost them, Sammy Waterson took Marybelle's death hard. She had been his best friend, his lover, his wife, and one half to their common whole.

One day, a year or more after Marybelle passed; the Junkman left his house, started his beat-up, old pick-up truck and took on the avatar he went by at present. He was tired of sitting inside all day, surrounded by memories of Marybelle in every room. The Junkman knew full-time employment was out of the question, not at his age. He trusted that the Father, the Son, and the Holy Ghost would take care of his wife until he caught up with her. Until then, the Junkman needed something to occupy his time on earth. He had always worked around metal. But his eyes were no longer as sharp as they once had been. Sammy Waterson's welding days, sadly, were over. But like his marriage to Marybelle as the years wore on, his relationship with metal took on new meaning. He went from the intimacy of marrying metal together to collecting scrap parts for profit.

The Junkman often used his time on the road to contemplate the more serious mysteries of life. He was thinking about his wife in Heaven when reality reared its ugly head and pushed to the forefront of his mind.

A tiny red Mazda Miata cut in front of the Junkman. Sammy Waterson let up on the gas, almost clipping the car's rear bumper. The Junkman believed that pumping the brakes

26

at every hint of danger was a sign of weakness. Soon, his pick-up truck slowed under the weight of the cargo he hauled in the truck bed.

In truth the Junkman disliked September. It was the month Marybelle passed away. It also marked the beginning of the fall semester for the Camden city college campuses. And with ever-increasing enrollments, traffic in and around the city worsened. That fact was like a nightmare come true for the Junkman; hundreds if not thousands of young people commuting to class every morning and each one no better behind the wheel of a vehicle than they were at taking exams. Sammy Waterson read the papers. He was well aware of the sad state higher education in America had reached. Such knowledge prompted the Junkman to purchase and prominently display a bumper sticker he'd discovered at a dollar store on Broadway.

Skip School, Learn A Trade, the bumper sticker read.

Presently, the Junkman eyed the Renault station wagon in his oversized side-view mirror. The college kid behind the wheel of the wagon was attempting to pass him. Sammy Waterson came down on the gas pedal. The truck's engine revved. The Junkman mustered all the energy he could from his old truck. That morning the truck's bed was piled high with scrap metal. And yet, despite the behemoth weight he hauled, the Junkman managed to switch lanes and remain ahead of the wagon. Thus, he trapped the green-footed, frantic driver between his truck, a concrete barrier on the left and a long convoy of subcompact cars moseying along the center lane to the right.

"That'll learn you," said the Junkman. He stared at the driver, now, with eyes wide as he added, "Asshole."

A rusted brake shoe atop the Junkman's load fell from the metal mountain. It bounced once on the road and ricocheted off the Renault's front bumper.

The wagon's driver cursed when he felt the sudden jolt. "God damn it!" he shouted, believing the end was near. "Fred Sanford wanna-be jerk-off motherfucker!"

Fortunately, for the Renault driver, Sammy Waterson did not hear the comment. He disliked being stereotyped;

27

especially, by college students. It was bad enough to live as a black man in America, seeing so much racial animosity in one's daily life when the country boasted about the great strides it made. Had the Junkman heard the insult he might have swerved left and right, thus liberating the bulk of his haul and allowing metal scraps to rain down on the station wagon. True, the Junkman would have lost a day's worth of profits; but rare were the moments in life when satisfaction felt better than money in the pocket.

Mel Talbott, the Renault's anxious driver, felt the balance of life lean askew. Throughout his existence, at least the portion he remembered, he'd never been late for anything. Anger consumed him as he watched the old man in the truck. Talbott was aware of the road, but his attention was pulled to the pick-up truck cab. He wasn't sure if the elderly black man was laughing at him or having a seizure. Talbott imagined the mountainous metal load falling off the truck. He was sure whatever scrap had hit the front bumper had left an indelible impression. A single dent to the Renault he could explain to his mother. Being crushed beneath the rest of the old man's heap was another matter.

Talbott's mother lectured him ad nauseum about taking care of her car. She didn't believe in speeding or reckless driving. But Talbott's tireless pursuit of punctuality conflicted with his mother's concerns. Thus, a vicious cycle had been born.

Talbott knew the furies had marked him. He saw it in the stars before he went to bed the previous night, he read it in his horoscope at breakfast and, as he shaved his face that morning, he detected it in his aura while looking into the bathroom mirror. Doom cast its dark cloud around him. Talbott decided that the malevolent angel charged with taking human life did not come to earth dressed in dark armor astride a pale horse, but as a hoary black man behind the wheel of a dilapidated white Ford pick-up truck.

"Stop this cruel torture," Talbott cried as four more brake shoes fell from the truck's bed. "I don't want to die! Not today! Not ever!"

28

The student did his best to avoid further catastrophe. He swerved left then right. As he maneuvered the vehicle he heard the brake shoes lay waste to the Renault's underbelly.

The convoy of subcompact cars to his right dispersed in a frantic push. Talbott darted into the middle lane, avoiding a fifth brake shoe as it fell onto the road.

The worn scrap missed Talbott's car, bounced off the road and crashed into another vehicle's windshield.

"Sorry!" Talbott shouted at his rearview mirror.

On any other morning he would have pulled off the road and offered his assistance to the victim. He was proud of the few instances where he volunteered to help others avoid life-threatening injuries. Talbott was the guy other commuters saw jogging down the shoulder of a highway searching for a call box. On that day, however, he feared his bad karma might rub off on the unfortunate soul whose windshield had been spiderwebbed by the errant brake shoe.

Sammy the Junkman Waterson jumped two lanes and headed for the exit ramp. He rolled to a stop before the traffic light at the foot of the ramp. Patiently, he sat, waiting for the light to turn from red to green, and watched the Renault pull up behind him. The Junkman waited for another vehicle to pull up behind the Renault station wagon before he made his move. At the precise moment, he slammed the truck's gear into reverse and rammed the wagon. Two large toaster ovens bounded down from the scrap heap and crashed first one then the other, onto the station wagon's hood. When the traffic light turned green the Junkman put his truck into drive and pulled away.

Talbott studied the two paint-chipped, cavernous dents on the hood. His hands trembled as he shifted into park. The hazard light switch provided some difficulty owing to the mental state Talbott had sunken into. He leaned forward and wrapped his arms around the steering wheel. His forehead came to rest on the horn.

The shrill honk that followed drowned the others that sounded behind him. A lamentable, collective cry, the blaring horns were, to the indifferent heavens above

29

Chapter Five

The fall semester was a week old, and Joy Felder failed to grasp the concept of punctuality. She entered her Western Literary Masterpieces class held in a large lecture hall disoriented, out of breath and nervous. At the back of the hall she bumped into an empty desk. While acts of clumsiness are commonplace in the academic world, one might argue even expected; Joy's presented a certain danger. The desk she knocked into slammed into another one and that desk hit a third desk. A domino effect resulted, causing an avalanche of prefabricated wood and tubular metal framing. The deluge of desks caught everyone's attention. One student was nearly trapped, but his friends pulled him to safety in the nick of time. Joy apologized in a weak voice as she descended; her head slung low, to the front of the class.

Joy preferred the anonymity and comfort of the back rows when it came to lecture halls. She had an idea that college professors were paid money to project their voices across a room, no matter the room's size. An added bonus was the quick exit one was able to make when class ended. But owing to the accident she had just caused, Joy hurried to the front of the lecture hall. She managed to make the acquaintance of a few students, despite the blunder upon her entrance, before the professor arrived. Beside her sat a young man who looked quite distraught although he slept soundly at his desk. She wondered what dreams he was experiencing to cause him to harden his face the way he did.

Joy did not hear the professor enter the hall from a side door. Nor was she listening when the professor commenced roll call.

Instead, she reflected on the many events that shaped her week thus far. Foremost, she resented not having normal parents. The only people who seemed to have cool parents fell into two categories for Joy: those whom she did not know and those who would never accept her into their social circles. Why was it, she often wondered, that the coolest people she knew had the strangest parents, and the people she deemed shallow or lacking intellectual substance worth any merit had parents that were amazing? Was it a generational thing? The more she thought about it, the crazier it seemed.

Her thoughts wandered as the professor droned on, calling out the names of students in the lecture hall.

Joy felt her jeans against her legs and her stomach. The sensation brought to mind another vexation – her body weight. She blamed only herself. Between the ages of eighteen and twenty she had coveted her body, a perfect 36-24-36, almost as much as the boys she knew who did so, too. Now, Joy didn't want to know her measurements. She still wore a 36D bra, but they felt tight against her chest. All her favorite panties had been replaced by boxer shorts. She kept telling herself not to worry. The weight gain was only temporary. Joy refused to buy into the myth of the 'freshman twenty'; the added pounds young women gained when they began their college careers. It was only a matter of time, thought Joy, before the old body came back.

The young student next to her began to snore.

What occupied the forefront of Joy's mind now was not her parents or her recent weight gain, but the harrowing experience she'd gone through on the first day of classes. And while the experience was already a week old, it left a grave impression on her.

It began the morning her father questioned her about angels. Joy drove to Camden during the rush-hour commute. As she neared exit 1 off I-676 she was nearly cut off by a Renault station wagon. Beyond the Renault she spotted a white pick-up truck swerving from lane to lane. There was a

31

brief delay at the exit ramp traffic light when she arrived there. The Renault she'd seen minutes before on the highway was now parked in the ramp's left lane. Joy pulled up on the right side of the car. As she passed she caught a glimpse of the driver. A dark cloud surrounded the young man's head.

Joy drove straight into Camden, ignoring her impulse to stop and see if the young man needed assistance. She parked her tan and brown Ford Maverick at the first empty space she found on Cooper Street. Parking was the worst part of the day for Joy. Camden was a small city. And parking spaces became more limited as the morning progressed.

It was the first day of classes on the morning Joy maneuvered her car down the pot-holed Cooper Street like a tank driver going over a bombed-out pasture. She wondered what lay in store, being a transfer student from a suburban community college. Her big fear was getting lost in Camden. Fortunately, just as the college course guide had promised, there were plenty of signs around directing new students toward campus. After Joy locked her car she studied the map board posted at the curb. Things aren't so bad, she thought.

As a young girl growing up in a small town that bordered the New Jersey Pinelands, Joy Felder had heard many stories about the city of Camden. They came from her father mostly. Mick Felder believed firmly that Camden should be annexed by the state of Pennsylvania and made part of Philadelphia. Joy's father had many visions for the socio-political landscape of the Delaware Valley. Fortunately, his kind was never taken seriously. Joy knew it took more than giving away an eyesore of a city to make things better.

When Joy announced her plans to attend college in Camden her mother didn't take it well.

"Mick," Annie Felder barked, "do something. You know you can't let our baby go into that city."

The argument carried on for several weeks before Joy reached an agreement with her parents. Mick and Annie Felder were reluctant, at first. They wanted their only child to have the things in life they never did. They wanted to protect their girl from the ugliness of the world. Joy knew that Rutgers University was a good school. She also knew she'd

32

save herself and her parents a small bundle if she commuted to the city campus rather than live in New Brunswick at the main campus.

Joy studied the map a few more times before she set off on foot. Once she had a fix on the Delaware River she figured finding the campus was no problem. With each step the map's directions faded from her memory. As she walked she took out her schedule and reviewed her class times and meeting places. The sun that morning was bright. Joy turned in a semi-circle to shield the piece of white paper in her hand. It was important to commit the schedule to memory. The last thing she wanted was to look like some doe-eyed freshman gawking in marvel at the campus surroundings and trying to make sense of it all. When she was satisfied that she knew where she was headed she continued along 4th Street. Joy walked south a few blocks. She thought she might see more students in the area, but she didn't.

Soon a multistoried brown-brick building came into view. Women of varying ethnicities dressed in suggestive clothing stood on the sidewalk facing the structure. A fence topped with barbed wire separated the women from the men inside the building. Several men gestured at the women from narrow windows.

Joy glimpsed one such man at a window close to ground level flailing his arms. At first, she didn't believe the way the man was shouting at her. But after a quick glimpse at the other women nearby, Joy guessed the man was addressing her since she was the only 'fat-assed blond bitch' on the block. She watched, numbed by the insinuation, as the man made a series of gestures. Some crude sign language, she thought. The man in the window pointed at her and repeated the same gesture.

A woman who stood beside Joy said, "I think he likes you."

The man in the window made a hollow fist with one hand. Then he placed the index finger of his other hand into the fist and pumped. He took turns pumping vigorously in that fashion and spreading his arms open as if waiting for a reply.

"Excuse me," Joy beckoned the young black woman who stood next to her. "This isn't the university, is it?"

33

Some women nearby laughed. One tall, corpulent, white female with teased, lacquered dark hair and tattoos on her arms approached now.

"This ain't no college," the black woman clutched Joy's arm and led her toward the curb. "You know what I'm saying? This here's the county—"

"Just who the fuck are you?" the dark-haired, tattooed amazon shouted at Joy. A good number of teeth were missing from her grotesque mouth. The few that remained were stained and rotted. "Hey, Blondie. I'm talking to you."

"Fuck off, Greta," said the black woman. "You don't know this girl."

Joy watched as Greta closed in. She guessed, judging by the woman's tree trunk thighs and breasts like half-deflated basketballs, that the woman outweighed her by one hundred pounds.

"Yeah?" the behemoth replied. "Hector sure seems to know her."

"I don't know anyone named Hector," said Joy.

"My guess is," Greta went on, "she's the bitch my Hector was fucking before he was sent up." She clenched her fat meat claws into huge fists. "I know all about you, Blondie. I heard all about those gangbangs up at Garcia's place. You cocksucking whore—"

"Who's Hector?" Joy asked.

"Greta," the other woman said. "Take it easy."

The huge woman retreated and took her place again at the fence.

"Like I was saying," the black woman told Joy. "This here's a prison. Those imbeciles inside, the ones acting like they've never seen a woman before, they belong to us. Now, you'd best take a hike. I can't spend my whole day protecting you from crazy jealous bitches."

"I'm lost," Joy admitted, eyeing Greta whose back was turned to her. "Maybe you can point me in the right direction?"

"Turn around and go the way you came," the woman told her. "You'll see the college once you get past Cooper Street."

"Thank you," said Joy.

34

"Unless you're blind," a smile formed on the woman's face. "Then you might miss it."

"Hey, I never got your name."

"What's that?" she shielded her eyes from the morning sun's glare.

"Your name," said Joy.

"Basima."

"I'd like to be able to repay you, somehow."

"Forget it," said Basima.

"No, really," Joy said. "I would."

"Can you break my man out of prison?"

"No, I doubt that."

"Then don't worry about it."

"You come down here often?" Joy asked.

"Two or three times a week," said Basima. "It depends."

"Maybe I could give you lift somewhere one day."

"I got my own ride," the woman explained. "He drops me off at the courthouse and I walk over here."

"But I thought you said—"

"My father," said Basima. "He told me Ray's no good. He was right. But what are you going to do? You have to learn love the hard way, I guess."

"I'm Joy," she told her.

"A white girl's name if I ever heard one," she replied.

"Thanks," said Joy.

"Hurry up," said Basima. "You're going to be late for class."

The two women shook hands and parted.

"Christophe?" the professor's voice boomed, catching everyone's attention including Joy's.

"Here," the young man seated next to Joy replied. Then he hunkered further into his seat to resume his nap.

Joy was grateful Basima had intervened during her confrontation with the gargantuan apple of Hector's wandering eye. She knew women like Greta from the bars she frequented in Lindenwold and surrounding communities. It seemed tattooed amazons like Greta always fought hard and dirty. When Joy saw Greta approaching she resigned herself to the inevitable truth of the situation. She knew she didn't stand a chance against the woman. Joy was no stranger to fights, but

35

those altercations happened at a younger age. And more often than not Joy ended up throwing down with some boy over something stupid like the way her body developed long before the other girls in her grade school class. As an adult, she had no interest in fist fighting.

"Felder!" the professor shouted, projecting his voice with full force.

Joy sat up and opened her eyes wide.

"Present," she replied, looking at the dozing student beside her.

Her classmate yawned. Next, he opened both eyes long enough to wink at her before he dozed again.

"Let me say this now," the professor announced, stroking his fiery red beard. His gaze fixed on the void somewhere between the middle and the rear of the lecture hall where PhDs and other eggheads of equal cerebral capacity focused when they struggled to choose their words. "If you should find yourself more than ten minutes late for my class, then use some common sense and courtesy and refrain from entering the lecture hall. Today, of course, was a reprieve. Starting next week if you are late for class and miss roll call you will be counted as absent. I don't want to treat anyone like they are still in grade school, but until you prove yourselves worthy I will have to enforce certain rules."

Jimmy Christophe awoke and rubbed his eyes. "Pinhead," he muttered loud enough for Joy to hear. "Do you think he treats his wife the same way?"

Joy smiled, keeping her eyes on the professor.

"Imagine him in bed," Christophe went on. "If you're going to come after me, then what's the point of coming at all?"

"You there," said the professor, "lounging like you don't have a care in the world. You wish to add something to our punctuality protocol?"

"I move to strike the protocol," Christophe said.

"Motion denied," the professor said. "Ms. Felder?"

"Yes sir?" said Joy.

"Are we clear on the future?"

"Is anyone?"

36

"Touché," said the professor as he grinned. "Try to be on time. And a little less physical drama when you make your entrance."

"Yes sir. Less physical drama."

"Good," he said. "Now, for those of you who don't know me, my name is Dr. James Freeman. Yes, the rumors you've heard are true. I don't give out 'A's in my course. To do so would mean you people didn't need improvement and I would soon be out of a job. But given no one of you is perfect and I am already tenured here at the university there is nothing to worry about.

"Some of you, judging by the sullen faces I see out there," he went on, "have already experienced the privilege of taking my courses. For you newcomers please do not be inclined to call me James, Jimmy, Bud, Dude or some other familiar address. I'm certain I've earned my credentials; so please, show me the respect I deserve. If you extend me that one simple consideration, I'll make sure you don't fail my course."

"Somebody stop this comedian," Christophe whispered. "I'm busting a gut over here."

Joy bent forward, pretending to search her knapsack for some item, and hid the smile on her face. Her mirth, however, was short-lived.

"On the first day of class I asked everyone to read Swift's 'A Modest Proposal'," said Dr. Freeman. He stroked his beard as a low murmur of discontent rippled through his audience. "Today we will review that work in preparation for your first test scheduled for our next meeting."

37

Chapter Six

On a cloudy spring day nearly two thousand years ago atop a hill site known as Golgotha, Gaius Cassius Longinus sealed his fate. Until that day Longinus, a Roman soldier who was forty years old, believed that after spending half his adult life in the military he had finally arrived. He had modest living conditions, an easy assignment in which he helped crucify enemies of the state, and the respect of his commanding officers. Life was good. Gone were the days of bloody campaigns into foreign lands. Rome maintained a chokehold on Jerusalem. Longinus no longer feared for his life. It was here, often while he chastised dying men as they hung from wood crosses, that he considered his future. The day was fast approaching when he would hang up his scabbard and leave the army.

Longinus considered going into business, perhaps livestock or the grain industry. His father had gone that route, maintaining a large farm outside of Rome, and had bequeathed his only son a sizable portion of land. Too many years had gone by since Longinus savored the place he believed was the center of the civilized world. It felt good to know he was returning home.

His plans for a grand homecoming were thwarted, sadly, when a single act sealed his destiny for all time. Longinus had performed the act countless times before during his tour on Golgotha. At first, he was unaware of the ramifications.

It all began on that fateful Friday when he showed up for duty. Longinus had a good night's rest and was ready to work. His superiors had promised him a weekend leave. The furlough was set to begin at sunset.

That the day was charged with an inexplicable energy did not seem extraordinary to the Roman. Friday was a busy day in the crucifixion business. There were quotas to be met, and, as of late, enemies of the Roman Empire stood up to be heard all over Jerusalem. And in so doing those dissidents kept carpenters, torturers and soldiers in business.

The afternoon progressed. Longinus maintained his position near the many crosses on the hill. One of the crucified begged for water. He was the one, Longinus knew, whose crucifixion Pontius Pilate had hastened at the behest of certain Jewish authorities. Longinus heard many stories about the man, odd stories that told of heavenly sovereignty, magical practices and things worse. For several minutes the Roman listened to the one who called himself the Son of God as the dying man begged for water. It was rumored throughout Longinus' garrison that the self-styled rabbi was so cunning that he nearly convinced Pilate that he was guilty of no crime. Tales concerning the man and his radical views, his vast knowledge of arcane metaphysics and his supposed healing powers circulated in and around Jerusalem even before he was apprehended.

When the dying Nazarene requested a taste of water Longinus and his crew thought they'd lighten the mood by substituting another liquid in place of water. One soldier suggested urine. The rest frowned on such a whim. The urine trick had been pulled so many times before it was beyond old hat. In fact, the urine-soaked sponge was reserved for those new recruits on other hills who knew no better. Talk then shifted to the supper the charismatic rabbi threw for himself on the night he was apprehended. There had been much talk about the dark magic the rabbi employed to change wine into blood. Longinus and his crew shared a good laugh over that one. Anyone in Roman society with half a brain in his head knew that Jews certainly did not master such feats of magic. Then, as if by unseen hands, a skin of vinegar was passed up

39

the hill. Longinus and his crew fell about laughing hysterically when the Nazarene sucked on the vinegar-soaked sponge hoisted to him on the end of a pike. The radical rabbi's eyes watered, his throat constricted. His body convulsed as he drew short breaths.

The merriment the Romans enjoyed did not last long. Not long after the vinegar trick the Nazarene found his second wind. Longinus had seen the phenomenon enough times during his tenure on Golgotha. Dying men often expended their last bit of energy cursing those responsible for their crucifixion. The Nazarene was no different. He pronounced many blasphemies against his aggressors. Suddenly, the dying rabbi spoke out in several different languages at once. Longinus and his crew lost their lust for foolery. Everyone was scared.

Longinus remembered the license Pilate allowed on the killing hills. He gripped his pike and stabbed a long spearhead into the Nazarene's rib cage. A voice rose from the crowd at the foot of the hill. Longinus heard something about slaughter and the Lamb of God. A wind gust blew over the hill as the Nazarene drew his last breath. Then, for the rest of the afternoon, silence reigned on Golgotha.

In the days that followed strange events occurred. Wild stories spread throughout Jerusalem. The people, caught up in the mass hysteria, claimed that the Nazarene had risen from his grave three days after his death. Many asserted they had already seen him. Others, intrigued by the rumors, rushed to the grave and found the heavy stone that once sealed the tomb cast aside. Within the tomb, another discovery had been made. The death shroud draped over the dead rabbi's face now bore his likeness.

The talk of dead men walking reminded Longinus of a similar tale he once heard about a man named Lazarus. The people told of how the Nazarene went to the dead man's tomb and raised Lazarus from his eternal sleep. They called it a miracle, proof of God's power. The occupying Roman force considered it a mere fabrication, a staged hoax meant to strike fear into the outsiders' hearts and fuel the hope of Jews who longed for liberation. A small, platoon-sized detachment was

40

sent to check out the story. As always, the Roman soldiers were armed to the teeth. They found Lazarus at his home, conversing with neighbors and curiosity seekers. The man was no doubt alive, although he looked under the weather. More than a few of the soldiers were spooked by the whole ordeal. And since the Roman soldiers had no formal training in dealing with a situation like this they did what they did best when faced with a threatening uncertainty. They charged Lazarus and cut him to pieces. In doing so they erased the sole evidence of the Nazarene's most infamous, egocentric and, considering Lazarus' zombie-like appearance, undoubtedly most slipshod miraculous handiwork.

Late in the afternoon on the Friday the Nazarene was dispatched to his heavenly kingdom a great storm broke. As promised, Longinus received his furlough. He and a few close comrades from the crucifixion detail retreated to a small apartment. Their initial plan before the storm was to visit as many whorehouses as possible and other places of ill repute that existed in Jerusalem's underbelly. Longinus insisted that everyone get drunk before setting out to the brothels.

Longinus and his crew were headlong into a bender when a few informants came pounding on the apartment door. The Romans learned of the unrest that spread throughout the city following the Nazarene's death. Small groups of zealots, some armed with homemade weapons, were ambushing lone Roman soldiers left and right. Pilate, the informants told him, was attempting to regain some control over the city. The temple elders had long since locked themselves away in their temple for fear of retaliation from the Romans as well as the Nazarene's followers. Upon hearing the news, Longinus and his comrades sobered up immediately when they heard the last of the informants' news. Christ, they told him, like Lazarus before him, had risen from the dead.

When his furlough ended Longinus returned to duty. Order was restored to the city, and the crucifixions continued. The Roman had almost forgotten about the Nazarene until word reached him that the rabbi's followers spoke in public about Christ's imminent return. Some believed that the Nazarene was returning from his heavenly kingdom with an

41

army of angels. Longinus heard little about the so-called angels, but what few details he had known were enough. Conquerors of the world or not, Rome didn't stand a chance.

Word reached Longinus while he was on duty at Golgotha. He was wiggling his pike free from another crucified criminal when a fellow soldier relayed the news. Terror seized Longinus. He recalled the Nazarene had spoken to him at the exact moment he sank his spear into the Nazarene's rib cage, but he could not remember what the carpenter rabbi said. That afternoon, feeling the pressure of an imminent change about to take place and losing his taste for his sadistic stabbing game, Longinus left Golgotha with his spear in his hand.

Later that evening, the Roman fled Palestine.

Longinus roamed the world for years, fearing the death-defying rabbi would catch up to him. The years went by and turned into decades. Slowly, his fear subsided. He met travelers along the roads Rome had built who told Longinus that the Romans had destroyed the temple of Jerusalem. The temple's destruction occurred in the first century following Christ's death. Longinus decided, when he discovered that Rome took on Christianity as its official religion, that the one God of whom he'd heard so much about possessed a peculiar sense of humor. By now, the Roman was no stranger to the cruel twists of history. The news of a Christian Roman empire disturbed Longinus. Where fear and dread once dwelled in his heart, certain emptiness now ruled.

Gaius Cassius Longinus wasn't aware, at first, that his life was an immortal one. The realization surfaced when he surpassed his one-hundred-fiftieth birthday. But throughout his travels Longinus had met men and women who had lived exceedingly long lives. That they looked a day older than dirt compared to his youthful appearance forced him to remain secretive about his own age. The centuries progressed along their linear march. In the late 1400s, his long-time suspicions were confirmed.

Longinus had returned to Italy. He settled in Florence where he overheard a conversation one day that settled the matter. A cardinal bishop and a young Swiss Guardsman were vacationing in Florence and shed the light that brought

42

Longinus out of the darkness. The guard wanted to know if the heresy concerning an object known as the spear of destiny was true. The young man demanded that the Roman Catholic official share any secret knowledge he possessed about the soldier who pierced Christ's side and the soldier's spear. The cardinal bishop immediately dismissed the matter of the spear. The young guard was used to the old man's antics, and he knew well that any church official that outright denied a thing's existence was, in essence, telling the uninitiated that there was more to the story than they were willing to concede. The cardinal bishop had other ideas that afternoon. The guard swore off intimate contact until the old man came clean. Yes, the church official agreed that the rumors of the Roman soldier were well known. No, he would not entertain the popular tale of man cursed by God to live forever. The cardinal bishop was at a loss when the young guard lectured him on the heresy concerning the sole instance when Christ reportedly used his divine power to curse someone. At last, the cardinal bishop admitted that the whole legend was indeed true.

Longinus, who had been eavesdropping on the cardinal and his companion in a secluded grove, felt his heart drop. But it wasn't until later in that century while living in Venice that the immortal Roman remembered sneezing after he thrust his spear into the Nazarene's rib cage. That involuntary action, the sneeze brought about by wind-born sand that irritated the Roman's nostrils, rendered Longinus deaf for a second. And in that instant as the soldier's heart quit beating for a millisecond the Nazarene called Jesus Christ decreed that Gaius Cassius Longinus would exist until the end of days.

Longinus learned early on that the curse of immortality, despite however attractive it may seem to those destined to die, had its faults; namely, living. The immortal Roman followed death around the globe through time. He made finding a means toward death the sole purpose of his unending life. The Grim Reaper kept his distance from Longinus. No plague, no war, no natural disaster could harm the Roman.

In the twenty centuries that followed that fateful day on Golgotha, Gaius Cassius Longinus crossed oceans, rivers and

43

deserts, traversed both poles and all four hemispheres, finding employment where he could. When there were no jobs to be found he begged for alms.

It was an early September afternoon in the latter part of the twentieth century when Longinus stepped off a bus at the Trailways depot in Camden, New Jersey. One quick look around coupled with a whiff of the hot, pungent air that assaulted his skin and clothes told the Roman that he had landed in a city devoid of hope.

Chapter Seven

"The dream's not the worst of it," Christophe cried. "Talbott, I think my mother's trying to poison me."

His face loomed over his beer mug like a sullen satellite.

"Dear God!" his friend exclaimed. "Are you serious?"

"She's putting something in my food."

"No."

"I had the runs every day for a week at the start of the semester."

Talbott did what any true friend would do when faced with a dangerous crisis. The severity of the situation was too much for him. He flagged down the bartender and ordered two shots of tequila.

"Let's go back to the dream," he said.

"Have you been listening?" Christophe asked. "I'm telling you my mother's trying to kill me."

"The dream, Jimmy."

"Do you remember 'The Pit and The Pendulum'?"

"Poe?"

"How the fuck should I know," he said, losing patience. "I'm talking about the movie."

"Vincent Price," said Talbott. "Of course, I do. A classic in my book."

"Last night," Christophe ignored his friend's zealous remark, "I dreamt I was on a slab, and when Vincent Price took off his hood he'd turned into my mother. It was horrible.

45

The closer the blade came to my abdomen, the more my mother laughed like some syphilitic harpy."

The bartender set the tequila shots down on the bar.

"That's it then?" Talbott asked.

"You ordered tequila, didn't you?" the bartender asked.

"Not you," he dismissed the old man. Then to Christophe, "That's the whole dream?"

"Yeah, Mel," his friend said, picking up his shot glass. "That's it."

Christophe drank his tequila and washed away the bitter aftertaste with beer. He contemplated the odds of his survival. By now, he was convinced the end was near.

It was during his freshman year in high school that his life began to change. His mother and his father had divorced the summer after Christophe's eighth grade graduation. His father was, according to Agnes and her close friends, the most unfaithful man in the Delaware Valley. Christophe knew his father spent considerable time away from home, but even if he had a girlfriend or two on the side, having him around kept Agnes Christophe from antagonizing her son. Once Christophe's father split, having moved to Fort Lauderdale with a young woman only ten years older than his fourteen-year-old son, Agnes Christophe let out all the stops.

At Christmas during his freshman year Christophe's father, Tommy Muldoon, sent him a Hallmark card. On the card's cover was an illustration inspired by Edward Hopper's 'Nighthawks' that depicted Santa Claus seated at a diner counter. The message printed within the card, in big bold red letters, read 'Happy Holidays'. Tommy Muldoon wrote no words of greeting or fatherly wisdom. He did, however, include a photograph of his new bride. The young woman in the picture wore a scant bikini that hardly covered her tanned, ample proportions. After the New Year holiday, Christophe threw away the greeting card, but he kept the photograph.

It didn't take long for his mother to find the picture. Periodically, Agnes Christophe rummaged through her son's belongings in search of anything she might use as ammunition against him. That afternoon Agnes tore the picture to pieces while Christophe helplessly witnessed the act. Of course, he

46

protested, reminding his mother that she had no right, etc. to go through his personal belongings. Agnes reminded him that if he worked hard, considered his own feelings above everyone else's and practiced his pick-up lines he might grow up to be just like his dad.

In those first years after his parents' divorce Christophe treaded dangerous waters. He marked time and waited for the day his mother would exact some twisted revenge on him that was meant for his father. Lately, however, his paranoia took on a new dimension. He believed Agnes no longer harbored any resentment toward her ex-husband. At present, Tommy Muldoon was one of many men who had walked into her life and exited just the same. In that respect, Christophe thought, she had come full circle. Now, he was convinced that Agnes was simply out to get him.

"Listen, Jimmy," Talbott was saying, "this obsession of yours isn't healthy. You cannot believe that your mother wants to kill you. I mean, come on, she gave birth to you, man. Didn't she?"

Christophe remained silent as he looked around the bar. Tatters, his favorite drinking establishment, was filled with patrons beyond the legal capacity. He eyed a group of young women across the room. He felt alienated by their carefree, animated gestures and intimidated by their radiant beauty. When it came to the female gender, especially in the realm of relationships, Christophe was a neophyte. Closing in on his mid-twenties, he could still count on two hands, without employing all ten digits, the number of women he'd known intimately. Above all, he viewed women as a mystery. Some, like his mother, he considered malevolent. Others he viewed as saviors. A small number reminded him that there was perfection in the world. These were the women he likened to beautiful princesses that dwelled once in enchanted realms. The first category, women in league with his mother, he avoided at all costs. The last category, the perfect females hailing from some chimerical realm, he also avoided since those women were no more substantial than a damp mist. Christophe sought the savior-type in a relationship. Sadly, the women who fit that role were dwindling in number.

47

"Are you going to class tomorrow?" Talbott asked.

The Coors Light Silver Bullet clock on the wall read 1:30am.

"I'll be there," said Christophe, regrettably.

"You said that last week," he replied, "and you missed two classes."

"I'm allowed six cuts per semester before my grades are affected."

"The semester is only three weeks old."

"Did you ever feel like none of it's worth it?" Christophe posed the question that had plagued him lately. "When I'm sitting in those classrooms I sometimes think there's no real point to it all."

"It's the game," Talbott reminded him. "That's all. Sure, we're not going to learn the secret of the universe in college, but it's a step toward—"

"I know, I know," he said, lamenting the hours he had wasted at the bar. "But to what end?"

"You want to pump gas the rest of your life?"

"That's as much a noble profession as any other," said Christophe. "In fact, I'm sure somewhere in the world there are people who aspire to be gas station attendants."

"So, go move to that part of the world. Honestly, Jimmy, everyone needs a college education nowadays. It's the only way to get ahead."

"I remember when…"

"What?"

"I can't believe I was just going to say that," he told Talbott.

"You're not making much sense," he said. "You need a college degree."

"A four-year degree today is the same as a high school diploma was fifty years ago."

"You need to rationalize less and prioritize more," Talbott advised him. "Everyone needs priorities, my man. It builds character. And that, in turn, will make you more appealing to others. That's the way of the world, Jimmy."

"The western world, maybe."

48

"Don't get all mystical on me. For all your dabbling in eastern thought, you're still the product of immigrants from the western world."

"In this incarnation."

"Jesus Christ!" Talbott exclaimed. "What did I just say?"

"You don't believe in past lives?" Christophe asked.

"No, I don't."

"You think our pathetic existence is a one-shot deal? That we don't get a chance to come back and do it again, perhaps make things right?"

"Since you put it that way," Talbott said, "I hope it is a one-shot deal."

"Do you believe in God?"

"Why are you torturing me with these questions?"

"Never mind," he said. "I was just thinking about something a homeless man said to me."

"You're conversing with the homeless now?" asked Talbott. "You may be right. You don't need a college education. You need your head examined."

"Christ rarely bathed."

"Meaning what?"

"If he showed up at your doorstep you probably wouldn't invite him into your home. Of course, even if you wanted to, your mother definitely wouldn't let him in."

"True."

"So, how about it?"

"How about what, Jimmy?"

"Answer my question. Do you think God the almighty created the soul just to dwell within the human body for sixty or seventy years before it returns to heaven?"

"Jimmy, you're my best friend," Talbott said. "But sometimes when you go on like this you make my head hurt."

"That's the booze."

"Whatever."

"You don't believe?"

"I believe in tangible things," he told Christophe. "I believe that the sun will come up tomorrow, and I believe that if you didn't spend so much time with your head in the clouds, communing with the cosmos, you'd stand a better chance of

49

getting laid occasionally. I believe that once we breathe our last breath that's it. I believe that all your talk about reincarnation, the afterlife and the soul is camouflage for your fear of death. A fear that manifests itself in weird dreams about your mother starring in that Vincent Price picture."

"The Pit and The Pendulum."

"Whatever," Talbott's frustration turned his face red. "Come down off the mountain, great mystic. The pussy in the valley is ripe."

"You don't get it."

"I don't have to. Besides, what's to get?" he asked as he signaled the bartender once more. "Another round."

"Joe believes in reincarnation," Christophe told his friend when the old man stood in front of them.

"Sure, I do," the bartender said.

"No!" Talbott cried. "It can't be."

"In my past life I was a schmoe," he said. "And before that, way back when papyrus hadn't been invented, I was a schlemiel. Now, what can I get you?"

"Two more beers," Talbott told him.

"No," said Christophe. "No more."

"Couple of shots of Irish whiskey?" Talbott asked.

"Mexican tequila and Irish whiskey," Joe the bartender said. "That's healthy, I'm sure. Listen, when you girls are finished bickering, get back to me."

"Come on," said Talbott, as he watched the bartender retreat. "One more beer won't kill you."

Christophe shot him a look. His friend understood that another drink, while not life-threatening, would certainly be disastrous.

"You want to leave?" Talbott asked.

"I wanted to leave an hour ago."

"Ah, you're pissed off because those chirpies across the bar left," he said, nodding toward where a group of young, good-looking women once stood. "There's more than one fish at the market. Didn't you learn anything from your father?"

"Mel, lay off that subject."

50

"Testy," Talbott drummed his fingers on the bar's edge like an anxious dandy. "Anyway, the Borelli sisters just walked through the door. Now we have to stay."

Angel and Gina Borelli lived in Bellmawr on Talbott's block. They attended the same grade school and junior high as Christophe and Talbott. Long ago, before cable television slowly crept into every Bellmawr home, neighborhood boys spied on the Borelli sisters through their bedroom window. It was better entertainment than the movies, and for some men it sparked a life-long obsession with live nude entertainment. What the sisters never knew was that Christophe and Talbott were among the pubescent peeping tom squad.

The Borelli bedroom window was the number-one attraction in those days. The best vantage point had been the tree in Talbott's backyard. The Borelli sisters were as curious about their bodies as those boys were who viewed them in secrecy. Yet, Angel and Gina's days of exhibitionism were numbered. Once Angel graduated the eighth grade, she realized the importance of modesty. Her 34-24-34 body was off-limits. None of the neighborhood boys figured out why Angel had a sudden change of heart. She was the one who first provided the most entertainment. Angel was often seen dancing around her room naked while singing to the radio or one of her Heart records. The young woman was developmentally advanced for her age, physically if not mentally. The day she caught on to the tree-dwellers, as she privately referred to them, was the final show. The curtains had been drawn. The bedroom burlesque theater, two open windows during warmer months that provided seconds of satisfaction to an eager audience after hours of waiting, was closed forever.

The prima donna stance Angel took had an adverse effect on the younger, more impressionable sister. Gina Borelli, perhaps driven by Angel's need for privacy, bloomed into a free spirit. Discretion was something alien to her. By the middle of her freshman year in high school she clinched the title of teen-aged town slut. True, Angel knew her way around the back seat of a car, the interior of a custom van and the many bedrooms of boys she had known. But Gina was

51

different. The younger Borelli girl developed into a predator. Whereas Angel knew how to manipulate men and cloud other people's perceptions of her, Gina never quite grasped the concept of being coy. She took no prisoners.

One inevitable fact of living in a small town is that certain people's paths are bound to cross. Gina and Christophe's certainly did. She was the first girl he had ever had intimate contact with.

It began during Christophe's senior year. Memorial Day was fast approaching and most of the graduating class, following the footsteps of those that came before them, cut class, piled into their cars and headed for the New Jersey shore. Gina, a sophomore, talked Christophe into ditching the senior gang and hanging out at her house. The two had been conversing for several weeks when spring broke. Christophe knew the girl's reputation. But he was powerless, he discovered, against her charm when he looked into her moody, big, dark brown eyes. Gina and Christophe met up when a wave of students rushed through an exit door. In truth, Christophe didn't feel like making the almost two-hour trek to Wildwood, New Jersey. When Gina herded him toward his car and suggested they go to her house he was flabbergasted.

His elation soon wore off. There were a few other girls his age that had joined the caravan for the Jersey shore. Christophe sensed that he had missed a great opportunity where romantic interest was concerned. The trip to the Jersey shore on Senior Cut Day was a rite of passage, a juncture that heralded an era's end.

Christophe's mood plummeted as he drove through the quiet town of Bellmawr. When he reached Gina's street he saw her father's Plymouth Fury III parked out front. Christophe felt Gina squeeze his thigh in quiet desperation. When she ducked her head into his lap he decided there might be a glimmer of hope.

"I can't let my dad see me," Gina explained, staying low.

Christophe, aroused by the current predicament, suggested they drive to his house.

"There's no one home?" Gina asked, sitting up when they had reached the end of the block.

52

Seconds after they entered his house Gina and Christophe mashed their mouths together. Their tongues came to life, darting around inside each other's mouths as they struggled for dominance. The competition didn't last long. Gina was victorious. Christophe accepted his defeat while his hands fondled and kneaded Gina's slender body through her clothes. Knowing the reputation of the licentious nymph made the experience all the more pleasurable.

"Maybe," Gina said at a whisper as Christophe continued to paw her body, "we could find something to drink."

Christophe let go of her long enough to produce a bottle of port that his mother kept hidden beneath the kitchen sink. Gina and Christophe took turns taking long swigs from the bottle. Soon, he guided her to the living room floor. Christophe sat lotus-style while Gina lounged with her legs spread out on the floor as she placed her head in on his leg. They talked in a whispery tone about their hopes, their dreams, their fears and the specter of parental ignorance that haunted their lives. Gina allowed him to pour wine down her gullet like some teen-aged Pan with one hand as his other worked his way into her shirt. Christophe felt Gina's nipples harden at his touch. She reached back and lazily stroked his cock through his jeans. Without speaking, they rose and retreated to Christophe's bedroom.

By the time they reached his bed Gina and Christophe had shed all their clothes. Gina laid him down on his back. She hovered over him a minute or two, allowing him to lick and suck her firm tits. Then she descended. Christophe gripped his pillow when he felt Gina's mouth on his cock. He drifted in and out of a dream state, envisioning Shambala, Heaven, Nirvana all rolled into one. For a moment as Gina's head pumped up and down in expert rhythm he thought he saw a nimbus around it. Then, as an orgasm shook Christophe's supine body, Gina experienced a gag reflex.

"Spare me the torture," said Christophe to Talbott as he remembered how Gina vomited in his bed that morning. "Let's get out of here."

The two young drunks staggered out of Tatters. Christophe and Talbott had a hard time locating the Talbott

53

family car. Minutes later, after searching several side streets near the tavern, they remembered Talbott had parked the car in the tavern parking lot.

Once they were on the road Christophe felt better. A cool breeze blew through the open passenger window. He watched the dark houses and empty yards as Talbott drove toward Bellmawr. His thoughts drifted to the time Gina had returned to his home a few weeks later.

Agnes had left the house hours before for a weekend excursion in Atlantic City. Christophe was left alone and free to come and go as he pleased. He heard a knock at his back door. When he opened it, he discovered Gina Borelli standing on his back porch. The first thing he noticed about Gina was that she wasn't wearing any lipstick or eyeliner. She looked more like a scared little girl than the vixen she was supposed to be. Gina and Christophe sat on the back step talking for an hour before he invited her in. Downstairs in the basement that Christophe's father had once converted into a 'recreation room' Gina and Christophe took up where they left off. All that was left of the old rec room was a card table, a sofa bed and two bookshelves crammed with Christophe's books. Their first attempt at intercourse was hurried. Soon after they both fell asleep, lying nestled in each other's arms. Gina woke Christophe with her hand. That night she didn't go down on him. Christophe wanted to feel her mouth on him again, but he feared a repeat performance of Senior Cut Day. They made love a second time. Afterward, Gina got up, dressed and said nothing as she left his house.

Sometime after midnight Christophe put on his clothes and left the house. He got in his car and drove all the way to Wildwood, NJ. At that hour there was no one out. Exhausted and not willing to face the drive back to Bellmawr, he walked across a huge stretch of sandy beach. When he neared the water, he sat down. The waves broke on the shore as he imagined the rhythmic sound washing away all the bad memories he kept stored within himself.

"All my life I never met anyone like her," he heard Talbott confess as his friend swerved away from on-coming traffic. Christophe learned that Talbott's latest object of desire was an

54

older, married woman. Talbott added, "If I could just sit her down and talk with her. I know she'd see how deep my devotion could be."

"You're dreaming," said Christophe. "Besides, your mother would never go for that."

"Jimmy," Talbott said, "she'd leave her husband. I know it. We could be together."

"What's her name?"

"Huh?"

"Her name? What is it?"

"Hell if I know," Talbott answered. He yawned. Then, "Maybe one day I'll work up the nerve to talk to her."

"You think a woman that you haven't even talked to will end her marriage to be with you?" Christophe asked.

"Stranger things have happened."

"You're drunk."

"On love."

"Every time you get drunk," Christophe reminded him, "this romantic monster rears its lovelorn head."

"The spirits consume me when I consume the spirits," he told him. "What's a guy to do?"

"You can pay attention to the road," Christophe gripped the dashboard as Talbott ran a red light.

Once at home Christophe felt safe. He unlocked his front door as Talbott pulled away and blasted his horn. Christophe winced at the shrill sound, wondering if his mother had waited up for him. In the past Agnes ambushed him in the dark the way she once did her husband. Christophe was convinced that his mother was an assassin in a past life. The way she utilized shadows and familiar surroundings to her advantage added definite weight to his theory. But it wasn't only Agnes' ability to camouflage herself in a domestic setting that supported Christophe's belief. Agnes, at a moment's notice, could turn any household utensil into a lethal weapon. Her arsenal included spoons, spatulas, chairs, lamps, fishbowls, pottery, lightbulbs, thumb tacks, ice cubes, uncooked rigatoni and frozen microwave entrees. Christophe felt like Inspector Clouseau anticipating Kato whenever he entered his house after a certain hour. Fortunately, his mother wasn't home.

55

Christophe went into the kitchen and found a note on the table.

Jimmy,

If you get home before me, please leave the parlor light on. I went to The Tide with the girls. Try not to make too much noise in the morning. I haven't been sleeping well.

Don't oversleep in the AM.

Mom.

P.S. I hope Mel Talbott didn't honk his horn like some crazy person when he dropped you off tonight. The neighbors have been complaining. Not that I give a shit about them. But it does bother me to have to apologize for your friend's immaturity.

Christophe tore up the note and threw it away. The clock on the kitchen wall chimed twice. Inside the refrigerator he found a can of beer and opened it. The beer tasted like water. It was a sure sign he had drunk too much that evening.

Chapter Eight

Agnes Christophe arrived home late. She rummaged through her purse for her keys as she stood on the front steps. The neighborhood was quiet. She noticed her son's car in the drive. Agnes staggered to the right. Her hip banged against the wrought-iron railing that bordered the small porch. In the morning a large bruise would mark the place that took the brunt of the blow. Agnes unlocked her front door and stepped into the dark living room. She was convinced that her son had rearranged all the furniture.

In the kitchen Agnes turned on a light and poured herself a glass of wine.

"Jimmy!" she cried, "are you home, honey?"

Agnes had to be dead drunk to use any term of endearment. Often, she experienced mood swings, melancholy and loneliness being two of the worst. Some nights she drank so much she believed that if her ex-husband returned home she would take him back no questions asked. As often as Agnes drank it seemed remarkable how well she could handle her liquor. But every now and then the dam broke. When it did she found herself possessed by alien feelings of love for her son. She expressed herself in a variety of ways; most of which were too hokey for even a greeting card company to take seriously.

"Jimmy baby," she called to her son, "are you home, doll?"

57

Above her she heard his muffled curses coupled with the squeak of the bed's box spring as he rose. A moment later Christophe's voice thundered from the second floor.

"Jesus Christ, mother!" he hollered. "Do you have to shout?"

"I just wanted to know if you were home," Agnes bellowed back from her place at the kitchen table. "You didn't leave on the living room light."

"I'm home! I'm home! Is it too much to ask that I might get some sleep?"

"Don't be a dud. Come down here and talk to your mother."

"Mother, I'm serious."

"And I'm Agnes. Pleased to meet you."

Christophe groaned.

"Ok fine," his mother said. "Go to sleep. Sleep your whole life away. See if I care."

"God damn it!"

"Jimmy honey," Agnes said, "there's no need for that kind of language. You never spoke like that when we were a family."

"Family!" Christophe shouted. "Family? If you're in one of your infamous kinship renewal moods, you can forget it."

"Jimmy."

"Mother, honestly, what would you do right now if he came back?"

"You don't have to be such a smart ass."

"As opposed to being a dumb ass?" Christophe offered. "Good night. We'll talk in the morning when we're both sober."

"I am not drunk!" Agnes shouted.

"Is this going to turn into one of those 'Home Is Where the Hurt Is' conversations?" her son asked. "I'd rather you stop before you say something you won't remember in the morning."

"Unlike some people in this house," she said, "I can hold my liquor. Ask anybody if you don't believe me."

"You mean the other drunks you associate with?"

58

"You're cruel, Jimmy," Agnes said. "Do you know that? Downright cruel."

"I've heard about how some people with chemical dependencies," he told her, "often project their own shortcomings—"

"I don't have a chemical dependency," she interrupted. "I don't even use drugs. So, don't start any of that psychology bullshit—"

"Psychology is not bullshit."

"Sometimes I wish you had moved to Florida with your father."

"Get real," Christophe said. "The entire state is culturally stunted. Florida's idea of high art is a strip mall that will stand up to hurricane-force winds."

"Burt Reynolds' dinner theater is down there," Agnes defended the Sunshine State.

"We're on the same wavelength, after all."

"Damn you, Jimmy Christophe," his mother cried. A piece of cork in the wine swirled in a counterclockwise motion. "You know I love Burt."

"I won't hold that against you."

"I wish I could have my life back."

"If only things were that easy," Christophe said. "Trust me, if I could snap fingers—"

"Oh, how I wish," Agnes' lament sounded.

"And oh, how I wish you'd check into a detox center," he said. "Good night, mother."

Agnes stayed in the kitchen. She finished off the bottle of Merlot in the three glasses. Her mood darkened when she recalled how happy Rosemarie Parillo was at The Tide. Agnes found out that Rosemarie had accompanied Darius Algernon to Atlantic City. Blackjack and dinner were nothing new to Rosemarie. When Agnes learned that Algernon preferred high stakes, even going so far as to give Rosemarie a few hundred dollars to bet with, she began to suspect something was wrong. Rosemarie and Algernon showed up at The Tide holding hands and acting like adolescents who mistook hormonal rage for love. Agnes couldn't believe it. And when

59

Rosemarie confessed that she had done something she hadn't done since she was in high school it proved too much.

"Please don't say any more to me," Agnes said inside the ladies' room as she and Rosemarie checked their make-up.

"Oh, Agnes," Rosemarie replied with a certain calm, "it was just a blowjob."

"What did I just tell you?"

"Like you never tasted Johnson?"

"Rosemarie."

"Agnes."

"Okay," she said, "you want to tell someone, you'd better get it out. You know how it will go if you tell Mary."

Rosemarie told Agnes about the long drive back from Atlantic City. When she finished her story, Agnes was reeling. The two women were about to exit the ladies' room when a stall door opened.

"You better get to church, girl," Mary said when she emerged from the commode stall.

They shared a raucous laugh, swapping tales of sexual conquest in their day, and returned to the bar.

Agnes went into her room and undressed. She studied herself in her full-length mirror and was unable to put aside the thought of being in Rosemarie's place during her friend's return trip from Atlantic City. More than that, she realized that Darius Algernon was all she thought about. Day and night, Algernon invaded her mind like sunlight through a window with no curtains.

Since her divorce Agnes knew men who wanted her. But the idea of consorting with them sexually did nothing for her. Algernon, on the other hand, proved to be a mystery. It was evident that he was after a good time. And yet whenever he was around Agnes he remained aloof.

At the bar there had been much talk about the man named Darius Algernon. For several weeks now, he had become a regular face in the crowd. During that time Agnes watched him leave the club at night's end with one woman or another. She wondered what he saw in Rosemarie that convinced him to lure her with dates to Atlantic City. And as far as the talk around the bar was concerned, Agnes played at being not

60

interested. She thought gossip and rumors were for narrow-minded people. But every time some story about Algernon cropped up in his absence she found herself listening. Some patrons believed he was an oil tycoon. Others said he had made his fortune designing war machines. And still another group maintained that everyone's favorite stranger Darius Algernon had amassed his wealth through even more devious means. From the fringes of The Tide crowd came talk about disgraced European royalty, government espionage, white slavery, drug trafficking and organized crime. It seemed one only had to mention Darius Algernon and a ripple effect took place.

Agnes didn't care where his wealth came from; nor did she desire to know how he had acquired it. She was practical-minded, after all. All Agnes wanted was to spend Algernon's money. It angered her that Algernon found someone like Rosemarie attractive. Sure, Agnes considered Rosemarie a good friend, a close friend whom she loved. But whether Rosemarie possessed the mettle to be some rich mug's mistress Agnes wasn't sure.

Agnes took careful inventory of her body that morning. At forty years old Agnes thought her body had seen its best years. She discovered years later that women who are determined could have just about anything if they set their mind to it. It helped that her breasts were full and in good shape. True, she had often been complimented on her shapely figure.

That morning, before the sun rose, Agnes gave herself one last look in the mirror and decided to take the bull by the horns. Her challenge didn't rest in luring Algernon away from Rosemarie. Agnes knew her friends too well. Rosemarie would take it in stride. What bothered Agnes was how her son would take it when he discovered her intention.

At last Agnes lay down in her bed and slept. A dreamscape unfolded. She walked along a quiet city street. Agnes heard a chain rattle as she looked up and down the deserted street, expecting to see a dog loose. A thick fog enshrouded the unfamiliar neighborhood. Agnes panicked as the rattling chain drew near. As a young girl she had suffered a dog bite on her rear-end. More than anything, she feared dogs, both in

61

dreams and in waking life. Soon a figure emerged in the fog. Agnes was relieved to discover that the shadow walked on two legs. She recognized the figure as he approached through the fog. Her son looked older in the dream, healthier. In his hands he held a thick chain leash. Agnes' eyes followed the chain and stopped. A hideous beast stood some distance away from her son. He wore a thick collar around his massive neck. Agnes wanted to run.

Christophe spoke to her. Agnes paid little attention to him. Her focus remained fixed on the monster. It stood a full head and shoulders taller than her son did. The beast's body was covered with coarse dark hairs. From the head of his long leathery cock protruded a blood-red thorn. Agnes recognized something familiar about the beast's hairy face. It was a visage she had seen before. The face belonged to Darius Algernon.

Agnes awoke a start. Sweat covered her body. She felt a strong presence in her room.

"Jimmy?" she called out.

Footsteps sounded on the stairs before her bedroom door opened. In the dimly lit hallway her son stood poised at the door.

"What is it this time?" he whispered.

"Someone was in here," Agnes said.

"Delirium tremens, no doubt," he remarked. Then, Christophe assured her, "There's no one here, mother. Go back to sleep."

62

Chapter Nine

Christophe returned to his room upstairs. He shook his head as he wondered about his mother's dreams. Her paranoia was not totally unfounded. Lately he had experienced certain phenomena around the house. There were definite cold pockets of air in rooms that were otherwise warm. Some nights Christophe thought he heard voices coming from other rooms in the house. But Agnes' recurring nightmares outweighed any of that. Christophe worried that his mother was going crazy. The idea that she might end up in an institution upset him. Many were the nights over the years that he sat at her bedside assuring her that the bad dreams she experienced were in no way linked to encroaching insanity. But what troubled Christophe even more than his mother's nightmares that morning was the pungent, sulfurous odor present in her room.

Christophe lay in his bed staring at the ceiling until sleep took him. A soothing peace settled within him as consciousness slipped away. What followed he later convinced himself was more a vivid dream than a near-death experience.

He left the world and his body behind and journeyed toward the absolute. Halfway to his destination he was detoured. Christophe ended up in Limbo. It was everything he had learned about in catechism when he was a boy. Limbo, a way station for the unbaptized dead, lacked any order. The inhabitants stood by; some of them had been there for eons Christophe discovered, waiting for something, anything to happen. From Limbo there was a perfect view of the light all the souls there longed to reach. The distance from Limbo to

Paradise, Christophe realized, was unfathomable; the road congested to the point where movement had ceased.

Christophe's visit to Limbo didn't last long. It was a good thing, too, because he had a thing about personal space; and in Limbo all the souls there wanted to be as close to him as they could.

The deep dark space he found himself a part of appeared no more familiar or hospitable than the terrain he had just vacated. Everything around him was pitch black. Christophe was aware of the light his own body gave off. It wasn't long before the darkness surrounding him became visible; distinguishable shapes took form before his eyes. An enormous gate stood in front of him. Far beyond the vast structure wrought with intricate detail voices sounded. Christophe was unable to make out the cries. His attention was then drawn to a neon sign suspended high above the gate that blinked its message in bright red:

THROUGH ME
THE WAY INTO
THE SUFFERING CITY,
THROUGH ME
THE WAY TO ETERNAL PAIN,
THROUGH ME
THE WAY THAT RUNS
AMONG THE LOST...

And on and on the sign buzzed until the last line.

ABANDON EVERY HOPE,
YE WHO ENTER HERE!

Suddenly, Christophe was seized by a strange sensation. He looked back and saw his supine body lying lifeless in bed.

Christophe approached the gate. The sounds beyond the great barrier became more distinct. The huge knockers hung from the colossal portal. Dogs barked on the other side. Just when Christophe was ready to knock, the gate opened.

64

An ugly little demon, all hunchbacked and sporting an unruly tuft of red hair on his ill-shaped head, fought back a three-headed dog as the hound lunged at Christophe. The demon cursed and shouted orders until the dog retreated. The three-headed hound let loose once more despite his master's warnings. For his insubordinate behavior, the canine received a blow to each head. The demon composed himself after he was sure his disciplinary measure had taken the right effect.

"Don't mind Cerberus," the redheaded demon advised Christophe. "His bark is worse than his bite. Now, friend. What can I do for you?"

The demon's breath smelled like a bad beer fart. Christophe winced when he caught a whiff.

"I'm not sure," he replied, bewildered by his experience thus far.

"Are you coming in or not?"

"I don't know."

The little demon stared at Christophe. He sighed and polluted the air once more with his noxious breath. A commotion erupted from a pit some distance behind the demon. The ruckus startled Cerberus. He pawed the ground and began barking again.

"A moment, please," the eggheaded demon begged Christophe.

He turned on the dog and planted a swift kick in the dog's stomach.

"Perhaps there's someone in a position of authority I can speak to," Christophe said.

"You're not dealing with small change here, chump," the demon warned. "I once held rank among the seraphim."

"Don't get me wrong," said the mortal. "I'm sorry. I didn't mean to imply—"

"Sure, I get it!" a crease furrowed the demon's brow. "Every now and then some smarmy wiseguy comes along thinking he can smooth his way out. I suppose you want to talk to the big guy?"

"No, no. Nothing like that."

"Good. Anyway, he's not here."

"What?"

"Are you deaf?"

"Where is he?"

"You're full of questions for someone in your predicament. Do you know that?"

"Never mind. It's none of my business."

"Bah, what's the use," the demon blubbered. "He had some harebrained scheme. All that stuff about the kingdom of Heaven within our grasp was bullshit. We could be gods ourselves, he told us. Do I look the kind of god you'd want to worship? Eh, shit. It doesn't matter. Why? Why did I ever listen to him? Say, are you okay?"

"Hold on," Christophe said, shuddering as he looked through a long tunnel where his body lay. "I'm confused. If he's not here, then where—"

"If then, if then!" the fallen seraph snapped. "What are you? A logician? His Excellency always did things his own way. That's his trademark. A long time ago, when things were different, he convinced us that we were equal to the Almighty. We lost that war, and it hurt. It was the mother of all ass-kickings, the one by which the very definition of defeat was born. And to make matters worse, the Morning Star refused to bow to Adam in the Garden. Given his origin, Satan considered such an act beneath him.

"Yeah, the Morning Star's a temperamental one. Between you and me, I'd say his disposition could still use a little work."

Christophe remained neutral; sensing the demon wanted to vent.

"Still," the redheaded monster went on, "he got to Eve. That bitch was a pushover. I know how sentimental humans can be. But seriously, kid, what kind of halfwit listens to a snake? I'll tell you a secret. All the literary critics on earth, regardless of their school of thought, they all lumped so much shit onto the matter of Eve and the serpent. When you get down to it, when you strip away all the speculative criticism, all cloaking spells of critical theory, it is embarrassing to think that she was so easily led astray. You'd think God in his infinite wisdom would have created Eve from a piece of Adam's brain rather than his rib.

66

"Speaking of the old boy," the demon changed gears now, "do you think Adam would have rolled over like Eve did? 'Do not eat the forbidden fruit of the tree of knowledge', that was it, right? Here's a kicker for you. After Eve was so easily persuaded, she first weighed whether she'd share the fruit with Adam. Had it been the other way around, do you think Adam would have heard the end of it? I doubt it. Women. What can you do? So, are you coming in?"

"What's your name?" Christophe inquired.

"Hey, I ask the questions around here. Me, the keeper of the gate."

"I was trying to be polite."

"Polite?" the demon said. "Stalling for time is more like it." Behind him Cerberus growled, causing the demon gatekeeper to jump. He turned on the dog. "Shut up, you retarded, three-headed bastard."

"Never mind," said Christophe. "Forget I asked."

"Forget you asked what?"

They stared at each other.

"Thought you had me?" the demon asked. "Don't sweat it, kid. Sometimes I get carried away. It comes with the position. My name's Asmodeus. Everyone around here calls me Azzy."

"Nice to meet you, Azzy. Maybe you can tell me what I'm doing here."

"You're shitting me, right?" Asmodeus clutched his stomach as he chuckled. "You're dead, for Behemoth's sake."

"No, no. I'm only dreaming."

"My ass," the demon argued. "Get a grip. Who dreams of Hell?"

"Maybe—"

The demon Asmodeus ignored Christophe. He pulled a small bugle from a gunnysack that hung at his hip. When the demon put the instrument to his lips a flatulent call echoed through the darkness.

A whirlwind of dust, fire and smoke arose from a pit some distance behind Asmodeus. Another demon approached the gate. He was tall, slender, and much uglier than his fellow ex-seraph.

67

"Presenting a member of the old order," Asmodeus shouted as he snapped to attention. "The infernal judge of all souls in Hell, Minos!"

"Listen," said Christophe, "all this isn't necessary."

"I am the great Minos," the tall demon vociferated. "Infernal judge and big boss man of the second circle."

The mortal regarded both demons with suspicion. Dream-state or alcoholic hallucination, Christophe thought his imagination could never conjure something so absurd as his present situation.

"Are you feeling…mmm…lustful?" Minos felt out the new arrival.

"No," Christophe's patience faded now. "Look, all I wanted—"

"Judge him, judge him!" Asmodeus jumped up and down, bugle in hand, like some primitive bushman exalting in a bountiful kill. His mouth frothed. "Judge him, judge him!"

"I will, bedlamite," his comrade cuffed the enraged demon. "By the power of Satan, Heaven's brightest angel now fallen, overseer of Hell, seducer of Eve, scourge of Adam and all his descendants, the thorn in civilization's side, the archangel ruined, the thief of Paradise, the…"

Minos drew a blank.

"The prince of the power of the air," Asmodeus whispered.

"Yes," Minos rejoiced. "The Adversary with a capital 'A', the first angel with balls enough to sin, the true child of light, I judge you…mmm…not damned…mmm…and free to go."

The thin demon turned into a wisp of smoke and disappeared. Cerberus barked as he followed the unseen power back to the pit.

"Beat it, kid," said Asmodeus as he closed the gate, "before he changes his mind."

Christophe somersaulted away from the gates of Hell. At first, he thought he would wake up in his own body; but his journey wasn't over yet.

The pearly gates of Heaven appeared tarnished. Christophe had grave misgivings about them. A thick golden chain, held fast with a silver padlock, secured the portal's two innermost rungs. A sign on the gate read: The Kingdom of Heaven. The

68

sign bore many scratches and dents. Beneath the inscription someone had rendered an addition to the address: Slum of the Saved.

Through the gate Christophe spotted a small guardhouse. He waited, suspecting someone would soon approach. When no one did, he rattled the chain on the gate. Thunder rumbled in the distance. A body stirred within the guardhouse. Christophe shook the chain once more.

"Pete!" a voice boomed. "This is J.C. The Old Man wants you to answer the gate, pronto!"

The figure occupying the guardhouse left his post and shuffled to the gate. His rumpled appearance suggested he took little pride in his position.

"Yes," he said as he neared the gate, "what is it?"

"Does the name Azzy ring a bell?" Christophe asked.

"I can't say that it does," St. Peter replied. "Now, what is it you want?"

"I think I'm dead."

"Oy, another genius."

"What I meant," he explained, "is that I've been told I'm dead, but I'd like a second opinion."

"Of course, you're dead," Peter said. "When was the last time anyone living ascended into Heaven?"

"Would a wrong answer affect my admittance?"

"Deeds, my good man. Not words."

Christophe recalled the ecclesiastical stage fright he had experienced when he made his holy confirmation in the sixth grade. A visiting bishop from Ecuador tricked him into giving the wrong answer to a question regarding St. Ignatius Loyola's ideas on the consolation and the desolation of the soul. Christophe counted on inquiries pertaining to the Stations of the Cross, or the names of the twelve apostles. His studies for the sacrament were concrete; the material spelled out as it had been for those who had approached the sacrament before him. When Christophe failed to enter a discussion thread on the spirit of charity regarding how it directly correlated to bringing Christ into the center of one's life, things took a turn for the worse.

69

The good priests at St. Bacchus the Initiate of Thyatira Church Holy were intimidated by the Ecuadorian eminence. They decided after conferring with the bishop that Christophe was not ready to receive the Holy Spirit.

Agnes wanted her son to have a solid foundation upon which he might reach his own conclusions about life and the absolute. Her parents provided her with as much, and Agnes intended to do the same for her son. Too often she had met young men who had no basis with which they could argue for or against the existence of God and everything such an existence entailed. When she heard the news about her son having to wait another year to receive the sacrament of confirmation, she went ballistic. There were, after all, only two other sacraments left in a Catholic's life, even if Jimmy Christophe chose to seek his holy orders. One way or the other, Agnes decided her son would be among his sixth-grade peers on the exalted day.

It was a rainy night when Agnes visited the rectory at St. Bacchus the Initiate of Thyatira Church Holy. Twenty minutes later Agnes was issued a citation by the Bellmawr Police for disturbing the peace.

That autumn rumors circulated in the community about what really happened the night Agnes visited the rectory. The stories included a tale about the Ecuadorian bishop who fled the rectory babbling endlessly about succubae and other horrors. Another rumor told of how a young, handsome priest left his vocation after being left alone in a room with Agnes.

Hearsay and heresies aside, only one truth was borne from the encounter. Jimmy Christophe never received the sacrament of confirmation.

"Fuck," Christophe gave up at last. "I don't know. Wasn't Jesus the last one who went to Heaven in body and spirit?"

Thunder crashed. Mortal and saint jumped.

"What is it you seek?" Peter was irritated now.

"Am I supposed to be here?" he asked. "I can't help thinking this is a dream—"

"Don't kid yourself," the gatekeeper advised him. "This is the real thing."

70

Christophe refused to let the old man's crotchety demeanor get the best of him. He understood how St. Peter must have felt. As far as jobs in Heaven go, manning the gate was a shitty detail.

"Assuming I'm dead," he said, "how about telling me if I belong here?"

"Wait," Peter advised him.

He turned, allowing his stare to linger a moment. Then he headed back to the guardhouse with laborious steps. Halfway there St. Peter stopped.

"MOVE YOUR ASS, FISHERMAN!" another voice boomed overhead, "OR YOU'LL BE POUNDING THE COSMOS LOOKING FOR ANOTHER JOB!"

"Say," Christophe called to St. Peter. "Was that—"

"That's Him," the gate guard assured him. He shuffled to the small stall. A moment later he returned bearing three thick ledgers in his arms. "Now, young man, tell me your name."

"James Michael Christophe," he said.

St. Peter glimpsed the spines of each ledger. A small table appeared next to him. He placed two volumes on the table and opened the remaining one.

"Let's see," he leafed through the thin pages.

Once more, Christophe glanced over his shoulder. He saw his body lying in bed.

"That's odd," the saint remarked.

"What?"

"Maybe you're right."

"Care to elaborate?"

"Are you sure you're not lost?"

"I'm not the one holding the goddamned book."

Another thunder crash sounded and shook the gate. St. Peter covered his head with the ledger.

"He's still big on people taking His name in vain," he waved a cautionary finger at Christophe.

"Well?" Christophe pleaded. "What now?"

"It appears," St. Peter snatched the two ledgers off the table and held them to his chest while he continued to cover his head with the third, "that there isn't a place reserved for you here."

71

"But I've been everywhere else," Christophe argued.

"It's simple, son," the saint was nonplussed by the mortal's anger. "You're not on the list. You're not on the list!"

Christophe drew a deep breath. The gates of Heaven vanished. He opened his eyes.

Chapter Ten

Blunt yelped. His thin upper lip stuck to his dry gums. Something in his otherwise tranquil dog dreams was amiss.

Joy woke up as her dog growled in his sleep. Disturbed by the noise, she gave Blunt a slight shove as he dozed at the foot of Joy's bed. The dog landed with a pronounced thud on the floor, let out a miserable groan, expressing his dissatisfaction with being kicked off the bed, and slipped once more into sleep. Joy lay awake for some time, listening to the sounds of the quiet house that surrounded her. Soon, sleep returned for her as well.

Odd dreams presented dead relatives, childhood chums who had met with tragedy and peculiar strangers who seemed like close friends. In every episode Joy heard someone calling her name. First, it began with a single voice. Then, as the dreams interfaced with one another, several voices clamored for her attention. Despite being surrounded by so many she knew, Joy trekked through the chimerical landscape of her dreams to find the first voice that continued calling to her.

Bizarre dreams were nothing new to Joy. Most nights when she lay her head against her pillow and slept her brainwaves and rapid eye movements worked in a high-speed, kinetic frenzy. Weird manifestations sprung from the deepest wells in her subconscious thanks to the stress she experienced in life. Her home life, her studies, and her love life all had an effect. Even the slightest action during her waking life spelled itself out in Joy's dreams. A simple maneuver like kicking

Blunt off the bed had, subconsciously speaking, dire consequences.

More than a year ago Joy had accidentally stepped on one of Blunt's forepaws. In the months that followed that incident her sleep was filled with nightmares. Every time Joy fell asleep she found herself at the mercy of an angry, bloodthirsty S.P.C.A. goon squad who wore big steel-toed boots and stomped around like Nazis in their heyday looking for the barefoot woman who dared to harm her dog.

On the night Joy nudged Blunt and sent him tumbling; there were no S.P.C.A. blockheads waiting for her in the dreamscape.

Outside the Felder residence vast amounts of electrical energy flowed. High-voltage wires that hung from huge metal towers ran parallel to train tracks. There had been much speculation over the years about the long-term effects that electromagnetic fields had on human beings and other animals who dwelled close to the power lines. Now and again citizen awareness groups sprang up, populated by concerned residents related to someone who had suffered some mysterious illness. Each time these groups approached the local town council at meetings they were told by town officials and representatives of the various energy companies who used the high-voltage lines that the matter rested in the county hands. When action groups took their fight to the county level, they were told the power lines were a matter for the state to decide. By the time any of the citizen awareness groups got an answer the fervor had already died away. All the while the electromagnetic fields emanating from the power lines continued to wreak their invisible havoc.

Of those affected by the electromagnetic energy blanketing the neighborhood Mick Felder often experienced memory lapses. Joy's father was especially prone to those bouts around birthdays and his own wedding anniversary.

The invisible waves of energy affected everyone differently. Compared to the retired pharmacist Irving Zinsser Mick Felder's affliction warranted little attention. Zinsser, on the other hand, was a favorite of children and the Lindenwold Police. Irving Zinsser lived up the block from the Felders. He

74

was convinced that aliens regularly abducted people from the area. In an effort to combat the alien abductions, at least on his homefront, Zinsser laced long strands of bare copper wire and sheets of tin foil through the trees and shrubs that spotted his yard. When he was out running errands in the neighborhood Zinsser wore a skullcap he fashioned from (you guessed it) copper wire and tin foil. He told elaborate tales of an alien culture that dwelled within the constellation Delphinus some 122 light years away from Earth. Otherwise, Zinsser was a respectable fellow who never forgot a person's birthday or anniversary, including his own.

As Joy slept in her bed strange hosts introduced themselves to the electromagnetic field blanketing her neighborhood. They were the very same hosts that Mick Felder had read about in his tabloid newspaper. But this time they made certain they had the right address.

The angels leapt unseen from the wires spanning the field some four hundred yards from the Felder residence. They treaded the radiant waves of electromagnetic energy. Soon they reached their destination and dropped one by one into the Felder residence.

The angels held court in the Felder living room, remaining invisible to the human eye while Annie and Mick slept in their favorite chairs. Several debates concerning the location erupted before the angels set out on their mission. In the end the living room proved, for reasons known only to angels and other non-physical entities, the best vantage point for eavesdropping on Joy's dreams.

That the angels' mission was a serious one did not keep them from seeking a little horseplay. The empyrean powers juggled knickknacks, coffee mugs and various beer steins, tossing them back and forth.

Mick Felder opened one eye as he sat nestled in his Lazy Boy recliner. He saw several statuettes, rag dolls, coffee mugs and tankards float through the air. To his tired eye the phenomenon had all the hallmarks of a classical poltergeist. But before he could react to the phantasmal circus act he was witnessing, sleep pulled him back into its clutches. Mick dreamt in vivid detail about the girls at St. Maria Goretti

75

High School that he so desperately wanted to screw when he was a teenager. The image brought back bittersweet memories for Mick. Annabella Staccato, the object of his desire in those days, wouldn't give him the time of day. She was a raven-haired, brown-eyed Italian-American girl who regularly had her pick of boys. And pick she did according to the rumors Mick had heard back then. He never got close to landing any of the Goretti girls, nor any other teenaged female who dressed in a Catholic school uniform.

That night, however, at least in his dreams, Mick Felder at last felt the warm, moist love of Annabella Staccato.

"Nice work, Gabriel," one of the angels said.

"Thank you," the angel of dreams replied.

Another angel stationed in the living room, Uriel, as he is known by name, wanted to divulge himself to Mick Felder. Uriel's comrades, familiar with his whimsical, often disastrous intuitions, feared the fire of God might burn down the Felder residence.

His mischievous designs extinguished, Uriel elected another archangel and a cherub for a game of monkey-in-the-middle.

The little cherub bawled as Uriel and another angel tossed a ceramic garden gnome back and forth. For an eternity now, the cherub had always been the monkey. No other angels were ever roped into the part of the short-armed simian.

The angel Gabriel intervened, snatching the ceramic garden gnome from the air. Thus, the game ended. Gabriel was hot for the mission they were called on to conduct.

"This dream reconnaissance bores me," said Uriel.

"You're free to ignore The Old Man's will," Gabriel told the angel of thunder and terror. Just do it outside Heaven's curtain.

Gabriel's warning snapped Uriel into line. All angels knew the severity of banishment. Uriel knew more than the others did, having spent a considerable sentence in the void long ago.

"Ok, everyone," said Gabriel as he looked toward the ceiling. "Quiet, please. The dream's starting."

Torrential rains bombarded Joy's car as she drove along a familiar, dark street. Overhead, the menacing high-voltage wires buzzed. The windshield wipers on Joy's car proved

76

worthless against the downpour. It was too late when she realized the intersection she'd driven into flooded with every rainfall. Severe storms were the worst. The flooded intersection was known for sucking the power out of the strongest vehicles. Joy's car stalled, stranding her in the middle of the intersection.

Lightning flashed.

Joy saw the railway overpass not far ahead. Water slowly seeped into her car as she listened for a train. But the only sound that reigned was the humming from the power lines suspended high in the dark. Joy knew she was a short distance from home. Although conditions appeared spooky enough she found comfort in realizing one quick wade through the intersection pond and she would reach her house in time.

When lightning flashed a second time it revealed a figure suspended upside down from the train bridge. Joy rolled down her window. The figure shouted to her, but she was too far away to understand his words.

The water inside Joy's vehicle was a few inches deep. Cautiously, she opened her door, exited the vehicle and climbed onto the engine hood. The rain diminished her view, so she slid off the hood and waded into the water. Her jeans were soaked. There was something familiar about the figure's form. Joy plowed through the rising water for a better look.

"Don't you," a grisly voice sang in the darkness, "forget about me."

Joy turned. Water sloshed against her shirt. Seated on the hood of her car, wearing a bright, rainbow-colored jumpsuit and toting an obnoxiously loud, jumbo-sized bicycle horn under his right arm, was Joy Felder's very own dream demon, Bootsy Spittle the Clown. The haggard harlequin reclined against the windshield; his oversized red shoes had dark gray soles that looked like tombstones as they pointed toward the sky. His face was painted a luminous white shade. A crescent-shaped magenta smile was smeared over his lips. Black tears ran down his hollow cheeks. Bootsy Spittle's eyes were like two fireflies flitting about in twin dark caves. His nose was a necrotic, swollen, dark brown abnormality. When Joy saw him, she screamed.

77

The psychotic circus ghoul laughed. It sounded like breaking glass bottles in a long tunnel.

"What's the matter?" his gruff voice caused Joy to shiver. "Did you miss ol' Bootsy?"

As a young girl Joy possessed almost no fear. Reptiles, insects, birds, rats and other animals harnessed her wonder. Dark rooms, abandoned houses, quiet woods, strange neighborhoods and quiet beaches were all places that beckoned her. She ventured into each one with a veteran explorer's gusto.

There was only one aspect of life that truly frightened her – clowns. Clowns in person, clowns on television and in the movies, clown paintings (black velvet renderings were the worst), clown photographs, clown drawings, clown masks, clown coffee mugs and clown dolls; especially the clown dolls with the ceramic heads, leering eyes and preternaturally long arms; no matter the representation, she abhorred them.

The seed of her fear and hatred was planted one day when Mick Felder returned home from his weekly trip to the Berlin Farmers' Market. Joy was napping in her bed. Felder had purchased a clown doll, a porcelain-faced, limp-bodied monstrosity nearly as tall as his six-year-old daughter. He entered Joy's room, intending to surprise her, and laid the doll down on the pillow next to her. Afterward, Felder retired to the living room where he drank four cans of beer before dozing in his Lazyboy recliner chair. He had nearly forgotten about the doll with its alabaster face adorned with a somber blue shade around its mouth and red-orange circles around its black eyes. Later that afternoon he woke to the sound of Joy screaming.

Annie Felder rushed into the house from her garden where she had been contemplating the mysterious forces that kept her tomatoes from ripening (she blamed the electromagnetic field from the power lines near her house). Annie and her husband raced to their daughter's room, fearing some sneaky villain had slipped in an open window with the intent of kidnapping their daughter. When the confusion settled Annie ordered Felder to get rid of the doll.

78

The seed planted that day nourished itself on Joy's fear over the years. Around the time Joy hit puberty the fear had taken on a physical manifestation when she dreamed in the form of the nocturnal clown hobgoblin Bootsy Spittle.

"I only have eyes for you," his voice sounded like croaking frogs being crushed under the weight of an Abrams tank. Spittle leapt to his feet. He held his bicycle horn to his crotch and thrust his hips. "Yeah, yeah, yeah! (Honk!). Ugh, yeah (Honk!). Come on, baby. (Honk, Honk, Honk!) Give me some of that slippery flesh flower!"

"Go away, Spittle!" Joy screamed. It was an incantation that rarely worked.

"Not until *(Honk!)* you fix my weary willie," he pumped away on his horn. "I want to be your bumpkin, Joy. You know what I'm saying? *(Honk, honk!)* Bump-kin? Get it? *(Honk!)* Oh sugar, can you feel it?

"Of course," he reflected as his gyrating hips stilled for a moment, "it might be more fun if we were brother and sister. *(Honk, honk!)* I'd settle for cousins. You know me, Mr. Flexible. How righteous would that be? *(Honk!)* The family that loves hard. *(Honk, honk!)* Just like in the good ol' south, huh? Oh, I wish I was in Dixie! Hot diggity dog! My loins are on fire! Come on, you big-knocker slut, *(Honk!)* let me till your soil, let me burn your Bunsen, let me hew your wood. My silly stick is getting stiff, baby. *(Honk, honk!)* Are you wet yet? Let me cap your geyser, let me scratch your itch, let me draw your bath, let me snipe your gutter, let me fulminate—"

A brilliant flash of spiral lightning descended from the dark sky. Joy shielded her eyes. A sharp thunderclap sounded as the luminous colors faded.

When Joy uncovered her eyes she expected to see the specter of her dreams, but Bootsy Spittle was gone. All that remained in the clown hobgoblin's wake were a blackened, twisted bicycle horn and two smoking red shoes.

"Uriel, that wasn't fair," the merciful angel Gabriel remarked.

"So speaketh the righteous," his fiery brother retorted. "What? You were hoping that vile thing won her over?"

"No, I expected nothing of the sort."

79

"Good, I'm so happy to hear that," said Uriel. *"It's done, Gabriel. Besides, the girl will thank me one day."*

Joy turned now and advanced toward the train bridge.

"What happened to you?" she recognized her lethargic classmate.

Jimmy Christophe snorted and spat. His inverted body was held fast to a wood cross by rope tied around his wrists and ankles. The heavy rain washed away the spit from his brow.

"They crucified me," said Christophe.

"Who?"

"My mother, my father," his plainsong rang out, reminiscent of a Catholic High Mass, "and my only friend. Ah-men."

Joy remembered her classmate well. She wondered about people like Christophe, always in a dolor and choosing to go through the motions rather than participate in life. Sad people like Christophe, she reasoned, needed only one thing – love. And one act Joy could not help playing was the role of the savior. She decided in her dream that she would give herself to him. There was only one thing lacking in her waking life, but she had never been good at making initial contact. Joy always believed that in matters of the heart if a spark were struck the flame would take care of itself. Once the vibe was put out, time acted as the wind that would make the fire grow. Her biggest obstacle was getting Christophe to snap out of his doldrums long enough to notice her.

"Help me down," Christophe pleaded.

Joy started forward, then she hesitated. Christophe's head was only a few inches from the water now. The physics of the known universe often had no place in dreams. Joy stood in water only waist deep. She knew the overpass was an easy twenty feet above the road.

"The water's too deep!" she shouted.

"I'm going to drown!"

"If I go too far, so will I. I can't swim."

"You won't drown. Come on."

"How can you be so sure?"

"No one ever dies in their own dreams."

80

"People die," Joy repudiated his claim, "in their sleep all the time."

"That's not what I meant," said Christophe. "I'm talking about seeing one's own death in a dream. It just doesn't happen."

"Says who? One of my professors dreamed—"

"Trust me, it's true."

"—about dying of hunger in a desert," Joy's voice trailed off. "Desert sands swallowed her lifeless body."

"Listen and trust me," said Christophe, "when I tell you no one ever sees themselves die in a dream."

"Why should I trust you? I hardly know you."

"Suit yourself. Meanwhile you get to watch me die."

"Let me ask you a question."

"Sure, make it quick."

"Promise to tell me the truth?"

"Yeah, sure. Why?"

"A little test, that's all," Joy explained. "It's something that helps me figure out who I can trust."

"Go ahead," said Christophe. A crown of water hid his forehead from view. "Ask away."

"Do you masturbate?"

"What?"

"Do you," Joy cupped her hands to her mouth and shouted, "masturbate?"

"Yes, yes, my little duck," cried Anael, the archangel of love. He ignored the taunts of his seraphic brothers when he exclaimed, "Open all ye gates!"

"What sort of test is this?" Christophe demanded.

"Answer the question."

"Answer, answer," the Evening Star cheered him on to the others' chagrin. "For the truth shall set ye free!"

"I'm waiting," Joy's melodic voice sounded like a song.

"Yes," he answered. "Are you satisfied?"

"Good answer," she congratulated him. "Let me go find help."

"Help?"

"To get you off."

"Huh?"

81

"The cross, you pig," said Joy, embarrassed. "One of my neighbors has a small boat—"

"No," Christophe argued, "there isn't time. You have to do this yourself."

"But I can't."

"You want to watch me drown?" he pleaded.

"What about lightning? That overpass has been struck nine times in as many years," Joy told him. "The first time—"

"Look," a spasm jolted his body. "Save the meteorological history of this old town for someone else."

Lightning flashed. Sonorous thunder followed.

Joy turned and saw a man steer a huge chariot drawn by four white horses. The charioteer circled Joy's car a few times. Then he charged toward her, stopping a yard short from where she stood. He positioned the vehicle, so the horses faced away from her. The driver was the tallest man Joy had ever seen. The harsh rain did not affect him. His white tunic and white cloak were dry, and so were his horses.

"Say!" the charioteer shouted. "Have you heard the one about the man and the woman in the garden? Neither of them had any clothes on and they'd never seen each other before that moment. So, the man sees the woman staring at his genitals as he takes in her naked form. The man says, 'Stand back, I—"

"Uriel," Raphael the watcher called to his brother. He was a sociable angel, but he never got over the hand dealt to the original couple. Ever since then Raphael took great offense over jokes concerning Adam and Eve. "Get out of the dream," he told Uriel. "Or you will ruin everything."

Joy blinked. The charioteer disappeared along with his horses and his carriage.

"Jimmy," she said, turning again to face the man on the cross, "I've been meaning to ask you this. Have you decided on a thesis for your Western Literature class?"

"I'd rather not discuss research papers, if that's ok," came his vehement response. "I don't give a damn about Dr. Freeman, his class or his thirst for intellectual domination."

82

The pouring rain tapered off to drizzle. A light mist rose from the floodwater. In the distance the steady hum of the high-voltage wires continued.

"I've watched you in class," Joy told Christophe. "For an English major your fervor for literature is lacking."

"What's lacking," his inverse, maniacal grin reminded Joy of Bootsy Spittle's malevolent sneer, "is your willingness to help me."

"You should stop feeling so damned sorry for yourself. Loneliness can get you only so much pity."

"Pity?"

"That's right," she crossed her arms over her chest. "You give people a certain vibe."

"You don't know me."

"And the longer you put out that vibe," Joy went on, "the more people will think that's where you're coming from."

"You're not going to help me," he said. "Are you?"

"Maybe tomorrow."

"Tomorrow?" he struggled against the ropes that held him in place. "Tomorrow will be too late."

"Or maybe the next day," said Joy, fingering her wet hair. "It doesn't make much difference. It's obvious you've gone this long without it.

"Oh shit, it can't be tomorrow. We don't have class together until the following day. Oh Jimmy, can you stand it?"

"I'm confused," said Christophe.

"You don't have to feel lonely anymore," she vowed. "I know all about pain and the walls we construct to protect ourselves. I've put up a few in my time, too."

"Now I get it," Christophe's mocking tone didn't cloak his exasperation. "You're going to figuratively save me. Is that it?"

"No one can save you," said Joy. "But I am willing to share myself with you."

"Fine, that's great," he accepted, with some resignation. "Exactly what do you mean by...Who's that?"

On top of Joy's car sat an old man. He was barefoot and dressed in rags. His cast-off garments were bedecked with flowers. He twisted his upper body with sensuous rhythm, keeping time to a silent beat, as he waved his hands in the air.

83

The old man glimpsed his audience and quit his trance-like dance.

"Methinks I should know you and know this man," he said as he lowered his arms, "yet I am doubtful; or I am mainly ignorant what place this is, and all the skill I have remembers not these garments, nor I know not where I did lodge last night. Do not laugh at me; for, as I am a man, I think this lady to be my child Cordelia."

"No, my name's Joy," she said, running through the water. She climbed onto her car and sat down next to the old king.

Joy engaged the feeble, old king in conversation concerning the genius of Shakespeare. She harbored the opinion that many other geniuses were hedged into obscurity because the Bard had won the favor of so many in his day.

"Doesn't every age see popular figures turned into cultural heroes?" she asked Lear.

The old king shrugged.

"Did Shakespeare really write those plays by himself?" she wanted to know. "I know of certain collaborations, but what about these rumors that the Bard lent his name to the works of anonymous playwrights?"

King Lear, what with his old age, encroaching insanity and inevitable death, admitted he knew little of his creator.

"And what of you?" he said to Joy.

"Me?"

"Are you fully versed in the designs your creator has for you?" the king plucked at a flower on his sleeve.

"Will somebody please help me!" Christophe screamed. He kicked and pulled at the ropes. "Help me!"

"When we are born, we cry that we are come to this great stage of fools," the king reflected, unmoved by Christophe's desperate plea. Then he leaned close to Joy, and he pointed at the sky.

The rain stopped falling. Abundant stars shone when the clouds parted.

"Did you know that every star is held by angels' hands?" Lear sniffed Joy's hair as his hand came to rest on her thigh.

84

"That's not true," Uriel said. He dropped all five Franklin Mint limited edition Elvis the Angel coffee mugs he'd been juggling moments before. "Where do men get such ideas?"

Once more, lightning flashed. After the blinding array receded, Joy found herself sitting alone on her car. Beside her a pile of burnt flower petals rustled in the wind. She heard another cry and looked toward the bridge.

Christophe plunged headlong into the floodwater. The inverted cross had been reduced to a smoking ruin.

"Flame of God or not," Gabriel announced, his words accentuated by the sound of porcelain mugs shattering upon the fireplace hearth, "you wait until Metatron learns about this."

Joy's dog Blunt awoke at the crashing noise that came from downstairs. He pawed the carpet and sniffed. Then he ran the length of the bedroom, searching in the dark for a way out. His bark filled the room as he scampered back and forth. On his last run Blunt jumped for Joy's window; but he missed the target by several inches. The dog collapsed against the wall below the high windowsill, his body a mammalian accordion, before he tumbled down and landed on a stack of loose cassette tapes.

"Damn it, Blunt," Joy cursed him, emerging from her dream.

Despite his mistress' plea, Blunt refused defeat. He slowly rose from the mess of cassette tapes and limped to the door. He sniffed, listened and barked until Joy crawled out of bed.

"Holy shit, boys!" cried Behemial, the angel over tame beasts. "The dog's made us. Let's roll!"

85

Chapter Eleven

Gaius Cassius Longinus sat on the edge of his seat. He waited for his name to be called.

That morning he had arrived early for his job interview. Four other applicants had gone into the office ahead of the Roman. Longinus was nervous. Immortality did nothing to settle the nausea he felt when it came down to finding a job. He realized that the Nazarene left out no small detail. But then only a divine son possessed the ability to see into the far future. Having been cursed by the Son of God never won Longinus any popularity contests. His immortality was something that couldn't be expressed in a resume. Whenever he faced the prospect of finding a new job, about every ten years as he moved from one place to the next, Longinus cursed the Nazarene. The Roman considered it unfair that he could be immune to death but susceptible to trepidation.

The minutes slowly ticked by. Longinus tapped his knees with his fingertips.

The first three applicants spent twenty minutes each inside the security director's office. When each exited his expression was grim. Longinus knew the look. He wore it often enough through the latter part of the twentieth century.

The fourth applicant, a short, muscular, light-complected black man, emerged from the office forty minutes after his interview began. The gleam in the man's eye spoke volumes about the self-confidence he possessed. The man's square shoulders, long neck and air of pride reminded Longinus of days from centuries past he had spent in Africa. The Roman fell in with Germans bent on settling the Dark Continent. The colonizers were hungry for the abundant resource of diamonds in the region, but Longinus knew from experience that colonization was wrong. The ensuing war between the German colonials and African bushmen proved horrific. At one point the Roman found himself a prisoner of the bushmen. Fortunately, his captors practiced an open bisexuality that made Longinus' captivity a tolerable one. The Roman reveled in those memories now as the young applicant smiled at him. Longinus smiled back, conjuring different scenarios with the young man. His focus was nearly wrecked.

Presently, the security director's secretary waved a sheet of typing paper. The vexing gesture brought Longinus around. He looked at the old woman. Her black dress was covered with lint balls. Over her shoulders she wore three sweaters of varying blue shades. Tucked into the innermost sleeve on each skeletal arm were wads of tissue paper. Her quivering, bony hand, long and chalk-skinned, reminded Longinus of the ever-elusive Grim Reaper's; a hand he longed to shake one day.

"You may proceed now," the elderly secretary said.

Miserable old wretch, Longinus thought. "Thank you," he told the woman as he rose from his seat.

"Don't thank me," she quipped. "You haven't gotten the job yet."

The interior of the security director's office made the Roman feel uncomfortable. The cinder block walls were painted gunmetal gray. A white, rust-edged, metal blind covered the single window behind the director's olive-drab desk. In one corner stood a coat rack. A mannequin dressed in Marine Corps dress blues stood in the other corner.

Longinus noted the director's stern expression. It was one he had become familiar with through various wars when he approached enemy soldiers entrenched in well-fortified bunkers.

"Good afternoon," the director said. He stood up, and the two men shook hands. "Please have a seat."

87

The Roman followed the director's cue. He sat down in a cold metal chair facing the desk.

"My name is Sergeant Joe Montrose," the director told Longinus as he looked over the Roman's resume. "I am a member of the campus police department, and I am the head of campus security."

"Guy Long, sir," Longinus replied. "Pleased to meet you."

"On your resume you use the initial 'C' in your name. What's it stand for?"

"Cassius."

"Ah hah," Montrose chuckled. "You mean like the boxer?"

"No, I mean like the Roman general," he replied. "My parents were big on history."

"Cassius, huh? What is that, anyway? Italian?"

"Latin."

"I see," said Sergeant Montrose. "You've spent some considerable time in the military?"

"I did," Longinus said. "And you will note," he took the opportunity to acknowledge the mannequin in the corner, "that I switched my branch of service."

"Left the army and went over to the Marine Corps, eh?" the director's eyes glistened.

"That's right, sir."

"Shit, Long. Don't call me sir," Montrose barked. "I work for a living. We enlisted men are a breed apart. Not like those scum-sucking officers."

"Are you in the reserves, sir?" he nodded at the mannequin.

"No," he replied, curtly. "Why don't you tell me what you did in the corps?"

"Force Recon."

"No shit?" Montrose's face lit up with envy. "See any action?"

"Lebanon, Grenada, some work in Libya," the Roman answered. He cleared his throat. "I'd rather not—"

"What do you think of this bullshit going on between Iraq and Kuwait?"

"I don't really see how that has—"

88

"I'll tell you what," Montrose said. "I think George Washington was right when he said we shouldn't meddle in foreign affairs."

"Washington, sir?"

"One of those guys," Montrose waved him off. "Anyway, it's not like it used to be."

"You don't believe we should fight in the Middle East?"

"Jesus Christ, Long," the director's face turned red. "I definitely think we should go there. It's time to kick ass and take names. I say let Uncle Sam level Iraq. Then we send the Disney Corporation in to build a huge amusement park. Maybe tack on a plush airport and a few sporting stadiums."

"That would probably misplace the innocents—"

"Innocents?" Montrose's voice boomed. "In Iraq they all follow Hussein. Don't you read the newspaper? There are no innocents when they all blindly follow an inbred sociopath—"

"Inbred, sir?"

Sergeant Montrose resumed the same suspicious glare he wore when Longinus first entered the office.

"Says here in your application that you were born outside the states?" he asked.

"That's true," the immortal answered. He had lost count how many times he had played the charade, reinventing himself to fit the times. "My parents worked for the government; in foreign service you might say."

"Oh ho," Montrose's expression lightened. His laugh was reminiscent of the kind Longinus had heard from village idiots the world over. "A cloak and dagger couple, eh?"

"My father never talked about his work," the Roman embellished for the amusement of his interviewer. "And my mother, well, she was even more secretive than my father. It seemed every time some politico in a foreign country where we lived met with an unfortunate demise we were whisked to an embassy. From there we were moved to a remote airfield and moved on to another country."

"Interesting," said Montrose. "You lived all over the world?"

89

"Indeed," he said. "East Germany, the Middle East, South America, China. You name the country; I've probably lived there."

"Tell me about how you first heard about this position?"

"A few months back," said Longinus, "I contacted the university employment office in New Brunswick. There were no openings at the time. But a few weeks later I learned about the opening here in Camden."

"I see," Sergeant Montrose doodled in the margins of the Roman's resume. "And what makes you think you would be an asset to the security force here at Rutgers University?"

"Now that I'm no longer in the military," he explained, "I'd like to put my experiences to use in the private sector. If I came to work for the university I'd utilize what I know for the good of the student body."

"Good God. Are you serious?" The director felt a knot form in his throat.

"Sergeant?"

"I'm ok," he waved the Roman off with a cautionary gesture. Then, "Why aren't you pursuing an occupation more suitable to your credentials?"

"I'm a civilian now," Longinus told him. "I'm not interested in—"

"Hell!" Montrose cried. "With these citations and awards, coupled with your combat experience, you'd make one formidable mercenary. Have you ever read Soldier of Fortune magazine? Damn near every issue there are numerous ads—"

"Forgive me," Longinus said, "but I am no longer a soldier. I harbor no ambition to sell my experiences anywhere."

"Just thought I'd throw that out. No harm done, am I right?"

"No, I suppose not."

"Now," Montrose fidgeted in his chair. "Here comes the bullshit part of the interview where the university's human resources department implores me to ask a few psycho-babble questions."

"Pardon me?"

"Don't take it seriously," he told him. "It's those fucking eggheads in New Brunswick who dream up this shit. It sickens

90

me to think those intellectual faggots expect me to ask a man like you these kinds of questions. All applicants go through it. It's policy."

"I'm ready."

"Describe some of your strengths," Montrose said. "In addition to what I've read here in your application packet."

Well, I'm immortal, Longinus mused. Then, "My experiences have helped hone my leadership skills. I have no problems following orders. Attention to detail is important to me—"

"Describe one weakness."

The young African-American male who had exited Montrose's office prior to his interview popped into the Roman's mind. Longinus felt his cock jump.

"I act before I think," he confessed. "My hasty initiative has spawned dire consequences."

"Eh?" Sergeant Montrose muttered. "Oh, I see."

Montrose paid little attention to the applicant as he scribbled on Longinus' resume. Tiny stickmen fought a battle in the margins of the page. Montrose was careful not to enunciate the sound of automatic weapons fire, as he was prone to do when he was alone, drawing the stickmen at war. Likewise, he was sure not to replicate the explosions resulting from the heavy artillery strike that occurred in every battle scene he rendered. As the two-dimensional skirmish reached its climax Montrose decided that the interview was over.

"I'm going to be honest, Long," he announced as he looked at the Roman. "You could do this job with your eyes closed. Here's how it works. I have a few more interviews to conduct. When I make my final decision, I submit it to the equal opportunity board in New Brunswick. Remember when only qualified people got jobs? It's all quotas now. Anyway, once those minority-ass-kissing, politically correct whores up north determine the overall ratio down here, they pick the best candidate from the handful of choices I recommend. Any questions?"

"No, sergeant," Longinus said.

"Good," said Montrose. "I'll be in touch."

91

The security director bid the Roman farewell. He waited until the Roman had exited the offices before he picked up the phone. Montrose had friends all over the place. He took advantage of those acquaintances whenever possible. Fifteen minutes after he made the call to New Brunswick he received a return call at his desk. His contact at human resources gave him a green light.

"Chloe," Montrose barked, stepping out of his office. "Have you completed those letters?"

The elderly secretary Chloe lifted her head from her desk. She didn't like being disturbed from her nap. As she focused on Sergeant Montrose, Chloe wiped saliva from her chin.

"Yes, sergeant," she said. "I mean no. What letters?"

"Bah," Montrose snapped. "Never mind."

"Suit yourself," she put her head down again.

"Damn it, Chloe," he shouted, causing her to sit up straight. "If you wanted to rest, you should have gone into a retirement home."

"You talked me out of retirement."

"That's true," he agreed. "How about utilizing your administrative support skills for me. Dispatch a letter to Mr. Guy C. Long at 615 Albert Street, Apartment 3H, Mount Ephraim New Jersey—"

"How do you spell Ee-fram?"

"Are you shitting me?"

"No!" she cried. "And don't talk to me that way."

"Sorry, Chloe."

"And don't call me Chloe. I'm your mother."

"Stepmother," he corrected her. "Besides, we're on the job, Ma. You know how it is."

"What's the gentleman's name?"

"Guy C. Long!" Montrose shouted. "He just left the office not twenty minutes ago."

"The black fellow?"

"Chloe, come on," the derision in his voice did not go unnoticed by his stepmother. "I'm talking about the man after him."

92

"I didn't like that man," she announced, gingerly placing a sheet of paper into her manual typewriter. "There was something odd about him."

"Why can't you use the computer?" her stepson pointed at the machine that had gone untouched ever since it was installed.

"Too high-tech for a gal like me."

"What was so odd about Long?"

"Fickle."

"Fickle?" Montrose shook his head. "The guy's practically a walking war machine."

"He was light in his loafers," said Chloe. "A fairy."

"Long's a decorated combat veteran, for Christ's sake."

"Combat vets can't be queer?" Chloe asked. "Or to be more succinct, aren't gays capable of fighting as hard as the next guy?"

"You have to stop watching the news," Montrose said as he retreated into his office.

He strode to the window behind his desk.

"Ok, marine buddy," Montrose conspired with the uniformed mannequin in the corner. Outside his window he espied six students all dressed in tie-dye t-shirts, faded denim jeans and Birkenstock sandals lounging on a small grass common. The students passed two joints between each other in plain sight. "It's time to strike back."

Montrose recalled Vietnam War protesters he had met up with when he returned to the States in the late 1960s. Not much had changed in years since then, he noted. Baby killer, the protesters had called him. Rapist and Fascist. He tried to explain that he served overseas in a support unit. But the protesters didn't want to hear about how he had been a Marine Corps truck mechanic stationed in the Ryukyu Islands. They spat on Montrose and beat him unconscious with their 'Peace, Not War!' protest signs. Montrose never forgot what happened that day.

"Let's see," Montrose said to the mannequin, "if we can't bring back some order to this lawless drug zone the liberals call a college campus."

93

Chapter Twelve

The average window-fitting air conditioner draws air through the unit's lower front panel. Once the air enters the unit it blows across evaporator coils. A compressor pumps heat-absorbing refrigerant through the coils where it sucks up whatever heat the room air carries. The room air drawn through the lower front panel comes out the top cooler if the air conditioner is working properly. Meanwhile the warm refrigerant pumped by the compressor circulates to a condenser coil where the heat is dissipated to the outside air. The moisture that collects on the evaporator coils falls into a pan, and it either drains off, falling to the ground outside, or it is picked up and used to cool the condenser coil.

Christophe possessed no knowledge of the simple mechanics behind such workings. He was content to discover that when he turned his air conditioner on it worked. Who needed a theory when cool air was being pumped into the room? Certainly not Christophe.

The air conditioner was an older model Kenmore unit. Christophe had purchased the machine at a yard sale when he was a sophomore in high school. He neglected to follow a few simple steps to ensure the longevity of the unit. Vacuuming the evaporator coils, spraying the coils with a bleach and water mixture when the air conditioner wasn't in use and keeping the pan free of foreign debris (e.g. algae, fungus, rotted leaves, bird nests and so on), all would have made a difference in the unit's performance. But Christophe let the machine go, allowing it to fall into a state of ruin. His neglect caused the machine to produce excess condensation that leaked from the pan into his room.

Every night the air conditioner bucked and gurgled as if the machine was afflicted by some bronchial infection. It continuously spat water out onto the carpeted floor in Christophe's bedroom.

One night while Christophe slept a gathering of angels appeared high above the permanent haze of artificial light generated by the cities of Camden and Philadelphia. The angels listened as the air conditioner in Christophe's window suffered its latest attack. When the noise abated they pressed on toward the machine.

"Ok boys, let's do it."

"Right on, Michael," several of them cheered.

"Whose idea was this?" Uriel demanded.

"Gabriel," his brother Michael informed him. "If you have any beef with the operation you can take it up with him."

"Such theatrics."

"Uriel," said Michael, "you know Gabriel's penchant for this sort of thing."

"Grandiose fool."

"Tell it to him, not to me," Michael advised him. "Listen up, everyone. You know the drill. Two by two formation. And let's not screw this one up."

If a thousand angels can fit on the head of a pin, then it seemed a cinch for six angels to gain entrance to Christophe's bedroom through the air conditioner. The half-dozen heavenly visitors faced tighter spots than a drain pan.

Christophe climbed out of bed. The air conditioner had woken him when it began a convulsive fit.

"Steady Tarquam," shouted Michael. "Steady."

"He's bonding," Uriel cried.

"A molecular snag," said Michael, freeing his brother Tarquam. "Nothing to worry about."

Christophe found a pack of matches on the dresser when he crossed the room. He'd been dreaming when the noise from the air conditioner woke him. Christophe folded the pack of matches and wedged it between the air conditioner

95

and the windowsill. He recalled his dream. A faceless apparition had told him that Satan had grown tired of the realm of exile.

"The Morning Star wants back in," the figure told Christophe.

Where? Heaven?

"That's right," the apparition announced.

No way, Christophe thought.

"Way," the shade countered. "It's true. The due's been paid. The return has already been set in motion."

Christophe was introduced to an image of his mother dancing with a tall, dark-haired man. The stranger in his mother's arms looked peculiar. The man's prominent eyebrows mesmerized Christophe.

The air conditioner continued its fit unabated.

Christophe decided he would go downstairs and sleep on the living room couch. Then he heard Agnes crash into the bathroom vanity shelf. The last thing he wanted was to deal with his mother when she was drunk.

Fuck it, he thought. Christophe reached for the air conditioner power switch.

"Don't touch that dial, kid," advised Guabarel, an angel of autumn.

"What the hell?" mumbled Christophe.

"We know this isn't easy for you," Tarquam, the other autumnal angel, told him. "But you have to listen to us. This thing is big. Perhaps bigger than you can possibly imagine."

"Ok," said Michael, "don't scare the man."

Christophe knelt in front of the air conditioner. He marveled at the glorious voices that spoke to him. His knees sank deep into the sodden carpet.

"Don't be so formal, kid," said Guabarel. "Overt sanctimony is frowned upon these days."

"It's so blasé," Tarquam agreed. "Not only that. Think of your poor knees. Ouch. That's why Adonai gave you an ass to sit on and two feet with which to stand."

"That's right," said the chief of the archangels, Michael. "So, pull up a chair or grab some pillows from your bed. I

96

assure you if you choose to stand you'll soon grow uncomfortable. This may take some time."

Part Two: Angels, Agendas, & Alley-oops

Chapter Thirteen

Autumn, the season of change. The season of the angel Uriel. Gold, brown, red, orange and yellow colors in nature all mimic his fiery presence. When the month of Uriel ends so does the light of day lessen.

Along with autumn comes Samhain, or Halloween. A holiday steeped in tradition and mystery whose magic touches everyone.

Sadly, there are those who remain immune to the glamour of autumn. The days between the September equinox and the December solstice seem no different than the rest of the year. One such person was Agnes Christophe.

Agnes wore a mask of fresh Pond's Cold Cream as she stood in the kitchen. Two eggs fried in a pan on the oven range. A cigarette dangled from Agnes' mouth, the ashes threatening to break off and fall into the cooking pan.

Where romance was concerned things began looking up for Agnes. Rosemarie Parillo's interest in Darius Algernon had waned. And while Algernon showed no interest in Agnes she still saw it as a sign of hope.

Recently, Darius Algernon was accompanied by women much younger than he was. Agnes guessed the young women were dancers, prostitutes or worse. Algernon spent much of his time when he showed up at The Tide seated at a table in the back of the club. Agnes attempted to spy on him and his small harem, but a cloud of smoke lingered about the table

98

thus thwarting her efforts. She knew that Algernon was trying to distance himself. Men were such strange creatures. Patiently she waited while Algernon surrounded himself with young, pretty, and decidedly intellectually stunted women. Agnes knew that Algernon would soon see the frivolity of chasing girls and seek out an older woman of substance.

Agnes took a drag from her cigarette. Her head hurt. The night before she and Rosemarie and Mary stayed at The Tide until closing time. Then they drove to Rosemarie's house where they consumed two bottles of Merlot. The wine's mellowing effect made the women confess many secrets. Agnes dropped Algernon's name more than once. She was surprised that Rosemarie wasn't upset by that fact. In truth, Agnes felt like a schoolgirl admitting to a crush.

Agnes' yearnings for Darius Algernon were temporarily replaced that morning by a dull pain between her eyes.

When the eggs finished frying Agnes slid them onto a plate. She extinguished her cigarette under running water at the kitchen sink. Next, Agnes left the kitchen to summon her son.

"Jimmy," she called from the foot of the stairs. "I made you eggs and bacon. Are you up? Come on, baby. You're going to be late for class."

"I was wondering what that pungent odor was," said Christophe when he appeared fully dressed at the top of the stairs. "What prompted you to make me breakfast?"

"An act of kindness," said Agnes.

Christophe took a step down and stopped. He stared at Agnes.

"What did you do with my mother?" he demanded.

"Jimmy," she said, "don't be like that."

"You never cook."

"That's not true."

"Sure it is," he said. "The last time you made me breakfast you wanted to borrow money, remember?"

Christophe descended the stairs. Agnes kissed him on the cheek when he reached her.

"Jimmy," she said, "I paid you back, didn't I?"

99

"It's more like I had to steal it back from you one night when you were drunk."

"Details," his mother dismissed the admission.

"It's true."

"Don't be a bore."

"You don't realize how much you complicate my life," Christophe told her.

"Your problem," said Agnes, following him into the kitchen, "is that you think you are a big, fat novel when all you're really just a slim volume of poetry."

"Sure mother," he said, wiping cold cream from his cheek as he went to the refrigerator. "Whatever you say."

"Jimmy, don't talk to me like that."

"What?" he grabbed a carton of orange juice. "In English?"

"You're not my son," said Agnes. She stomped her foot to emphasize her point and regretted the action when the jolt increased the pain she felt in her head. "You're a changeling. That's what you are."

Christophe took the glass of juice he had poured and sat down at the kitchen table. He poked at his food with a fork. It was a habit he had formed as a child, a habit that grated his mother's nerves.

"What?" Agnes inquired.

"Nothing," he said.

"Try lying with a straight face," she said. "It works better."

"These eggs," Christophe pointed out. "They're fucking raw."

"Stop that."

"No, really," he went on, poking the eggs, "look at them."

"I don't care about the eggs."

"What then?"

"That cursing. I detest it."

"Let me get this straight," he threw one arm over the back of the chair. "You renounce religion and God, calling them, if my memory serves me, the hoax and the fear—"

"Don't bring that up."

"No, let me finish," Christophe argued, ignoring his mother's mischievous grin. "You said that God and religion

100

were the hoax and the fear the ignorant forged to keep themselves down."

"What's that have to do with anything?"

"Where is the morality by which you find it necessary to lecture me about cursing?"

"A foul mouth has nothing to do with morality or God or religion," said Agnes. "Besides, how long ago did I say that?"

"I was in the sixth grade."

"Communion?"

"Confirmation."

Agnes lit a cigarette.

"Whatever," she said. "I didn't like that Argentinean monk anyway."

"He was Ecuadorian," Christophe reminded her. "And he was a bishop."

"Yeah right, Jimmy," his mother flicked ashes into the kitchen sink. "Anyway, Central America is a big place."

"South America," he said. "That's where Argentina—"

"It doesn't matter," said Agnes. "My point is I've done everything possible to ensure that you don't sound like you're from the gutter. Vulgarity shows how limited one's vocabulary—"

Christophe held up his hand. "Enough," he said. "I don't need a lecture from you about the horrors of an insufficient—"

"Fine," she countered. "Let's drop the subject."

Agnes prepared a pot of coffee. When the coffee finished brewing she poured two cups and sat down at the table.

"We're out of milk and sugar," she shoved a cup toward him.

Christophe nudged the cup back toward her.

"What did you do last night?" Agnes asked. "Where did you go?"

"Camden," Christophe told her. "Mel and I bought some crack and met up with these two five-dollar whores—"

"Be honest."

"Ten-dollar whores," he went on. "They were amazing. You'd be surprised what a woman would do to satisfy her craving—"

"Don't be filthy," Agnes said.

101

"Mel and I went to a bar near the campus."

"Did you have a good time?"

"Me? No. But Talbott did. He hooked up with two sorority chicks."

"Chicks?"

"Don't get all Gloria Steinem on me," Christophe warned. "When a young woman values the material over the spiritual and possesses shall we say decidedly less than average intelligence then one can call them anything he likes. I can't help that Talbott goes for women like that."

"And you two are regular Nobel laureates," Agnes said. "Is that it?"

"It's a sure thing," her son said. "When you strip away all the shit society heaps on you, whether you're labeled a quantum physicist or a farmhand, you're still a sexual animal. It's Talbott's gift. He's able to see past all that."

Agnes sipped her black coffee.

"What did you do last night?" Christophe bit into a piece of bacon.

"Mary and Rosemarie—"

"Aged harlots."

Agnes crammed her half-smoked cigarette into the ashtray. She looked hard at her son as she took another cigarette from her pack and lit it.

"What's your problem?" Agnes blew smoke at her son.

"I don't have any problems," said Christophe. "Maybe that's my problem."

"How much bullshit can a mother stand?"

"What do you find so interesting about The Tide? That den of ill-repute you call your second home."

"Well," said Agnes, "it's classier than the dives you frequent."

"It's a cruising ground—"

"The Tide?"

"No," said Christophe. "Church. Of course, The Tide. It's a cruising ground for middle-aged—"

"Who are you calling middle-aged?"

"I find it offensive that my mother would be seen in such a place."

102

"But it's ok for you to slum through the streets of Camden?" Agnes exhaled smoke from her nostrils.

"That's different," Christophe argued. "The places I go to in Camden are college bars. There are only three worth going to."

"Excuse me," she said. "You get an even dose between the high-brows you meet near campus and the working-class stiffs who haunt the suburban firetraps where you and Talbott go trolling. Is that it?"

"Point taken," he told her. "I suppose our pathetic lives will never change."

"Speak for yourself," said Agnes. "I still have hope."

"Did you get lucky last night?"

"Jimmy!" she cried. "What a thing to ask your mother."

"Well," he said, "my friends' mothers are all married. It wouldn't be proper to ask them."

"How did you sleep last night?" Agnes changed the subject.

"Not good."

"The air conditioner?"

"You got it."

"Honey, face it. It's dying. Buy a new one."

"It's not my air conditioner," said Christophe.

"But—"

"It's the dreams I'm having."

"Dreams?"

"More like one continual chimerical narrative," he told her, not sure whether to admit the loosening grip he had on reality.

"Tell me all about it."

"Angels came to me and said—"

"I'm sorry," said Agnes, lost momentarily as she thought about Darius Algernon. "Did you say angels?"

"That's right," he said. "A few weeks ago they visited me and told me something strange."

"In your dream?"

"No," said Christophe. "In my bedroom. Anyway, they told me the devil is trying to get back into Heaven."

Agnes stood up and went to the kitchen sink. She stared out the window that overlooked the backyard.

103

"Weird, huh?" Christophe focused on her back. "The dream was so real. I hardly knew when I woke up. It was like they were really there in my bedroom. I wish you could have experienced it."

Agnes shrugged her shoulders. She believed that dreams were the exhaust produced at night by a mind that worked hard during the day. And while she plotted her day according to her horoscope, Agnes gave little heed to the notion that some people were given messages through their dreams. Then there was the whole Darius Algernon question. How was it that a strange man like him showed up in her dreams? Agnes could not recall a time when a man crept into her dreams; her bed perhaps, but the dream world of Agnes Christophe was off-limits.

Agnes' throat constricted as she silently pledged to forget about Algernon. It was enough that he occupied her thoughts when her mind was idle. She prided herself on never obsessing over a man. And yet there was Algernon, slinking his way through The Tide and the landscape of her dreams as if he was at home.

"Drink this," Christophe slid his coffee mug toward Agnes.

Agnes took the cup in both hands and raised it to her mouth. She gulped down the coffee.

"Jesus Christ!" she screamed, dropping the mug into the sink as her coughing fit worsened. Agnes turned on the faucet and fed herself handfuls of cold water. "Are you trying to kill me?"

"I wanted to help," Christophe offered.

"Don't."

"Fine," he said.

Agnes coughed one last time and spat into the sink. Then she reached for her cigarettes.

"I want you to get rid of that air conditioner," the lit cigarette bobbed in her mouth as she spoke.

"It doesn't bother you," he said, astonished at the notion. A few weeks ago he might have considered it. But ever since the voices arrived there was no question about keeping the dilapidated machine.

"It does bother me," Agnes said.

104

"You can't hear it at night."

"It keeps me awake."

"How come you never complained before?"

"It makes too damned much noise," she said. "Get rid of it."

"The noise can be fixed."

"It's leaking water," Agnes added. "I'd hate to see what all that moisture is doing to the floorboards beneath the carpet."

"As soon as I save some money," Christophe told her, "I'll get the air conditioner repaired."

"I don't want it repaired," she told him. "I want it out of my house."

"Air conditioners cost money," he argued. "Am I supposed to sweat my nuts off without one?"

"You and that mouth!" Agnes puffed hard on her cigarette. "You work, don't you? Go out and buy a new one. It's a wonder the thing hasn't fallen out of your window already. Not to mention the freon that is no doubt leaking into the atmosphere. What? Do you plan on destroying the…uh…"

"Ozone layer," Christophe reminded her.

"Don't interrupt me."

"How can I afford a brand-new air conditioner," he said, "when I'm going to school full-time and making next to nothing?"

"Don't use that argument with me," said Agnes. "College is a privilege. If you expect me—"

"An orgasm is a privilege," he countered. "What's your point?"

"The last time I checked I still owned this home," she said. "I don't have to take this shit from you. It's my roof you're living under. And I say the air conditioner goes."

Christophe stood up and exited the kitchen. When he returned he carried his knapsack over his shoulder and his car keys in one hand.

"I'm going to class," he announced.

"Finish your breakfast," Agnes demanded.

"I'm not hungry."

"Eat, Jimmy. I went through all the trouble—"

"And don't do that."

105

"Do what?"

"Talk to me like I'm a child."

"I never said you were."

"That's right," said Christophe. "I stopped being a kid when you stopped caring, remember?"

Agnes followed him to the front door. She stood on the front porch and watched him get into his car.

"I always cared about you!" the cold cream on her face hid the reddish tinge to her skin as she screamed. "It was you who never cared. Just like your father, Jimmy. Just like your father!"

Christophe started his 1988 model Ford Mustang. The automobile's body was leopard-spotted with body-fill. He slammed the car into reverse and looked at the rearview mirror.

The newspaper delivery girl was seated on her bicycle behind the Mustang. She sneered at Christophe when he slammed on the brake. Then she maneuvered her bike out of his way, keeping an eye on Agnes as she continued her angry litany from the porch.

Christophe backed his car into the street. He gave a sympathetic smile to the twelve-year-old girl. In return the newspaper girl opened her mouth and made lascivious motions with her tongue. The sight was unsettling for Christophe. It brought to mind a day he had spent with Gina Borelli. Fortunately, the vulgar display did not last long. Christophe watched as the young girl drew a folded newspaper from the bag tied to the bicycle handlebars.

"Throw it up here, sweetie!" Christophe heard his mother call out.

The girl cocked her arm, brandishing the newspaper as she winked at him, and launched the projectile in a forceful, parabolic arc.

Christophe didn't wait for the sound of breaking glass. He knew by how fast the young girl had peddled up the block that she'd hit her target. As he put his car into drive he laughed, hearing his mother's voice fill the quiet street.

"You little cocksucker!" Agnes shook her fist at the newspaper girl as she sped away. "That was my living room window."

106

Chapter Fourteen

The Rutgers University Camden campus turned out more business majors than it did any other. The Business and Science Building, a steel and glass monolith standing several stories high, had been erected not only to meet the needs of the ever-growing number of business science majors but also to pay homage to the pursuit of commerce.

Across campus the Paul Robeson Library looked more like a complex military bunker than a place where students went to study and to do research. The squat structure of red brick and smoked black glass consisted of three floors that housed books, periodicals, on-line catalogues, audio and visual resources and a small computer lab. Compared to the modern monument of business science the library served as a dreary reminder of what little stock people put into actual learning.

Students of varying disciplines, including a small number of business science majors, used the library for a variety of reasons. English majors lost themselves in the stacks of classic literature. Graduate students at the School of Social Work armed themselves with ammunition for the day they would become overqualified bureaucratic desk jockeys and tell poor people the future looked grim. Math and science majors worked themselves over mentally on a regular basis. Psychology students were easy to find. They were among the most troubled individuals on campus. The confined space of the library often brought out their worst attributes. But for all the activity going on inside the library it was apparent to everyone that money changes everything. And for the library that meant minimal renovations and expansions over the years.

107

When a student entered the library there was a tense feeling; as if the administrators were waiting for the day when all resource materials would be on-line in cyberspace; thereby doing away with mildewed books, outdated periodicals, shoddy microfilms and all the other physical materials that fared poorly with age.

Jimmy Christophe loved the Paul Robeson Library. The smell of old books welcomed him on the basement floor whenever he had free time. It was there that he perused various books that never made it to the assigned reading lists. His pursuit of forbidden and forgotten knowledge was a perilous one.

At that time there were few search engines in the library computer catalogue. The most accessible and widely used was IRIS – Integrated Rutgers Information Systems. Even the most computer-savvy students discovered that IRIS was a crazed bitch most of the time. Either she worked too slowly, or she closed herself off completely from the outside world leaving the user feeling unfulfilled.

Christophe remedied that obstacle by doing his search the old-fashioned way. Four huge card catalogue cabinets graced the first floor. Shuffling through the card catalogue Christophe looked like a caveman lugging a flaming torch through a lighting store. He was surrounded by computers that in milliseconds could do the work that at times took him several minutes. But he gained a certain satisfaction by doing it his way. The worst-case scenario he had ever faced was getting a location down within the library and then seeking out a book by scanning titles and call numbers in a given section.

The monotony of keeping up with required reading plagued Christophe. When he grew bored with the books his professors assigned he found solace in the library. Christophe concentrated on texts dealing with religion, philosophy, theosophy and metaphysics. There were several questions that came to mind since he started communing with the angels in the air conditioner. The answers he sought were never found in the books he pored over at the library. Still, the very act of

108

reading a work that wasn't on a syllabus quieted the madness that plagued him.

When faced with the unpredictability of IRIS most students turned to the reference librarian for help. But it was never easy. The elusive secret sharers of knowledge were notorious for their vanishing capabilities. When that magic wasn't possible the reference librarians implored the circulation department members to maintain the gap between themselves and the student body. The librarian aides, the women who worked at materials loan, provided the first line defense against the onslaught of unbridled, undergraduate inquiry. The aides pledged their allegiance to the reference librarians. They believed the reference librarians possessed an Essenic quality, an embodiment of all that was good and true in an environment of confusion and absurdity.

It was that very attitude Joy Felder faced, while Christophe sat brooding in the bowels of the library, when she stopped at the circulation desk and asked for help. She was promptly ignored. Prior to that Joy chased a librarian's shadow through the government document stacks.

Familiarity with one's surroundings contributes greatly to the effectiveness of stealth. Armed forces special unit members, assassins, and librarians the world over share that knowledge in common. Going into the government document stacks was Joy's first mistake. The librarian eluded the persistent student with ease.

"Excuse me," Joy said. She leaned atop the circulation desk. "Could I get some assistance?"

An overweight woman, younger in years than her spinsterish appearance projected, ceased her clerical duties long enough to look over her thin eyeglasses and down her nose at Joy. She wore a long gray skirt and sweater of the same color. Her gray hair was secured in a tight bun at the back of her head.

"Is there a problem?" the woman inquired.

"I need some help locating—" Joy started to say.

"It is not the library's policy to allow the librarian aides to assist students, faculty members or alumni in locating any research materials," the corpulent aide explained. "That is why

109

the university in its infinite wisdom saw fit to hire reference librarians."

"I understand that, but—"

"Did you not attend any of the library orientation meetings?"

"Sure, I did."

"If you wait by the reference desk someone will be along shortly to assist you."

"That's the problem," said Joy.

"Oh?"

"I've already waited nearly thirty minutes."

"Patience," the gray-haired woman announced as she resumed stamping forms with a rubber stamp, "is a virtue. You know, young lady, there's a lesson learned from every experience. I know you think your time is precious, but the truth is every student that walks into the library feels that their needs come first."

Joy watched as a student passed the circulation desk. Then she grimaced when that student blindsided a librarian and they both moved toward the computer catalogue.

"That's not to say you shouldn't remain steadfast in your pursuit," the woman behind the desk went on, slamming her stamp down every other word to stress her point. "Why, I remember when I was your age attending Smith College. There was a certain English literature professor—"

"Thanks," Joy waved good-bye as she spoke. "I'll wait by the librarian's desk."

Ten minutes passed before another librarian appeared. He was a tall, gaunt fellow who loomed over Joy as she sat atop the reference desk. His expression darkened when she started kicking both feet against the metal skirt below the desktop. Though he affected the style of the French writer Louis-Ferdinand Celine, tattered dark sweater, stained and worn pants and a haircut that spoke volumes of his personal barber's hyperopia, the librarian bore an uncanny resemblance to the mad, debaucherous monk Rasputin. He disliked people, having read too much existential philosophy and related works of literature to have any faith in his fellow human beings. Day in and day out he reminded himself that the student body at

Rutgers-Camden would never rise above the superstitious beliefs and mundane, television-addled interests of their working-class parents. Seeing Joy seated atop his desk threw the librarian.

"May I help you?" he asked.

Joy noted the librarian's faded black sweater. Next, the man's face. She saw beneath the full dark beard and decided that the man's skin had once been ravaged by acne. Joy shifted her weight from one buttock to the other. She tapped the heel of one foot against the desk as she studied the librarian's cold blue eyes. Embarrassed, Joy couldn't help thinking about the man as a sexual creature. A band of gold around the librarian's ring finger on his left hand told her that somewhere there was a Mrs. Rasputin.

"I'm doing a paper on Homer's Iliad," she told him.

"I know who wrote it," the librarian remarked.

"Yeah, anyway," Joy's foot became still. She stood. "I need recent material on the subject, anything with a deconstructionist bent to it."

"The library is virtually littered with information," he said, yawning, "with the bent you're looking for."

"Virtually littered?" asked Joy, surveying the area.

"Do you have a thesis?" he asked. "An angle from which you plan to approach your topic?"

Rasputin frowned as he called to mind a girl he once knew during his undergraduate days. Like Joy, the young woman he remembered now had always corrected him when he spoke. Clear, concise speech was never one of Rasputin's strong points. When he was pursuing his own baccalaureate degree times were different. It was the dawning of the Age of Aquarius, the advent of hippie free love. The soon-to-be librarian leaned toward romanticism as a young man. He wrote poetry, painted still lifes and read nineteenth century pastoral novels by the pound. The existential bug had not yet bitten Rasputin the librarian. It was only after he tried to get close to the flower of his desire, the grammarian with a penchant for poking fun of him in public that he lost faith in others and shut himself off from the world. After his attempts to get the young woman he knew into bed failed, he stalked

111

her for the better part of two semesters. All around him non-committal love reigned (read: sex with no strings or incurable health risks attached). Rasputin the librarian bedded about as many women as a leper did in a germaphobe retreat. He shuddered now, thinking about the coldhearted girl he once knew, and concentrated on the shape of Joy's breasts.

"So I thought I'd read a few essays," Joy was saying, "and see what I come up with."

The librarian folded his arms across his concave chest.

"Plagiarism," he announced, "is a serious crime in the academic community. It could ruin your college career."

"Career?" Joy said. "I don't plan on being here that long."

The librarian sighed. Sorrow filled his heart as he looked into the young woman's pretty green eyes. Her hair reminded him of the auburn autumn afternoons he'd known while attending Umass at Amherst. He conjured the small coffee shop where he situated himself every day, hoping to glimpse the one he loved. His devotion was envious, writing love poems to a woman who belittled him whenever she could, singing passionate original ballads in a time when his peers fashioned themselves after Bob Dylan, Janis Joplin and the like, but his approach, fueled by unrequited love, was obsessive.

"Come on," he said, at last. "Let's go."

While a transfixed librarian guided Joy through the use of the computer catalogue on the ground floor, Jimmy Christophe labored over a book concerning the devil's origin. All he knew until that day was based on his Catholic upbringing and what he had seen in movies. Christophe learned that man once saw God and Satan as one, that the devil was the angry side of an otherwise benevolent god. Each new piece of information he uncovered that afternoon filled him with dread. The angels of God that present-day people shaped into post-modern pixies who watched over human beings and protected them from their own blundering mistakes (car wrecks, failed relationships, suicide attempts) weren't always so kind. Christophe discovered that he rather liked the angels of the Old Testament. The kinder, gentler

112

heavenly messengers of the New Testament seemed weak by comparison.

Female voices broke his concentration. Two doe-eyed, beautiful females sat at a table nearby. Since the devil question had consumed him Christophe had paid little attention to the opposite sex. The ceaseless chatter between the two girls sounded foreign to him now.

Christophe hunched his shoulders. He lowered his head and shut out the rest of the world as he continued to read.

Upstairs, Joy gave up on the librarian. She searched the literature stacks until she found shelves crammed with various copies of Homer's Iliad and numerous critical texts.

The librarian had suggested she create her thesis first, and then find information to either support or dispute her claim. But Joy had other ideas. A product of the university undergraduate environment, Joy understood all too well that shortcuts counted in college. She removed a dozen books from the shelves and retired to a small table. There she skimmed the essays that filled the critical texts. Some names she recognized. Others were penned by scholars long since turned to dust. An hour passed. The mold and dust that clung to the books wreaked havoc on her respiratory system. Joy suffered an allergic reaction. She remained seated at the table long enough to write her thesis. Then she gathered up her books and headed for the circulation desk.

Half blind and short of breath, Joy passed a stairwell entrance that led to the basement. It was there that a collision occurred. She bumped into another body. Books crashed to the floor like broken-wing birds falling from the air. Index cards, pens and highlighters were loosed from her grip. Gasps of surprise and mild grunts of embarrassment sounded.

"I should watch where I'm going," said Joy as she recognized the culprit who bumped into her. She squatted down to retrieve her belongings at the same time he did.

Christophe averted her gaze. He was struck hard by her beauty.

"You should see me drive," Joy went on, noting the sensation she felt when her hand touched Christophe's.

113

"A treat, I'm sure," he remarked. Then, "You're in one of my classes."

"Western Literature," she said. "We sat...I mean I sat next to you on the first day."

"My memory is slipping," Christophe admitted as he studied the titles on the spines of each book he retrieved for her.

"I'm doing my paper on Homer's Iliad," her attempt to come off looking studious did little to mask her nervousness.

For weeks after the dream Joy had in which Christophe hung on an inverted cross she tried to win the young man's attention. It was important not to look like a sex-starved floozy or a lovesick stooge. Thus far she had succeeded. What she didn't count on was meeting up with Christophe the way she did now.

"How about you?" she stood up slowly.

"How about me what?" said Christophe. He held her books in his hands, showing no intent to hand them back to her.

"We have a paper due in Western Lit next week," she said. "Remember?"

"No," he answered. "I mean sure I do."

Christophe followed her to the circulation counter. A tall, reed-thin woman dressed in varying shades of earth tones had relieved the librarian who had dealt with Joy earlier. She wore round, metal-framed eyeglasses and hunter orange socks and Birkenstock sandals on two large feet that rested atop a low desk behind the counter.

"This identification card hasn't been validated," the woman informed Christophe when she waited on him. She pushed aside the books he meant to check out.

"So what are you telling me?" he sneered and gave a wink to Joy. "I'm not valid?"

"Unless your card is validated," the librarian aide explained, "it's as good as expired."

"I'm expired?"

"Didn't you receive the addendum for your student handbook in your campus mailbox?"

"I have a campus mailbox?"

114

"Every student has one," said the woman. Then added, "That is, everyone who's been validated."

"But how do I get a campus mailbox if I'm not validated?" Christophe asked.

"Good question."

"Listen," he said, "when I get a chance—"

"Sorry," she cut him off, wielding her authority like a homophobic, corn-fed, steroid-abusing, conservative national guardsman brandishing a riot baton at a gay rights rally gone awry, "I can't check these books out to you unless your card has been validated."

Christophe moaned.

"That's ok," Joy intervened. "Let me check those books out for him."

The librarian aide regarded both students with suspicion. Long ago she had considered herself a radical, offering a hearty 'right on!' to anyone who revolted against the system. But with age comes wisdom and complacency. Nowadays the woman harbored low tolerance for anyone that bucked the system.

"Well," she conceded at last. "It's not against the rules. But you do understand that you will be responsible for this material?"

Joy nodded and smiled at the woman.

Outside the library students crisscrossed the campus. Christophe watched the ritual with little interest.

"Do you have class right now?" he asked Joy.

"No," she stood beside him on the library steps.

"How about getting a cup of coffee?"

"Together?"

"No," said Christophe, "I thought I'd sit here while you hustle on over to the campus center."

"Very funny."

"I was being serious."

"Are you buying?" Joy asked.

"I planned on it."

"Good," Joy beamed as she nudged him. "We'll both walk over to the center. And you can carry my books."

115

Chapter Fifteen

"Good evening, ladies."

"Darius!" Agnes clutched her throat as he approached.

"Look at you," Mary said.

"I missed you so much," Agnes ignored Mary as she hugged Algernon and kissed his neck.

"You little devil," said Rosemarie. "Why didn't you ever call me again?"

"Alas, Rosie, there are worse things to be than a devil," Darius Algernon said. He gripped Agnes around her waist.

"Drinks," Mary shouted as she pounded on the bar.

Indian summer took its final bow a few weeks beforehand. Cold winter winds crept across the Delaware Valley in its wake. The Jersey shore bars were all closed; the summer rentals all locked up until the following year. Business boomed once more at The Tide.

Algernon explained to the women at great length the reason for his absence. Old business concerning his previous job had taken him out of town.

"It was all quite vexing," he noted.

"Were you able to air out your grievances?" Mary asked.

"Yes, I suppose so."

"That's what's important."

"Did you behave while you were away?" Agnes asked.

Algernon raised his long bushy eyebrow. "What do you think?"

"Oh, Darius," Rosemarie patted his forearm, "you are such a dog."

At The Tide that night entertainment was provided by The South Philly Five. The ten-member group had begun its second set when Algernon had entered the club. Phil Mazzanone was the group's leader, a part-time radio disc jockey, a father of six, a wannabe wiseguy and an all-around raconteur. Mazzanone's group performed nothing but bonafide oldies. It was during the second set that The South Philly Five paid homage to the Holy Trinity: Sinatra, Dino and Bennett. They also performed renditions of hits by Bobby Rydell, Otis Redding, Bobby Darin, Fabian and a host of others. Part of Mazzanone's shtick during the sets his band played was telling short tales of his youth in south Philadelphia. The youthful Phil Mazzanone was preoccupied, much like any other young man in any era, with sex and making a quick buck without doing much work. Intermingled with stories concerning his dead-end jobs and his various romances were ones about his Catholic upbringing. Mazzanone also went on at length about different 'benefactors' of the old neighborhood who were now either dead or doing time. At the end of the night The South Philly Five closed with 'Many Rivers To Cross'. Mazzanone always invoked the memory of his late father, Antonio Luigi 'Tony Pick-up Sticks' Mazzanone, the saint of south Philadelphia, a 1950s capo who was gunned down in front of a Paterson, NJ diner by two heroin-addicted beatniks. Mazzanone offered a solemn 'salud' to his dearly departed father before he sang the opening verse to 'Many Rivers'.

Presently, The South Philly Five kicked off their second set with 'Mack The Knife'. The crowd applauded and cheered like mad as Old MacHeath's story unfolded.

Algernon took the opportunity to grope Rosemarie while everyone faced the stage. The big-breasted bon vivant sucked up to his advances. Her willingness, however, proved boring for Algernon. He turned his attention to Agnes, setting his sights on a proper target, one worthy of the pursuit.

Rosemarie adjusted her blouse. The top buttons had come undone while she was in Algernon's arms. When she saw

117

Algernon and Agnes share a secret joke she darted for the ladies room.

Mary Reilley chugged down the rest of her drink. She had been drinking vodka and orange juice all night. The screwdrivers already began to turn in her stomach. The sight of Algernon's brazen play for her friend almost caused her to puke. Mary shot Algernon a reproachful glance before she lumbered off to check on her friend.

"What are you afraid of?" Algernon took Agnes by the arm when they were alone.

Agnes felt uncomfortable. She knew that Algernon had already figured out that much about her. Why, she wondered, did men always want women to say to them what they already knew?

"Come on, Agnes," he said. "You must know it's you I want."

"I'm not sure about that," she played him now. "And even if what you say is true, then you have a strange way of showing it."

He moved closer to her. The South Philly Five shifted into melody mode, coasting through a series of Sinatra tunes. Inspired, Algernon raised an eyebrow.

"Care to dance?" he took hold of Agnes' hand.

"I don't know, Darius," she said. "That was a shitty thing to do to Rosie—"

"Slut."

"Excuse me?"

"Rosie," he said. "Not you."

"I know who you meant," said Agnes. "I won't stand for you to talk about my friends like that."

"She threw herself at me."

"I didn't see it that way."

"Your friend is a floozy," he said. "It's all a matter of perception. And while I'm on the subject of friends, let's talk about that moron Mary Reilley."

"Darius."

"Do you think her mother drank while she was pregnant with her?" he let the question hang in the air. Then, "Mary looks to me what some refer to as alcohol fetal—"

118

"You're a horrible man."

"You don't know the half of it, sister," Algernon glared at her. "Some would hardly consider me a man at all. However, I won't bore you with that. You realize that Mary lusts for me, as she does for most moderately attractive men, but she's too stupid to come to grips with her sexual self."

"You think Mary's a lesbian?"

"Judging by what Rosemarie said in her sleep," Algernon held up his hands. "Nothing more, nothing less."

"Darius," his name dripped from her mouth like venom. "You have no right to talk about them like that. What you're saying is not true. It's not true."

"You're right," his expression lightened now. "Who am I, after all, to talk about your friends?"

"You're goddamned right."

"My dear Agnes," said Algernon. "I've wondered these past weeks why you surround yourself with drunken mediocrity."

"Please, Darius. That's enough."

"Look around," his hand swept over the crowd. "Idiots. Idolaters. They've forgotten why they are here. And not one of them has had an original thought throughout their entire lives. They'll do whatever their church and their government tells them to do so long as they can get drunk and fuck every now and then. When I think of you with these people, Agnes, I weep."

"Save the bleeding-heart poet shtick for the young girls, Darius."

"I'm serious."

"So am I."

"These people are imbeciles. They know nothing of true love and friendship. The men will bang anything with a wet hole and a pulse. The women will give birth like animals dropping their litters. That includes your precious Rosemarie and Mary. The only reason you're keeping company with them is to give yourself a sense of superiority."

"Keep talking," said Agnes, "and see if I don't cause a scene."

"Go ahead," he said. "Just remember that I had nothing to do with the intellectual decomposition going on in this room."

119

"You're an asshole, Darius."

"And you remind me of Eve."

"What?" Agnes put down her anger when she heard another woman's name. A woman she did not know. "Who's Eve?"

"Eve," his eyes opened wide as his eyebrows danced. "The first woman of Old Testament fame."

"Got it," Agnes felt relieved. Her mood lightened. "Why would you say that?"

"You think for yourself," said Algernon. "And so did she. All the trouble in the Garden came about because Eve fooled Adam, the angels and God. She was created from something that the Almighty thought would keep her bound to Adam. Boy, was He wrong. It was evident from the beginning that she had a mind of her own. That's not to say He set out to create a twit as Adam's companion. On the contrary. But when God figured out that He had created something from man equal to him, if not in physical strength then intellect at least, He freaked out. If you ask me, the Creator's mind was already made up. The forbidden fruit had nothing to do with it. Eve had the knowledge before the apple came along. God just used the tree of knowledge to set her up. You follow me? The original sin we hear so much about was actually original wisdom, but God, seeing that curious strength He created in woman, put a mark against it. In turn, he chose to shut out future generations from ever knowing what Eve did.

"Yes, Eve's genesis was wrought with wisdom. Divine wisdom. Recollection of the true light. Call it whatever you want. Any way you cut it, that wisdom set the Big Guy's teeth on edge. And He who giveth saw fit to taketh away lest she know herself fully and through that knowledge come to know God unconditionally. They say that with greater knowledge comes sorrow. That's because the more you know, the closer you come to God. And believe me, He punishes those that get too close. That's the meat of what happened in Eden. Everything else, I'm afraid, was drama."

"You really get into that whole bible thing," said Agnes, "don't you?"

120

"I'm passionate about it," Algernon admitted, "only because so much of me is there. As are you and the rest of us."

"So," she said, "you like me because I have a head on my shoulders?"

"Precisely," he answered.

"Thanks for the compliment," said Agnes. "But you shouldn't tear down my friends just to prove a point."

"They put themselves down long before I came to town," Algernon extended his hand. "Why won't you dance with me?"

Agnes attempted to smile, but instead she only bared her teeth.

"Come then," he pursued her. "Wow me with your feminine intellect and show me I'm wrong about Rosemarie and Mary."

Algernon led his partner through a throng of people to the dance floor. He shuffled a coked-out couple performing The Bristol Stomp out of the way and commandeered the dance floor.

Agnes felt secure in Algernon's arms. Suddenly, the faces of those around her on the dance floor blurred. Even the music she had known seemed foreign now. In her stomach she felt a wave of nausea. Had someone slipped her a mickey? Was it Algernon? Though she had heard about men slipping different substances into women's drinks, Agnes doubted that Algernon had to resort to that kind of tactic. She leaned close to her partner for support. Her body felt weightless against the hold he had on her.

Slowly, the dancers descended through darkness. The familiar noise and sights of The Tide had slipped away, giving way to a soundless void. Thus Algernon and Agnes journeyed through Chaos until they reached another domain.

Pandemonium was the most beautiful place Agnes had ever seen. The city rose up to meet them as they floated downward. Agnes noticed a stark change in Algernon's appearance the closer they got to the city. Sorrow filled her as she realized that the priests and the nuns she had known as a little girl were all wrong. Satan was not something sinister and

121

ugly. Seeing him in his true form Agnes understood now how he had once been God's favorite.

They walked the majestic boulevards of Pandemonium. Agnes marveled at the spirits that moved through the air. Not one of them offered the slightest salutation as they went about their business.

"You wonder why they don't acknowledge me," he said, reading her thoughts.

"Yes," she gripped his hand. "I do."

"They know it's over."

"Over? Look at this place. What are you talking about?"

"A long time ago it was easy," Satan explained to her. He squeezed her hand back. A dim expression clouded his face. "But it wasn't until recently that I realized what direction I should take."

"I don't—"

"Understand? You don't have to. I'll be going back to Heaven on my own. My office will be vacant, and I will need someone to fill it while I'm gone. I'll set him up with everything he needs. It's important that I can trust him while I go to the bargaining table with God."

"What do you expect to gain?"

"His ultimate act of forgiveness."

"And what is it," said Agnes, hesitantly, "that you want from me?"

"I was getting to that," a smile formed on his radiant face.

The nether city faded into darkness. Agnes awoke with a start and found herself inside a dimly lit hotel room. Beneath the coarse bed sheets her body was naked. A toilet flushed in the bathroom next to the bed. Through the thin walls she heard the unmistakable sound of synchronous grunts made only when two people were engaged in sex. The bathroom door opened. A shaft of fluorescent light spilled into the room. Agnes squinted. She saw Darius Algernon standing naked beside the bed with a towel wrapped around his head.

"What happened?" she wanted to know.

"You passed out on the dance floor," he answered. "Hospitals are so depressing, what with all those sick people,

122

so I brought you here. Rosie and Mary wanted to come along, but I didn't think that was such a good idea. You slept well?"

"I'm naked, Darius," said Agnes. "And so are you."

"Touché," he taunted her as he placed his hands on his hips and swung his long, pallid penis around. Agnes heard his cock slap against first one thigh then the other. "I read somewhere that clothing is restrictive."

"Did we—"

"No, I wanted to wait until you were feeling better," Algernon said. He smiled as he knelt down on the bed beside her. "Are you feeling better, Agnes?"

Chapter Sixteen

Gaius Cassius Longinus studied a painting over the hotel room's dresser. His accommodations at the Admiral Wilson Motel & Honeymoon Suites were much like the countless other ramshackle rooms he had rented. The portrait he contemplated, a rendering of a lithe matador caught in mid-pirouette, his red cape billowing, as he barely missed being gouged by a bull's huge horns, was indicative of the netherworldly quality low-rent hotels were guilty of. That the painting was slipshod at best meant nothing to Longinus. In his time, he had known innumerable so-called artists who were more suited to painting houses than portraits and landscapes. The Roman supposed that the artist who worked on the matador painting was past his prime when he set brush to canvas. Still, something about the arc of the matador's back called to mind the days Longinus had spent in Pamplona. It was before the Spanish Civil War. The Fiesta de San Fermin – the running of the bulls, the running of the boys.

Longinus always felt sentimental when he drank dark wine. And the four empty gallon bottles of Gallo Bros. Burgundy stirred many memories as he continued to ponder the matador painting.

Next to the Roman lay a young blond named Alan Cooper. Longinus had met him that same evening at Mint Julep's, a gay nightclub on Route 70 in Cherry Hill, NJ. Mint Julep was a retired 'stage actress' who bought the property when disco finally crashed and burned. Longinus had heard about the club

124

through contacts on campus. He liked the club, he liked Mint Julep and he liked young Alan Cooper for being so receptive to his advances while maintaining an innocent air. Cooper looked out of place compared to the rest of the men at Mint Julep's. And Longinus never liked forward men. For two thousand years the Roman prided himself on being the one in control. But fifteen minutes alone with Alan Cooper in a secluded booth on the second floor led Longinus to believe that perhaps he had found a wolf beneath Cooper's sheepish veneer.

The taxicab ride from the club back to Longinus' room on Admiral Wilson Boulevard cinched it. Alan Cooper's face lit up when the Roman reluctantly admitted the location of his temporary living quarters. The more decadent, Cooper told him, the better. Inside the taxicab the young man went down on Longinus with the ferocity of a starving vulture swooping down on carrion prey.

Ordinarily the taxicab union and the local law enforcement frowned upon such public displays of affection.

Longinus studied the driver's face in the rearview mirror while Cooper worked his magic. The Roman decided, judging from the maniacal glint in the driver's eye, that the driver was a man hardened by life. He had known men like him. The driver was a product of his environment, tipping his hat to things all-American like baseball and Bruce Springsteen, summer weekends at the Jersey Shore and harboring suspicions against anyone who spoke with an accent.

What Longinus didn't know was the finer details of the man's life.

The taxi driver favored the right to bear arms against enemies foreign and domestic. For him gay men fell into the latter category. He despised all that was wrong with the world; namely, homosexuality and the mongrelization of the races, liberal agitation under the guise of free speech, atheism, minority special-interest groups, tree-huggers and eco-faeries. The sound that reached him now, the ineluctable sound of a man sucking off another man in his cab, tested every shred of willpower he possessed. He wanted nothing more than to reach into the glove compartment, pull out the nickel-plated

125

.45 caliber pistol he kept there and shoot both men dead. But traffic was light that night and they reached the Admiral Wilson Hotel & Honeymoon Suites before the driver could strike a blow for God-fearing, homophobic losers everywhere.

Longinus heard the hysterical cries of a woman accompanied by the steady box spring squeak that had sounded next door throughout the night. The racket imposed upon Longinus' silent reverie. Throughout the early morning the Roman, Cooper and the occupants of the room next door combated to see who could make the most noise. When young Alan Cooper finally passed out Longinus accepted defeat like a good sportsman.

His thoughts drifted, as they often did in times of repose, to the Nazarene. Longinus was thankful that the Son was remorseful to the extent that He did not render the Roman immortal and impotent. His curse was a dark one, to be sure. Having sex through ages was the one thing that made everlasting life more bearable.

The woman in the next room commanded her lover. Longinus leaned his head back and listened. In his time the Roman had loved women. He considered the female sex a curious enigma. The curve of a woman's hips, the symmetry of their breasts, the feel, the smell and the taste of their precious fleshy rosebuds. Their bodies and their minds were extraordinarily different. Fate saw fit to make the Roman's luck run better with men. His quiet ruminations came to an end when the woman in the next room climaxed.

A few minutes later, Longinus heard the couple next door leave their room. The woman's high heels clicked by on the tier outside. A private joke passed between the man and the woman, evident in the man's hollow laugh that left the immortal feeling cold and empty.

Longinus leaned across Alan Cooper's sleeping form and turned on the bedside lamp.

He rubbed his hands over the young man's buttocks. No response. Longinus leaned back, considering, as he stared at the lamp, how human beings took so many things for granted. Sadness filled him whenever he thought about the light of man's inventions with regard to the darkening heavens.

126

Alan Cooper woke up. He squinted against the light and looked with scorn at the Roman. Then he turned over and buried his head beneath a pillow.

Longinus savored how the soft light accentuated the young man's fine body hair. His gut stirred. He had concluded at about the time the Dark Ages settled over Europe that love was a notion conceived by those destined to die. He likened it to leaving a candle lit in the dark. People could saturate themselves in love, just as they could with light, but death, like darkness, always lay waiting.

The curse Longinus lived with not only gave him everlasting life but the capacity to love forever. Up until the Roman Empire collapsed, and perhaps once during Charlemagne's rule, the immortal knew love. But after leaving behind the corpses of various lovers that he had known over a few centuries Longinus began harboring misgivings. Over time he learned not to let his heart rule. It was better to live with boundaries and barriers than face the pain associated with the alternative.

When Longinus allowed himself to think of human emotions, the broad spectrum by which those feelings portrayed themselves, he always remembered how the people around Galilee felt about Christ. When the Son of God walked the earth those who knew of the Nazarene, pagans, Jews or otherwise, considered him a lunatic. In time a select few discovered, however, that his madness had little to do with the moon. And, despite the public's view of self-styled messiahs, Christ did have a following. As time wore on the powerful and the influential, Roman and Jew alike, saw the Nazarene as less a descendant of the divine as they did a seditious thug who sought to band the poor together. They saw through the smokescreen of spirituality he professed. In the rabbi's rhetoric of love and forgiveness they heard the seed of destruction.

Temple elders in Jerusalem knew there was no room for a self-styled prophet whose message spoke of rebellion. Their relationship with Rome was a volatile one. And they weren't willing to risk losing their hold over the community by allowing someone to stoke the fire of discontent in others;

127

especially a non-traditionalist who, in their eyes, did not come from Davidic lineage.

Despite the bad press history had given Pontius Pilate, Longinus knew that the man did what he could. Pressed by temple elders, Pilate gave up Christ in order to avoid civil unrest. The deaths of an indigenous few always worked favorably in getting a message across to the remaining native population. The elders wanted to keep their temple. Rome wanted to keep the peace. Killing Christ and other dissidents sent a warning to those who lurked in the shadows contemplating the same course of action.

When Christ first set out to spread his message the Israelites refused to take stock in him as the messiah. A commoner would never suffice. They expected their messiah to come in glory. Jews with power and influence scoffed at the flock the Nazarene had gathered about himself in the early days: the diseased, the poor, and the illiterate. What spurred their fear more than the notion that Christ might be the messiah after all was the specter of total defeat. No one was about to stick his or her neck out for a carpenter's son and risk having Rome obliterate all that remained of their culture. Only a successful coup resulting in the defeat and subsequent expulsion of all Roman forces could make them believe in the true messiah. When all the mystery and intrigue was swept aside only one real truth remained. Rome continued to administer its chokehold on the lands she had conquered.

On the day Longinus picked up his orders at Golgotha he didn't care whether the Nazarene was the real McCoy. His mission was a simple one. Hasten the death of the crucified in order to make room for more enemies of Rome. The immortal often wondered since that day if he'd been born an Israelite would he have followed the carpenter rabbi or been among the crowd who shouted for the thief Barabbas.

Cooper stirred and lifted his head. He squeezed his eyes shut against the light.

"For the love of God," he said, "will you turn off that light, please."

Longinus regarded his latest conquest. His interest in the young man waned as the hours had passed.

128

"I think it's time you left," he said.

"What?" Cooper shouted as he sat up in bed. "I can't leave now. Do you know what time it is?"

The Roman saw Cooper's cock peek over the bed sheet.

"I need solace," Longinus warned. "I wish to be alone."

"A moody drunk," the young man's voice filled the room. "Great. It's like sleeping with my uncle Warminster all over again."

"I'm not moody," said the Roman. "And I'm no crusty, dim-witted relation of yours."

"Fuck you!"

The immortal climbed out of bed. He scratched his ass and walked to the door. Cooper had told him about roving bands of queer bashers disguised as comic book superheroes that prowled Admiral Wilson Boulevard. Longinus unlocked the deadbolt. Outside he discovered an overweight Captain America crouching by the door. Longinus delivered a swift kick that rendered the man unconscious. When the Roman stepped out onto the tier he saw two equally unfit superheroes, Superman and Batman, charging at him with baseball bats.

"Guy," Cooper called out when the immortal stepped out of view. "What's going on?"

"Nothing," he answered as he snatched Superman by the neck and threw him over the railing.

Witnessing the man of steel being bested, Batman fled.

Longinus looked over the railing. The man from Krypton lay motionless atop a huge metal dumpster. The caped crusader, meanwhile, jumped into a van parked close to the stairs. Longinus saw the driver for only a moment. A bearded boy wonder Robin flipped Longinus the middle finger before he sped off into the night. The man of steel atop the dumpster looked dead.

When he returned to the room Longinus found the bed empty. He turned his attention to the bathroom door. Beyond it he heard Cooper whimpering followed by a loud retch.

"You bastard!" Cooper cried. "I'm sick because of your cheap-ass wine."

"You're sick," Longinus replied, "because you can't handle alcohol."

129

He heard him vomit a second time, envisioning, as he did, how he would leave Cooper's body in the room if the young man died.

"How can you stand this rotgut," Cooper's weak voice filtered through the closed door. After he threw up a third time the jags began. "Oh, for shit's sake. Why did I ever leave Massachusetts? Look at this place...There are cockroaches beneath the tub...I'm in Hell...I'm in Hell..."

Longinus found his clothes, dressed and went outside. Superman was gone. The Roman suspected that some sinister party snatched the unconscious hero from where he lay and was now sodomizing the man of steel in an anonymous room below. At the edge of the parking lot he saw a half-dozen prostitutes gathering around a Renault station wagon.

"What's your fucking problem?" the tallest prostitute called out to the Roman. He wore a tight shirt that revealed his d-cup breasts and bicycle shorts that showed off the impressive length of his manhood. A short stogie protruded from the whore's painted mouth.

"No problem here," Longinus announced.

The driver behind the wheel of the Renault wagon looked up and saw Longinus. He slid the vehicle's gear into reverse. The prostitutes fanned out when he barreled out of the small lot and sped away.

"A girl's gotta make a living, asshole!" the cigar-smoking she-male shouted. "My customers don't like negotiating in front of an audience. If you're looking to cruise some college ass, go do it somewhere else."

Longinus started down the stairs. He wasn't sure what he would do. Punch him out? Kick her in the balls? He wasn't worried about the other prostitutes. Even if someone shot him he'd get back up again. The confrontation, however, never came to pass. All eyes before him were on the tier he had just descended. Longinus looked back.

"Guy honey!" Alan Cooper stood naked on the tier outside the room. "I'm all better! Come back!"

The immortal shoved his hands in his pockets and started for the stairs. He endured the chorus of catcalls instigated by the she-male prostitute.

130

"Guy honey!" the prostitutes sang. "Guy honey!"

Inside the room, Longinus found a refreshed Alan Cooper waiting for him.

Chapter Seventeen

Joy Felder and Jimmy Christophe hit it off over their first cup of coffee together. The weeks passed. Joy and Christophe saw each other every day on campus. On weekends they were inseparable. On week nights they spent some time apart, pursuing their studies or catching up with friends, but at least one night during the week they went out together, going to movies, eating in small restaurants, or going out for drinks. Everyone they knew mutually thought they were good together.

Joy soon came to a point in the relationship when she felt the initial spark had gone out. The romance had faltered. Still, she harbored compassion for Christophe. When she described him to others she used words like complicated, intelligent, and acerbic to conjure for others the image she had of him. Christophe knew things, Joy realized early on in their relationship, that other people didn't. At odd times he thought nothing of spouting some obscure historical event as if he had experienced it himself. Whenever they spoke of books they had read, either for class or through their own endeavor, Joy heard in Christophe's musings a certain, rough-edged genius. But for all his intellect she saw in Christophe signs of self-destruction. Joy knew it was her curse, picking up with young men who cared little about themselves or the world in which they lived. But with Christophe it was different. He didn't despise the world so much as he appeared to be bored with it. Joy had the uneasy intuition that told her Christophe might have passed through the world before, perhaps more times than memory cared to remember.

The lack of faith Christophe held was evident in every aspect of him. Joy remembered one night when they had gone out to see a movie. The title of the film escaped her, but the story was fresh in her mind. A 300lb transvestite falls for an androgynous beekeeper living on a small farm outside Paris. The movie, a French production with English subtitles, touched home with Joy in its attempt to portray unrequited love. By the film's end the beekeeper never acknowledges the obese transvestite. Even when the transvestite stumbles into an angry swarm of bees and dies as a result of numerous stings, the beekeeper continues to go about his business (mainly, tending to his bees). Joy cried at the end of the movie. Her tears went unnoticed.

Christophe complained about the film's banal plot. He didn't see anything redeeming or interesting in the two main characters that warranted the story to be told. He droned on about America's fascination with foreign films, usually subtitled, that viewers perceived as art on a higher plane than the assembly-line productions that came out of Hollywood. For Christophe it was apparent that Americans would eat whatever cinematic waste the French could cook up.

Joy disagreed with him. But Christophe wasn't having any of it. By the time Joy had formed a sound argument in defense of foreign film Christophe had already moved on.

"The entire world," he hypothesized that evening, "or at least three-quarters of it, has a working knowledge of English."

Joy resisted the conversation's tidal pull, fearing he might lash out at her.

"Even in the most destitute parts of the world," he went on during the drive home, "places where war and famine and disease ruin life every day, the poorest people know enough English to beg from tourists."

"I don't know about that," said Joy, wanting to drop the subject and talk about John Donne or Andrew Marvell – two poets she and Christophe were studying at school.

133

"Here in American cities," he said, "we watch a bad foreign film subtitled in English and we call it art, we fool ourselves into thinking that we've just experienced a beatific phenomenon. Some of these films are mere forgeries and yet we consider ourselves more cultured for having looked at foreign landscapes while struggling to keep up with the subtitles."

"Knowing the English language has nothing to do with culture," Joy felt confident enough to share that point. 'Plenty of ignorant people can speak more than one language."

Christophe gave her a look. He shook his head and said, "So, you agree with me?"

"No," Joy told him. "I don't."

"Fine," he said.

Christophe belabored his point until Joy was nearly overcome with the urge to steer into oncoming traffic. Some nights it was the only way they communicated, driving each other mad. Joy couldn't decide which she disliked more, Christophe's desire for silence when he didn't want to be bothered by other people or the unceasing soliloquies she endured whenever he opened his mouth.

Joy now sat at a picnic table on campus. Christophe was seated next to her. More than anything Joy wanted the spark back. How far into darkness she would have to travel to retrieve that sliver of light was anyone's guess. For now, she worked on keeping his attention.

"What's eating your brain today?" she asked him.

Christophe remained silent.

Mel Talbott sat across the table from the couple. He was engrossed by some activity going on behind them.

"Dude," he said at last, waving a notebook in the air, "what's going on here? Look at all the bees."

The bees he observed buzzed around a nearby trash can. They paid little attention to any other stimuli except the scent of half-empty soda cans that brimmed over the trashcan's lip.

"Be careful," Joy warned him. "Bees get testy this time of year."

Talbott assessed the situation. He put down his flimsy notebook and armed himself with a biology textbook. Feeling

134

the weight of the book in his hand, he was confident that he would emerge victorious if the battle ensued.

"Listen Jimmy," said Joy. "Something's bothering you. I can tell."

"Die!" Talbott slammed the textbook down on the table. The noise bounced off the student center. When he lifted the book he saw bee remains smeared across the cover.

"He's the one you should be concerned with," said Christophe. "Not me."

"Why?"

"There's a violent streak in him."

"But it's you I love, Jimmy."

"Whoa," said Talbott, holding his hands over his heart when he put down the biology text. "Joy, baby, what are you saying?"

"I'm saying," she replied, "don't be an ass."

"Whatever you say, my sweet."

"And don't kill any more bees."

"A percentage of them will die anyway," Talbott countered. "I'm facilitating a basic rule of nature."

"Yeah? Well, don't."

"Fine."

"Jimmy?" Joy cocked an eyebrow at her beloved. "Tell me what you're thinking."

"Nothing," he answered.

"Come on," she nudged him with her elbow. "You must be thinking about something. Even a stooge like Mel thinks all the time."

"I don't think!" Talbott cried. "I act!"

He climbed on top of the picnic table.

"Mel, please don't," Christophe said, but it was too late.

"The time to rise is now!" Talbott announced to the indifferent student body. "The revolution begins right here! Smash the state! Workers of the world unite! End the reign of corporate tyranny and government corruption! Rise up! Rise up and follow me!"

A voice from the people rose up to greet him. "Shut up, asshole!"

Next, a campus security guard approached the table.

135

"Get down from there," he said, watching as Talbott hastily removed one shoe. "Get down from there before you hurt yourself."

Talbott jumped to the ground. He squared his shoulders.

"Don't you want to see my Khrushchev bit?" he asked.

"No thank you," said the guard.

Talbott tapped his shoe on the table.

"We will bury you," his accent sounded more like the nefarious cartoon character Boris Badenough than Nikita Khrushchev. "We will bury you."

"Your vulgar parody," the guard said, "ruins the memory of a great man."

Talbott sat down and put back on his shoe.

Christophe stared at Longinus the security guard. He felt Joy's hand grip his arm.

"Do I know you?" he asked. A dim flash jarred his memory.

"No," the immortal replied, "but I know you." He stared at each of them, allowing his gaze to linger until his point was made. "All of you."

"Tool," Talbott muttered when the security guard had walked away.

"That guy is creepy," Joy let go of Christophe's arm. "He was in the library last week and a girl in my post-Inquisition poetry course said she had heard that guy tell someone that he knew Descartes. And that he knew Francis Bacon."

"The painter?" Talbott inquired.

"No, the other one," she said. "Talk about delusional. Isn't there some kind of psychiatric evaluation that a guy in his position should undergo? After all, he is supposed to be responsible for the student body's safety."

Christophe and Talbott shrugged their shoulders, expressing their indifference.

High atop the campus center building, unseen by the numerous students making their way to and from class, a host of angels stood at the roof's edge. There they had a perfect view of the campus quad.

"Who's the douche bag with the big mouth?" Raphael inquired.

136

"Mel Talbott," the angel Gabriel told him. "He's a slacker. A dabbler in politics, metaphysics, science, and philosophy."

"Another Francis Bacon, eh?"

"Yep. A regular moron. He'll be no problem."

"And the girl?"

"Joy Felder. She's on our side."

"You're certain about this?"

"Mihir," Gabriel beckoned his brother.

The angel weaved his way through the ranks until he stood before Gabriel and Raphael.

"Yes?" said Mihir.

"Tell Raphael what you know," Gabriel instructed him.

"Talbott has eyes for Joy," said the angel of love. "He won't admit it to anyone, but he thinks she's the goods. Why, the other night he was lying in bed and"

"Spare me the details," Raphael told him. "Will this cause a problem? Talbott's infatuation with the girl?"

"It's only lust," Mihir said. "In the grand scheme it doesn't matter. My advice would be to let the infatuation run its course. It will be of no consequence."

"Granted," said the healer of the earth, "but I don't want that imbecile distracting the subject's attention with something as trivial as coming between the subject and the girl."

"Not to worry," he assured him. "Our agents have it all worked out."

"The Old Man's concerned with the subject's fortitude," said Gabriel as Mihir retreated into the ranks. "He wants to be absolutely sure Christophe's right for the position."

"Do you truly believe He's going to let the traitor back into Heaven?" Raphael asked.

"Well," said Gabriel as he cast his gaze at Uriel who busied himself by throwing stones at the quad flagpoles, "he did let someone else back into the Kingdom."

"True, true."

"Not even Metatron knows all of Yahweh's thoughts," the spirit of truth reminded Raphael. "If He wants Christophe, then Christophe it will be."

"And the fallen one?"

"What choice does he have?"

"It's the way of things," Raphael concluded.

"There's still the matter of the test," said Gabriel.

All the angels on the rooftop concurred.

"I had a dream," Christophe was speaking.

"Sorry," Talbott said. "My man Dr. King used that one."

"Mel?" Joy leaned across the table. She stopped when her face was only a few inches from Talbott's.

"Yes?" his voice croaked.

"How much of your own brain matter have you destroyed already?"

"I don't...uh..."

"How'd you like me to beat you about the face and neck so hard," Joy went on, "that you end up living the rest of your days in a coma?"

"Jimmy," said Talbott, "how can you stand this she-demon?"

"Tell us about your dream," Joy leaned against Christophe.

"Someone came to me," Christophe began, "and told me that the devil was vacating his post. The stranger who told me this news didn't give a reason why the devil decided to do it. He went on at length about everything that would and would not happen as a result of the fallen angel's decision."

Joy and Talbott stared at him as he continued relating his dream to them. Both knew that Christophe wasn't the only one subject to strange dreams.

Talbott had known Christophe since they were children. He always knew his best friend had a dark mysterious side. There were moments during the course of their friendship when Talbott experienced the eerie feeling that Christophe was less human and more ethereal somehow. Talbott could not recall a time when his friend showed his anger. Even when Christophe and his mother had arguments at home, and Talbott had witnessed plenty of them, Christophe resorted first to sarcasm rather than raise his voice. Both young men shared secrets the way friends do. Talbott suspected that Christophe suffered depressive bouts from time to time. The fits came and went, but never once did Talbott ever see Christophe shed a tear over the thoughts that coursed through his mind. With Christophe it wasn't so much that he didn't

138

want to live his life. Talbott was convinced that his friend harbored no suicidal tendencies. It was more like Christophe fully understood the physical reality around him, that the face he saw in the mirror every day was only one aspect of a many-faceted existence, and that he had been waiting for something more his whole life.

Joy looked up at the campus center roof. In her mind she went over the content of her recent dreams. She was unable to recall the last time she remembered her dreams with such vivid detail. Some mornings she woke up wondering whether she was living a multitude of lives in separate but parallel realities. More and more now she wondered if Christophe didn't feel the same as she did. Joy crossed her arms as she continued to study the rooftop edge. She shivered at the notion that the man she had become intimately involved with was slowly withdrawing from the world. It was something new to her. Until then it had been her experience to witness young men lose their grip on reality and act out their frustrations. With Christophe it was different. She didn't know how to handle it. Joy continued to stare at the campus center. Something shimmered at the edge of the roof for a brief moment.

"Impossible," Talbott spoke up first.

"Did you see it?" Joy asked.

Talbott looked at her. "See what?"

"Never mind."

"Why do you think it's impossible?" Christophe asked.

"How much of 'Paradise Lost' did you read over the summer?" Talbott wanted to know.

"Mel," Joy said as she slapped his arm.

"Forget it," said Christophe. "It was just a stupid dream."

"No, you're wrong," Joy argued. "Think of the consequences of such a thing."

"Like what?" Talbott's sarcasm cut deep.

"If you believed the devil was responsible for all the ills of the world," she said, "and he suddenly was out of the picture, then we would be held accountable for our own actions."

"We already are."

"To a degree, sure," said Joy. "But if there's grace in the world then there must be a propensity toward sin."

139

"Granted," Talbott said as he rubbed his hands together. He was a self-proclaimed agnostic, despite his mother's plans to make him a model Catholic, and he was always ready for a fight when it came to matters of faith. "But if the devil no longer exists then where does evil come from? Maybe God isn't dead. Maybe He's just misunderstood."

"What do you think?" Joy turned to Christophe.

"I told you already," he replied. "It was a stupid dream."

"Sure," she said. "Come on, honey. There have been many mystics who have visions in their dreams."

"Name one," he said. Then, he added, "I'm no mystic. And in my dream no one said anything about evil."

"No way," Talbott picked up the notebook he had armed himself with a few minutes beforehand. "The whole thing is absurd."

"What's absurd?" Joy asked.

"It goes against the grain."

"What grain would that be, Mel?"

"Say for a moment that things are as the Christian church tells us," he said. "In that scope it could never happen. What's the point of Heaven if there's no Hell to fear?"

"Maybe there is no suffering," Joy offered.

"And maybe this is all bullshit because there's no God anyway," Talbott argued. "Anyone with half a brain, a shred of intellect, can see through the—"

"Who said anything about Hell?" Christophe asked.

"What's that?" Talbott waved his notebook at a passing bee.

"Hell," he repeated. "I never said anything about Hell closing up shop."

"I suppose next you'll be telling me—"

"Drop it, Mel," said Joy. She looked up at the roof again.

"She's onto us," Raphael announced.

"Don't be ridiculous," Gabriel told him. She's a human being.

"It's happened before."

"In third-world countries where people are starving," said Gabriel. "This is America. These people are too self-centered and well fed to see us."

Raphael shrugged, letting the matter drop.

140

"I suppose," Talbott pursued his next point, "you think that matter is dependent on antimatter? That one doesn't need the other in order to define itself?"

"You're talking about the physical reality of our universe," Joy remarked. "There are different rules that govern all things spiritual."

"So what's the push here?" Talbott demanded. "You're saying that physics doesn't permeate everything?"

"It's different in other realms," she told him.

"You can't be serious."

"I am that and more."

"An English major should stick to what he or she knows," Talbott advised her. "Don't pretend to understand the workings of science."

"Mel," said Christophe, "lighten up."

"We're not talking about that," Joy ignored him, her sights focused on Talbott. "We're talking about the devil's influence. Without him in Hell that would leave us to sin on our own. No temptation. Get it? Just us humans left to our own devices."

"Dreamer," said Talbott. "Go read some more William Blake."

"Blake's got nothing to do with this," she said.

"Without darkness there can be no light," Talbott pontificated now. "Jimmy said that the devil is vacating his position. Now, I'm hardly the mystic stock, but to me that sounds like Hell will still be there."

"He knows too much," Uriel said to Gabriel. "What will it be? Lightning? A little fire from Heaven? A meteorite? A bath of acid rain?"

"No, Uriel, let him be," Gabriel warned. "The buffoon must remain alive."

Uriel rolled his golden eyes. Then he retreated into the ranks.

Talbott jumped to his feet. He gathered up his books and shoved them into his knapsack.

"Shit," he said, "I'm late for class."

"Jimmy," Joy said. She snapped her fingers in front of his face. "Come on, honey. We're going to be late too."

141

"You go," he said, coming out of his trance. "I don't feel like it."

"Don't start ditching classes now," she begged him. "It's too early in the semester."

"Too late, you mean," he said and grinned. "Take decent notes so I can copy them."

"You ass," Joy said. "You're really ditching class?"

"As we speak."

"You owe me," she said. Joy stood up and hitched her knapsack over one shoulder. "Now give me a kiss."

After Joy and Talbott went their separate ways Christophe looked north. Beyond the campus gymnasium loomed the Benjamin Franklin Bridge. He gathered up his own knapsack and headed off in that direction.

Christophe didn't know that Longinus, the campus security guard, followed several yards behind him. Closing the gap between the two men was a host of angels eager to see Christophe perform a leap of faith.

Chapter Eighteen

In the most comfortable beds inside the humblest homes in quiet neighborhoods all across America the most horrid dreams occur. Being immortal didn't make one immune to such experiences.

Gaius Cassius Longinus awoke in a cold sweat. It was early morning, and images of brutish women clung to the fading dreamscape in his mind.

Lately, he dreamt of strong women who not just ran with wolves but left the canids in their dust. In each chimerical landscape Longinus felt his life threatened. One night he ran helter-skelter through the trees that covered Mount Cithaeron. Women pranced naked, screamed and sang psalms of praise to Bacchus. Longinus slowed his flight long enough to glimpse Pentheus the Theban king. The Roman tried to warn him. As dreams go Longinus discovered that every time he opened his mouth his voice failed him.

"I will be the first to strike the wild beast!" a shrill cry filled the woods.

Pentheus' mother claimed the kill, mistaking her son in her enraged ecstasy for a fat pig.

Longinus watched as the king concealed himself in the hollow of a dead tree. Poor Pentheus, he thought. The naïve king never knew what hit him when his mother attacked him. Pentheus was torn to pieces.

The bacchanalia of femme fatales gathered strength. Longinus witnessed several women devour chunks of the dead king's body. Then Pentheus' mother Agave, her box-shaped face twisted with kill-rage, set her sights on the Roman. Longinus hid behind a tree, frozen with fear. With animal swiftness Agave set upon him.

In another dream Longinus saw the cult of Cybele copulate while the Great Mother looked on with quiet satisfaction. Longinus' presence in the secluded grove where the cult met threw off the rhythm of the all-female orgy. They sniffed his male presence long before they saw him. When the Great Mother learned of the intruder she ordered her lions to attack. Longinus was brought down as he ran deeper into the never-ending woodlands that made up that nightmarish landscape.

On another night the Roman was present for the stoning of Mary Magdalene. In real life he had heard stories of the epileptic whore turned bride of the Nazarene. In his dream she turned out to be as ferocious as the other women he had encountered. Longinus stood in the crowd at Mary Magdalene's stoning. Someone handed him a rock. Even when the whore ridiculed him, calling him weak and impotent, he could not bring himself to cast the stone.

Another dream dropped Longinus into a labyrinth of immense proportions. When he first started his journey through that structure he felt sunlight on his back. But as he twisted through the many corridors of that maze the day faded into night. When he at last emerged from the labyrinth bright stars shone in the dark sky. Longinus found himself in a forest much like the others he had already dreamt about. A high wind blew through the tops of tall fir trees. The Roman was made delirious by hunger and fatigue. What he wanted more than food and rest was to meet up with someone, anyone who would show him that there was a way out of the forest.

Just when Longinus felt as if he would collapse a black elf jumped out from behind a tree. Her face was brown like the earth, and her eyes looked like two pieces of round coal. When she smiled at the weary traveler Longinus saw her rotted green teeth that reminded him of olives.

The little elf cast a handful of runes at the Roman's feet. An ill feeling consumed Longinus. He stood motionless, waiting for a gang of elves to jump him. The dark elf told him

144

that horrible misfortune was inescapable. All that he had wished for, she read the message from her runes, would never be. All that was he never wanted in the first place.

"There's only one way out of this," she told him. The elf produced a pair of bikini briefs constructed of wood, metal and leather. "Put these on."

Longinus remained still.

"Don't look at me like that," the elf said, aware of his scrupulous stare. "You remember Skidbladnir don't you?"

Longinus confessed ignorance. Norse mythology was of no interest to him given the curse he lived with. He had discovered early on in immortality that lesser gods than Yahweh could not cure his affliction.

"How about Thor's hammer?" the elf persisted.

Longinus nodded. He had heard of that one.

"You don't think a lowly spirit like me would steer the god of thunder wrong, do you?" she twirled the briefs on her finger.

There was a hint of mischief in her smile. Longinus took the briefs from her.

"Go on," she said.

No sooner had the Roman put on the contraption he felt a sharp pain in his groin. He woke up screaming.

The small bedroom where he slept was bright with morning light. Outside, someone honked a car horn. Longinus heard the sound through an open window.

"Guy!" a woman shouted. Her voice was deep and raspy.

Longinus jumped out of bed. Looking out the window he saw Margie Schlitz, a fellow Rutgers campus security guard leaning out of her 1976 Chevy Impala. Her ruddy complexion was visible from the second floor where Longinus' apartment was situated. When he first met Margie her permanently bloodshot eyes scared him. The woman's nose was splayed across her face. The Roman wondered about that. If ever he had seen a boxer's nose it was Margie's. One day, he promised himself, he would work up the courage to ask about the altercation that produced such a wound. Whoever it was that punched Margie hard enough to ruin her nose knew what he or she was doing. Still, whenever he looked dead-on at his

145

fellow worker Longinus couldn't help equating Margie Schlitz's face with a sack of wet grain.

"Come on!" Margie beckoned him. "We're going to be late!"

Minutes later, Longinus exited the apartment building and climbed into Margie's boat on wheels. Raindrops dotted the windshield. The car's interior reeked of stale whiskey, fresh cigarettes and recent sexual conquest.

"Good morning, Margie," Longinus said, and yawned.

"Look sharp, Guy," she told him. "Rumor has it that some students are staging a demonstration today."

Margie kept her left hand on the steering wheel as her right hand gripped a long black nightstick. She rubbed the brutal instrument against her meaty thighs. Her black skirt revealed more leg than Longinus cared to see.

"Get this," she said. "The students are accusing the security force of brutalization tactics."

"You don't say," came his reply as he recalled an isolated incident he was involved in recently. Then, "It won't amount to anything."

"Listen, Guy," Margie slammed the Impala into drive, "lately your indifference has contributed to the substandard quality of campus security. I'm telling you this because you're my friend. Ok? Attitude is contagious. And yours is hardly worth catching. Sergeant Montrose mentioned charges of insubordination, failure to follow procedure—"

"Montrose is a moron."

"That's your opinion," she said, "and you're allowed to have one. That's what makes America so great."

"Freedom of speech?"

"Exactly."

"Like those kids today?"

"That's different," Margie stepped down on the gas pedal. "No one wants any snot-nosed peacenik bleeding his heart on campus. My sources tell me they want to turn this into a human rights issue. Fuck that fucking Amnesty International. Oh boy, don't get me started."

"I won't," said Longinus.

146

"Those pot-smoking scumbags," she went on, "with their patchouli-drenched, vegetarian bodies don't have the right to expect protection from us and then question the manner by which we keep order. You want to know something? It makes me all sick inside. Anyway you cut it those faggot-ass frat boys had what was coming. Besides, guys like that would as soon spit on those neo-hippies than ask for their help—"

"Margie," he cut her off. The memory of the incident was fresh in his mind. "I think we instigated that whole scene."

"That's nonsense, Guy," she argued as she sped through the quiet streets of Mount Ephraim. "They provoked us. Get your story straight. A hostile force outnumbered us. We were perfectly within our rights."

"All those boys did was flick beer bottle caps from the porch of their frat house," said the Roman.

"Bodily harm," Margie countered. "We could have been blinded."

"I don't see it that way."

"Guy baby," Margie continued to press down on the gas pedal. The Impala sped through a stop sign and past a school. "It's us against them. This is how it always starts. Some little incident is blown out of proportion. When you become a college student you give up certain inalienable rights. It's just like when you join the military—"

"I don't think it works the same way," Longinus said.

"It does," she said. Margie slammed on the brakes to avoid a pack of schoolchildren crossing the road. The Impala fishtailed around the terrified boys and girls. "Students don't count, Guy," she announced. "Like soldiers they are at best second-class citizens."

Longinus gripped the dashboard with two hands. Crushed beer cans and empty half-pint whiskey bottles slid out from beneath the passenger seat.

"You should take it easy," he warned her. "The roads are slick. You might live longer."

Margie Schlitz straightened out her vehicle. Then she resumed the speed she'd been travelling when she lost control.

"Slow down, Margie," said Longinus in a calm voice. He hated daredevils. At times humans made him sick. They didn't

147

know how fragile and fleeting their lives were. "You're going to get into an accident."

"Slow down?" Margie looked at him as if he'd just spoken Aramaic or some other dead language. "Fuck that noise. I don't want to miss all the action.

Chapter Nineteen

"Jimmy," Agnes called from the bottom of the stairs. "What are you doing?"

Christophe didn't answer. Agnes waited. Then she started up the stairs.

Agnes found Christophe kneeling in front of the air conditioner. It had been another in a series of long nights at The Tide. Agnes wasn't in the mood for games. Lately she had been worried about her son. His behavior was odd. Christophe didn't go out of the house much anymore. Agnes worried about that. It used to be that her son couldn't stand being under the same roof with her. She stood behind him now and listened as Christophe mumbled to the air conditioner. Agnes wondered how long it would take her son to realize she was in the room with him. She remembered something Darius Algernon had said to her.

It happened a few nights after Agnes and Algernon bedded down together at the Admiral Wilson Motel & Honeymoon Suites. Algernon entered The Tide alone. He abused customers and staff alike, making fun of them with the kind of coy arrogance that intellectually inferior types mistook for good-heartedness, flirted with Mary and Rosemarie as he spouted off perverse acts that bordered on the grotesque and ordered three shots of bourbon that he downed one after the other. Then he took Agnes in his arms and whisked her into a dark corner of the nightclub. There Algernon's demeanor changed. He sat her down at a table. Agnes soon forgot

149

Algernon's antics when he had first entered the club; overwhelmed she was by the sincerity he exuded when he spoke to her.

"How's your son?" he looked into her eyes.

Agnes didn't recall mentioning that she had a son.

Algernon went on at length about time, matter and space. He talked about human life and what it meant with regard to the soul. Agnes remained silent through it all. Algernon's soliloquy touched on Heaven and Hell, offering several ideas that Agnes found rather confusing. Paradise and the Abyss as different aspects of the same place? Agnes didn't buy it.

"Anyway," he concluded, "take care of your son."

"Ok, sure," she responded, feeling slighted by the knowledge he possessed concerning a matter she wasn't quite sure she wanted to share with him.

"His purpose will soon be revealed," Algernon added.

Agnes stood up and walked away.

"Jimmy," she said, frustrated. "Did you hear me?"

"I'm listening," Christophe answered.

"Good."

"To the voices," he told her. "Do you hear them? Aren't they beautiful?"

Agnes stole a glance around her son's room. There were no signs of drug paraphernalia.

Algernon's words echoed in her head. "Jimmy," she said, "come on, baby. Go to bed. You have class tomorrow."

Agnes took him by the arm. Christophe offered no resistance when she helped him to his feet. His body felt incredibly light to her. Agnes stood by Christophe's bed after she laid him down. She remained there until she was certain he had fallen asleep.

A glass of red wine put her mind at ease. The house was quiet. Agnes' thoughts drifted.

"Damn you, Darius," she mumbled.

An hour later Agnes lifted her head from the kitchen table. She finished off the wine in her glass and retreated to her bedroom. After she shed her clothes Agnes crawled into bed.

"Agnes," a voice called out in the dark.

150

Agnes knew that the voice was too close to be part of some dream. Someone was in the room with her. The two strong hands that gripped her shoulders confirmed her fear. Agnes didn't scream, however. She recognized the face that loomed a few inches from her own.

"Don't act like you weren't expecting me," Algernon said. "We have to talk."

"How did you get into my house?" Agnes demanded.

"Agnes, really," he dismissed her question. He waved his left hand as he laughed. "I'm the devil, for God's sake."

"You want to know what I think?"

"Please," said Algernon, "indulge me."

"I think you're a bullshit artist," Agnes announced. "I think you get off on fucking with people's heads."

"Bravo," he congratulated her. "You hit it on the head, I think. However, I am looking to reshape my image. I'd like to go back to the old me."

"How dare you break into my house, you sick bastard," she said. "You honestly expect me to believe you are the devil?"

"You forgot our trip to my fair city?"

"That was a dream."

"Was it?"

"You've committed a crime, Darius. You've gone too far."

"No I haven't," he said. "But don't let me stop you. Go ahead. Call the police. I'm sure that when they arrive they will be convinced that we're just two old lovers having a little quarrel. You know as well as I do how much the police hate domestic calls."

"Keep your voice down," said Agnes. "My son's upstairs."

"Splendid," Algernon said. "But I'd rather meet him when the time is right."

"I think I'll take your advice," she said. "Hand me my phone."

"9-1-1, that's the number," he picked up the receiver on the nightstand and handed it to her. "In case you're too drunk to remember."

"Smart-ass," she said. "We'll see how all your lies stand up when the police show up."

151

"The law was invented because of my lies," said Algernon. "That goes for every civilization in every time period."

"What do you want?" Agnes sat up against the headboard.

"While we were in that seedy hotel that night," he told her, "you agreed to be my slave."

"Whore," she corrected him. "I told you I'd be your whore. And if my memory serves me—"

"You said you'd do my bidding."

"That was different," Agnes blushed as she let her bed sheet slip from her chest.

"Never mind," Algernon said. "You made an agreement that night."

"Did not."

"Yes," his voice saturated the darkness, "you did."

"Darius," she said softly. She reached out and placed one hand on his thigh. "What do you really want?"

"I want what you promised."

Agnes moved closer to him. Her bare breasts brushed against his arm.

"Agnes," said Algernon, "not now."

"Come on," she purred. "I want it."

"You do remember what you promised, don't you?" he said as Agnes gripped his crotch.

"Why didn't you choose Mary or Rosemarie?" Agnes whispered. She drew her hand away.

"Because they don't have what you've got."

"Darius, you flatter me."

"I'm talking about your son!" the room shook as he shouted. Algernon despised cheap theatrics, he always had since the fall. He considered such antics the mark of a lesser evil. Still, he needed Agnes' undivided attention.

Agnes smelled the sulfurous stench that filled the room as Algernon stood. When he took the shape she had known him from in her dreams Agnes squeezed her eyes shut. Her bed bounced up and down. Algernon's cloven hooves struck the floor. Agnes cried as she tried to remember a prayer, any prayer that might save her.

152

Chapter Twenty

"Your boss called today," Agnes announced when Jimmy Christophe sat down at the breakfast table. "He said you never made it to work yesterday."

Christophe pondered the green, purple and blue hues that swirled on the surface of the coffee within the cup before him. When he looked up at his mother he started at the sight of the smeared mascara that bordered Agnes' bloodshot eyes.

"He said you missed work three times in the last two weeks," Agnes told him. "No phone calls, no explanation."

"He's right for once," Christophe said of his boss. "So what?"

"He left a message."

"Let me guess."

"You're fired."

"I told you to let me guess."

"Jimmy," Agnes said, "this isn't a game."

"I know."

Agnes grimaced.

Christophe saw the look in her eyes. "I hated that job anyway."

"Sometimes," she said, "I think you inherited your father's best traits."

"What's that supposed to mean?"

"You're just like him," said Agnes. "Don't be so stupid. It doesn't matter why you were fired from your job. The point is you're finished. On the bum. Get it?"

153

Christophe examined the cheese omelet his mother had prepared for him. The egg and cheese were saturated with grease.

"You're going to come down on me for being out of work?" he asked.

"Jimmy," Agnes said, "you lost a job that pays ten bucks an hour—"

"Eleven bucks an hour," he reminded her. "But telemarketing is not all that it's cracked up to be."

"Not many college students make that kind of money."

"When was the last time you had a job?"

"Don't start, Jimmy."

"Don't worry," he said. "I have more important things to do."

"Like what?"

"Things that matter more than work."

"What could be more important than working?" Agnes demanded. "I think it's imperative that you work while you are going to school."

"Look who's talking," Christophe pushed his chair back from the table.

"You know I can't work with my back the way it is," she said. Her face reddened with anger. "I don't have time to explain myself to you. I have to get ready—"

"The Tide's open this early?"

"You're always so quick with the smart remarks," Agnes said.

"Sorry."

"Don't look for pity where there is none," she told him. "You find another job, young man, or you will be out on the street."

"I can't."

"What's this I'm hearing!" Agnes shouted. "Did you develop some handicap overnight? Explain this to me!"

"I have a higher purpose," he said.

"Oh? Like what?"

"They won't tell me," Christophe revealed. "Not yet."

"Does Talbott have anything to do with this?"

"No, he does not."

154

"Has he gotten you into drugs?"

"No."

"You are aware that his parents dripped acid—"

"Dropped acid," said Christophe. "People drop acid, mother."

"The point I'm making," Agnes went on, "is that back in the sixties the Talbotts did more acid than most folks thought was humanly possible. Goddamned deadheads! Beatnik freakniks, that's what they were!"

"Talbott has nothing to do with it," he assured her. Then, "nor do Mel's parents."

"That remains to be seen."

"Do you remember the dream I told you about?"

"Which one? You've told me about so many dreams lately."

"The one about the devil."

"Sure I do," Agnes lit a cigarette. She tried hard not to think about Darius Algernon. "What about it?"

"It's confusing," he said, after some consideration. "But I think something major is about to happen."

"Something major is you finding another job," Agnes proclaimed.

"I feel like God is trying to tell me something," Christophe ignored her proclamation. "But the way dreams go you never can tell."

"Oh God's telling you something," she said. "He's saying 'James Michael Christophe, find a job before your mother kicks you out'. It's very clear to me."

"I'm serious about this."

"So am I, honey. Besides, they're just dreams."

"Prophets had dreams."

"Jimmy, you're no prophet," Agnes said. "If you were you would be just as crazy as those Old Testament headcases like John the Baptist—"

"The Baptist was a figure in the New Testament," Christophe told her.

"Don't correct me," she warned him. Then, "Moses, for example. Since you're such a stickler for accuracy. Honestly, a burning bush? If you murdered someone and fled into the desert you'd hear voices, too—"

155

"Mother, wait."

"Voices from the most peculiar places," she continued. Agnes then spoke in a voice that more resembled Gregory Peck's Atticus Finch than it did God's, "Look upon me. I am a burning bush. Isn't that peculiar? I must be the Lord Almighty. I can make a bush burn."

"That's—"

"Not true, I know," said Agnes. "That's another point I'm trying to make. Of course, if old Moses had come across an ice-covered bush in the hot desert that spoke to him then I might be persuaded."

"Will you hear me out?"

"Not another word," she held up her hands. "You know how upset I get talking about religion."

"I'm not talking about that."

"Go to school today," Agnes told him. "Then do yourself a favor this afternoon and go get another job."

She saw the quiet despair in Christophe's eyes. She wanted to reach out and touch him, to let him know that despite all their differences he was still her flesh and blood. But Agnes knew that making any motherly, protective gesture now would only appear foreign and forced. Worse, if she put a name to Christophe's insanity, if Agnes acknowledged that he was indeed losing his grip on reality, she feared she might hasten his descent into madness.

Sadness, Agnes thought as she cast a glance at Christophe that was meant to show pity, was being surrounded by countless people, but still feeling utterly alone and lost in the world.

156

Part Three: Councils, Gossip, & Invisibility

Chapter Twenty-one

"Are you out of your mind!?" Agnes shrieked the moment her son opened his eyes. "What's wrong with you?"

Christophe wished that he had never come out of the quiet, dark place where he had found peace. With each passing second now he realized that the test he had performed had not been enough. Before making the leap of faith Christophe remembered reading something about angels being charged with folly. The heavenly messengers, he discovered, often toyed with people for sheer entertainment. He hoped that his near-fatal test of faith wasn't for entertainment's sake alone.

"You've pulled some stupid stunts in your time," Agnes scolded him, "but this one takes the cake. What were you trying to do? Kill yourself?"

Agnes took the opportunity to remind Christophe of everything he had ever done that bordered on stupidity. What she failed to realize, during her rant, was that the dangerous acts Christophe had performed over the years were all attempts to gain attention.

"For all intents and purposes," she said, "you should have been dead a long time ago."

Christophe doubted his mother really felt that way. The thought crossed his mind that he wasn't alive at all during that

157

moment, that somehow he had failed the ethereal messengers who coaxed him into his current predicament and as a result was sentenced to a private Hell where he would spend an eternity listening to Agnes chastise him. He was paralyzed by that fear as the seconds passed. Then, to his relief, Christophe saw a doctor and a nurse enter the room.

The nurse set about taking Christophe's vital signs while the doctor spoke to Agnes in hushed tones. Then the doctor examined Christophe's eyes with a penlight, pressed her fingers with clinical certainty against various parts of his body and listened with her stethoscope to Christophe's faint heartbeat.

As the examination progressed the nurse began looking pale. Christophe's withered condition did not assuage the nurse's uneasiness. The young man's face turned a few shades shy of white. The doctor suggested to the nurse that he go out into the hall and collect himself. The nurse exited the room and never returned.

The minutes ticked by, and the doctor's excitation increased. She had seen many physical conditions and afflictions in her career, but none came close to what she saw happening to Christophe. For lack of a better term the doctor called it transubstantiation, the act of changing from one substance into another. The doctor knew the connotations surrounding such a claim, and for that reason she kept her observations to herself. She wanted to get to the truth of the phenomenon unfolding before her. Her diagnosis for Christophe wasn't good, at least not as it pertained to his human physical condition. The doctor wondered if the young man's mother was aware of what was happening. If she was able to maintain Christophe for a little longer, to prove to the world that what was happening inside room 545 at Lady of Lourdes Hospital was real, then there was no doubt the research grants would come pouring in. There would be books to write and publish, interviews in and out of the scientific community and international acclaim. Her ambition to become the next household name, the storyteller of a modern-day miracle, was short-lived, however. For even as the doctor plotted her fame regarding the changing Christophe there

158

were powerful entities that had already laid claim to the young man.

"This is a most interesting case," the doctor announced. "With your permission, Jimmy, I would like to run a few tests. I have a friend who might be interested in what's going on here. He specializes in what you might call paranormal anthropology. Granted, the field is young and purely theoretical. I'd like to have my colleague conduct an examination—"

"Not a prayer, doc," Agnes snapped. "Paranormal anthropology. Who ever heard of such a thing?"

"Ms. Christophe," the doctor said. "There are many people who believe the human body and spirit are still evolving. I think Jimmy might benefit—"

"You're not running any tests," said Christophe. "I want to get out of here, right now."

"Shut up, Jimmy," Agnes said. "Let me talk here."

"Ms. Christophe," the doctor pleaded. "Your son—"

"Has recently tried to kill himself."

"Mother," said Christophe, "I didn't try to kill myself. If you would just hear me out. I'm sure you would—"

"Stay out of this, Jimmy," said Agnes. To the doctor she warned, "I'm pissed off, doc. Will you please tell me what's going on?"

"Rainey," the doctor told her.

"Excuse me?"

"Dr. Tina Rainey," she said. "That's my name. You may call me Dr. Rainey."

"Fine, Dr. Rainey," Agnes said. "Now would you kindly explain to me why my son tried to jump off the Ben Franklin Bridge?"

"Why? That I cannot answer. Perhaps one of my psychologist colleagues might be able to, but let's not get ahead of ourselves."

"I want what's best for my son."

"As long as Jimmy is in the hospital's care," Dr. Rainey said, "there are rules governing a patient's well-being. I cannot allow you to subject Jimmy to any amount of stress. I don't care how angry you are."

159

"Both of you," said Christophe, "bickering like little girls. Neither of you understands what's at stake here."

"Jimmy, for the love of God," said Agnes. "Don't start with all that fire and brimstone shit."

"Ms. Christophe," the doctor said, "I'm warning you."

"Dr. Rainey," she stepped close to her. "Do you have a son?"

"No, I don't."

"Then you wouldn't have any idea of what I'm going through right now."

"I suppose you are correct," the doctor conceded. "You should be thankful Jimmy's in fairly good shape. You're lucky to have him here."

"Not for long," Christophe said.

"I just want to know why!" Agnes turned and screamed at her son.

"I'll give you a few minutes alone," Dr. Rainey said. "Jimmy, if you need me I'll be right outside. Ms. Christophe, if there are any more problems from you I'll have hospital security remove you from the building. Do I make myself clear?"

"Don't let the door hit you in the ass," Agnes said.

"Your selfish insolence," said the doctor, "will only jeopardize your son's condition. Think about that before you lash out again."

Satisfied that her point was made, Dr. Rainey exited the room.

"So," Christophe said when the doctor was gone, "I'm alive after all."

Agnes pulled a handkerchief from her pocketbook. She removed the wet mascara from her cheeks and chin. Her body shook as she fought back more tears, struggling to find a way to express how she truly felt.

"Yes," she said, "you're alive."

Christophe looked at the ceiling. In the cracks that lined the surface there he saw faces of angels looking back at him.

"It's begun," he announced.

"What's begun?" Agnes asked. "You're not making any sense."

160

"I tried to tell you a few weeks ago. You didn't listen."

"Damn it, Jimmy," she stomped her foot. "A woman my age doesn't need this shit."

"Besides," Christophe ignored her, "they told me there would be many who wouldn't understand. They said people would act as if nothing's changed—"

"What's to understand?"

"For you?" Christophe stared at her. "Nothing, it seems."

"I spoke to Joy and Mel today. They told me you haven't been to class in almost three weeks."

"I had work to do."

"Work? What work? You never found another job."

"How are Joy and Mel?"

"They wanted to see you," she told him, "but they aren't allowed up here yet."

"How long was I unconscious?"

"You came to briefly after you were pulled out of the water," said Agnes. "Dr. Rainey believes there may be irreversible brain damage. It's a miracle you're not a vegetable."

"So it seems."

"Dr. Rainey said that when the human brain is deprived of carbon dioxide—"

"Oxygen."

"What?"

Deprived of oxygen," said Christophe. "I think Dr. Rainey was talking about oxygen and the brain."

"Whatever," Agnes flapped her handkerchief. "The paramedics told the emergency room staff that a campus security guard followed you—"

"How long was I out?"

"Three days," she answered. Agnes pulled a chair close to the bed and sat down. "If you needed help why didn't you tell me?"

"I did," he said. "You ignored me."

"That's a hell of a thing to say," Agnes wiped her eyes. "Jesus, Jimmy. What could I have done? My son quits college, hangs around campus like some derelict drop-out and begins preaching nonsense about dreams and the apocalypse—"

"There isn't going to be an apocalypse," Christophe said.

161

"I'm just repeating what Joy and Mel told me," she said. "And then, as if acting like some street corner preacher, you go ahead and jump off the Ben Franklin Bridge.

"Face it, Jimmy," she went on, "you have some serious problems. It's all beyond me now. You need professional help."

"I don't need anyone's help. I need people to hear my message."

"You may believe that," said Agnes, "but before this is all over I'm going to see to it that you go visit a shrink."

"I don't doubt you," Christophe said. "But it won't do any good."

"Let the shrink determine that."

"It's useless."

"What makes you say that?" she asked. "You don't know. It might do you some good."

"The only thing that matters is the test," he said. I have to know if I've proved myself worthy."

"What test?" Agnes slammed her fists down on the bed.

The door opened. Dr. Rainey stepped into the room.

"Is everything ok?" she asked.

Christophe nodded.

Dr. Rainey gave Agnes a look. Then she stepped back into the hallway.

Agnes gathered her coat, her purse and her magazines that she had thumbed through while waiting for Christophe to awake.

"Everything is going to work out," she said, quietly. "The worst is over."

Christophe closed his eyes. Agnes left the room.

"Can you believe it?" said Tarquam to Guabarel as both angels stepped out of the woodwork.

"He did it," Guabarel replied.

The angels stood by the bed while Christophe slept. Soon a third angel joined them.

"How's he look?" Raphael inquired as he approached.

"His body's weak," said Tarquam, "but that's to be expected. He won't need it much longer now."

"That's true," Guabarel agreed.

162

"Everything's going as planned?" Raphael asked.

"So far so good," Tarquam assured him.

"And the Morning Star?"

"His case has been heard," said Guabarel, "and his claim is deemed legitimate. But intelligence says there are many among him who would rather not reform. Those who are against the shining one claim that humility is not an angel's trait."

"Don't sweat it," Raphael advised his heavenly brother. "Opposition can always be easily persuaded."

"You're certain of this?" Tarquam asked.

Raphael praised him. "Gracious autumn spirit, even Gabriel himself asked for forgiveness when he stood outside Heaven's curtain. Has it been that long? Do you no longer remember those days?"

"Only too well, I'm afraid," said Tarquam as he gazed at Christophe's sleeping form. "Only too well."

Chapter Twenty-two

"I thought you were gone for good," Agnes greeted Darius Algernon when she opened her front door.

"I will be," he said, raising the continuous eyebrow that separated his forehead from the rest of his face, "but I wanted to see you one last time."

"What do you want, Darius?" Agnes felt uneasy as she recalled their last meeting.

"Let me in," he said. "I'll only take a few minutes of your time."

Agnes hesitated, then she opened the door wide. She had trouble piecing together the details of when they saw each other last. On that sunny afternoon when Algernon came calling on her for the last time, Agnes no longer believed that she had seen him turn into a grotesque monster in her bedroom. One event that stood out in her mind she would never forget. It was an unspeakable act. And she doubted she would forget it any time soon.

"Something to drink?" she asked, following him into the living room.

"No thanks," he told her.

Agnes sat down beside Algernon on the sofa. The living room was decorated with mementos of her son that had stayed tucked away in the basement. There were pictures in new frames, awards and certificates from various school functions and artwork that Christophe had rendered when he was a little boy. Agnes remained still as Algernon stood and studied the framed photographs.

"He's handsome," Algernon remarked.

"Jimmy's in pain," said Agnes.

"Not for long."

"Darius, please. You know I don't like it when you get all weird on me."

"My apologies."

"Look, I can be your friend, lover or whatever you want," she said. "I'll even French kiss your ass—"

"Anus," Algernon quipped. "Say it after me. A-nus. Come on—"

"Darius don't be like that," Agnes felt sick to her stomach. "What can I say or do to make you realize how much I hate when you talk about my son as if you've known him for so long."

"I think I'll take that drink now."

Agnes left the living room and went into the kitchen. She took two glasses from the cupboard. The only liquor she had in the house was an old bottle of Southern Comfort. She poured two double shots straight and returned to the living room.

Algernon stood in front of the fireplace mantle. He held a marble crucifix, shifting the object from one hand to the other as if determining the weight of it.

"I thought you didn't believe in God," he said.

"I don't," Agnes handed him a glass. "A long time ago I bought that piece in Mexico—"

"On your honeymoon," Algernon said. "The artist was an old blind man. I was there."

"It's the only thing from my marriage I haven't destroyed," she said. "And don't do that."

"Do what?"

"Did Rosemarie tell you about the blind old man?" Agnes asked. "Hell, I probably did and probably don't remember. So, don't act like you were there."

"It's a pity you don't believe."

165

Algernon took a long pull from his drink. He put the crucifix down on the mantle, caressing the tormented face of Christ as he did.

"I came to say good-bye," he announced before he polished off the drink and placed the glass down next to the crucifix. "At any moment I could be called away."

"When will you come back?" Agnes asked.

"With any luck? Never."

Agnes went to the sofa and sat down. She finished her drink off in one take.

"I suppose you do this sort of thing often?" she asked. "You walk into a woman's life, upset the order of things, fill her head with empty promises and then simply walk out? Is that it?"

"Something is happening to your son," said Algernon. He touched the crucifix once more. "Something wonderful."

Agnes leapt to her feet. She cocked her arm back and threw the glass at him.

The tumbler pinwheeled centrifugally before it struck Algernon. A deep long cut formed on his forehead and ran down his nose. Algernon touched the wound.

"Get out of my house!" Agnes scanned the room for other objects to hurl at him. "Get out and don't come back!"

Algernon wiped his left hand over his face. The wound Agnes had caused disappeared, leaving in its wake a space between the man's eyebrows. Algernon offered Agnes a sheepish grin. Then he complied with her wish and disappeared.

166

Chapter Twenty-three

"Mel Talbott!" The raucous barroom din drowned out Joy's cry. She stood up and cupped her hands around her mouth. "Over here, Mel!"

Talbott moved through the crowd like a clean man amidst contagious lepers. The faces that met him appeared hostile and drunk. He did his best not to knock into anyone, but it wasn't easy. Talbott knew that the regular patrons at Tatters Bar swayed like swamp reeds in strong winds when they were loaded. Three times he came face to face with large men who were aged beyond their years by alcohol, cigarettes, demanding wives and uncaring children. Each man cast his gaze on the thin college student. Talbott understood the look. He had seen it many times before that night. The men were all dressed the same. They wore paint-speckled flannel shirts, blue jeans coated with drywall dust and Timberland boots. Talbott discovered early on when he first began frequenting Tatters that the construction worker types were in the majority at Tatters. They fell into two categories as far as he could tell. Those with advanced stages of pattern baldness that wore their remaining hair long in ponytails and those who sported cheap baseball caps. The baseball caps were not Major League merchandise, but rather crude imitations that sported such catchy phrases as "If I'm Not Fighting or Fucking, I'm Fishing" and the ever-popular banner of overweight blue-collar types who frequented Tatters "God's Gift to Women". Every time Talbott set foot into Tatters, passing through the

167

ranks of such men, he was riveted with fear. When he saw Joy he breathed a little easier, sensing that the lowbrows who surrounded him were eyeing her.

"Did you have a hard time getting here?" he sat down on a stool next to Joy.

"No," she answered. "Your directions were right on."

"I would have met you around your way," Talbott offered, "but my mother won't let me take her car too far these days. She thinks I'm at the library."

"Were you in an accident?"

"Plural, I'm afraid," he said. "Some asshole driving a pick-up truck on I-676 started my run of bad luck. The karma scales have been tipped against me ever since. That was last semester. Then a few weeks ago I was involved in a minor collision in the parking lot behind Armitage Hall."

"Anyone I know?"

"Not unless you consort with campus security bull dykes."

Joy patted Talbott's forearm. "Sorry," she said. Then, "Have you been to the hospital?"

"I went this afternoon," he told her. "They moved Jimmy to a semi-private room. He slept the whole time I was there."

"Did you talk to any of the doctors?"

"Everyone there seems so secretive about his condition. How about you?"

"I didn't go today. Work, you know?"

"Only forty more years to go," said Talbott. He made a face and pointed at a pack of cigarettes on the bar next to Joy's drink.

"Go ahead," she said.

"Thanks," he lit a cigarette and passed it to Joy. Then he lit one for himself.

"Did you notice anything odd about Jimmy when you saw him?" Joy exhaled smoke through her nostrils.

"Not really," he recalled the way Christophe looked as if he was on death's doorstep. "No more than anyone else who's attempted to commit suicide."

"Do you think that's true?"

"What you don't know about Jimmy could fill volumes."

168

Talbott signaled the bartender. He ordered two frosted mugs of Budweiser and two shots of Cuervo tequila.

"Purely medicinal," he told Joy. "It's been quite a day."

"Make mine a bourbon," Joy said.

The bartender possessed as much charm as a junkie at a methadone clinic did. He was tall, gaunt and pale. He wore his receding hair long and pulled back in a ponytail. The permanent sneer on his face became more enhanced when he spoke.

"You're not driving mom's car tonight?" he asked Talbott.

"Stop busting my ass, Mark," Talbott said. "Do your job."

The story of Talbott's vehicular bad luck spread through Tatters Bar at terminal velocity. Among the regulars there was a small contingent of Rutgers students who knew Talbott from campus. Once they caught wind of the string of accidents Talbott had been involved in, they leaked the story to Mark the bartender. Not since the tale concerning Gina Borelli, a set of fake deer antlers, a little league dug-out and four members of the Tatters Bar softball team had a story gained as much attention. For most patrons Talbott's motor woes proved more entertaining. The Gina Borelli sexual exploit stories were becoming old hat. And many patrons at the bar found an ironic humor in the fact that Talbott didn't even own the car to which he had caused considerable damage. People felt safe talking about Talbott. Whereas with the Gina Borelli sexual escapades, people were more inclined to feel ill-at-ease as if invoking her name meant acknowledging the strength that motivated such prowess. There was no escaping it. Talbott was the Johnny-come-lately of barroom gossip. Contrary to his protestations, Talbott's fifteen minutes of fame were far from over.

"Here he comes, here comes Speed Racer," Mark sang as he poured the shots. "He's a demon on wheels."

"Your tip diminishes as the seconds pass," Talbott said.

"I guess I'll have to send the kids to Cornell instead of Harvard," Mark set the shot glasses down on the bar.

Four women at the other end of the bar, all of them drunk, overweight and menacing with their hard faces and close-cropped hair, broke into a fit of laughter. They idolized Mark

169

the bartender. The four drunks considered him a luminary on matters of love, sports and money. But the bartender's real strength, his gift, as far as the sodden hefties were concerned, was his comedy craftsmanship. All four women hailed from Collingswood, NJ. Nothing favorable had ever come from that small town of suspicious, backward people. And the four females, like so many residents in their community, rarely set foot beyond town limits because of that stigmatization. Despite the smear that marked them as Collingswood residents, namely their ignorance, the butch women had on occasion ventured to the city of Philadelphia in search of something different (i.e. lipstick urban lesbians). Sadly, their provincialism marked them as dull and half-witted. Gradually they developed a genuine hatred toward the more sophisticated lesbian community in the city. Instead, they attended tractor pulls, drag races and motorcycle rallies with the hope of finding temporary but satisfying liaisons. When there were no 'hunting parties', as the four women referred to the drag races at Atco Speedway and other equally low-brow forms of outdoor entertainment, they found solace at the unassuming Tatters Bar in Westmont, NJ. The idolatry they shared toward the bartender had nothing to do with his being a man. On the contrary, the butchers despised anything with a penis. In Mark they saw the perfect blend of comedic genius and non-invasive asexuality.

"Troglodykes," Talbott doubted the women heard his cry, much less understood the cave-dwelling lesbian reference. His heart seethed with anger.

"Did you hear me?" Joy asked as the four women shared some private joke and elbowed one another with jocular abandon.

"What?"

"Do you think Jimmy will ever make it back to school?"

"That's hard to say."

"You think he needs counseling?"

"Let me have another cigarette."

"Go right ahead," said Joy. "But you didn't answer my question."

170

She handed him the cigarette pack. The bourbon tasted good as it went down. She set the shot glass down on the bar. The liquor didn't quite hit the spot, however. Joy needed to be close to someone.

"Did Jimmy say anything weird to you?" she looked at the Coors clock on the wall.

Talbott drank down his shot of tequila. "No," he said. "I mean, he was always saying weird things. Did you know he believed in aliens?"

"Jimmy believed in many things," she said. "But I'm talking about recently."

"He did mention something about a dream. There was a demon in it."

"That qualifies, don't you think?"

"Don't take it too seriously. He also told me that in the same dream he met St. Peter."

"Well," she said. "That's comforting."

"Agnes swears he's nuts," Talbott said. His eyes focused on Joy's ample cleavage revealed above the undone buttons on her shirt. "Maybe if I paid more attention. I wish there was a way I could have seen it coming."

"Everyone wishes they could play the hero every time someone close to them commits suicide," she said. "But that's not the way life is. Once someone gets it into their head that they want to kill themselves there's nothing we can do to prevent that. Suicidal types will always find a way."

"But I'm his best friend," he argued. "It's not fair."

He looked Joy in the face and added, "do you really believe it was suicide?"

"Attempted," she made the distinction. "He is still alive, after all."

"I suppose there's that to be thankful for," he said.

Joy sipped her beer and studied Talbott's face. In the dim barroom light he looked almost handsome. He reminded her, or his spirit did at least, of the cavalier poets she admired so much. Until that night she had never given Talbott much consideration. She had already made up her mind that she could no longer devote herself to Christophe. One more headcase was sure to break her. True, Talbott's nervous

171

recklessness made her feel uncomfortable. But in him she saw the qualities she admired most in men. Namely, loyalty, compassion, honesty and a certain lack of fortitude that would make manipulating him all the easier. The realization came upon her like an epiphany. Talbott was the man she'd been after all along.

"The whole situation makes me feel hopeless," he was saying while the four lesbians at the end of the bar tossed drink coasters at him. "I'm not sure I can handle this. We're supposed to grow old together, work, find wives, have families, and leave a legacy. I used to kid Jimmy that despite how we felt about ourselves we'd end up in some warm climate living in a retirement community where the uniform du jour consisted of plaid Haggar brand slacks, white belts and white shoes. Now, he's dying in a hospital and he's not twenty-five years old yet. It's not supposed to be like this."

Joy watched his lips as he spoke. If tears form in his eyes, she thought, I'll kiss him right here and now. Watching his mouth, the way his soft lips formed various shapes, she felt driven to experience the company of another kindred lost soul. She felt nervous. For a moment she thought she might cry, listening to him. Instead, she sang.

"Worry," she followed Patsy Cline's lead as the CD played on the jukebox, "why do I make myself...worry?"

"Ah...um," Talbott stammered, not knowing how to react.

"Wonderin'," she looked into his eyes, "what in the world did I do—"

"Joy," he said, "are you listening?"

"Sorry," she grabbed her beer mug and hoisted it into the air. "To happy times."

"He's almost gone," he told her as a tear fell from his eye.

"Hey," one of the female bruisers called from the end of the bar. "Quit your belly-aching over there."

The four heavyweights let rip cacophonous laughter.

"If you really want something to cry about," the taunting lesbian shouted, "look between your legs!"

"Do you want to get out of here?" Joy whispered.

"No," he said. "I don't mind."

172

"Well I do," Joy slid off her barstool and stood in one fluid motion. "Let's go. We're going for a ride."

"Where?"

"What do you care?" she took his hand and kissed his cheek.

A cold rain fell as they exited the bar. Talbott's head was reeling. He was happy Joy decided to drive, but he was reluctant to leave the Renault in the parking lot at Tatters Bar.

"You worry too much," Joy told him as they pulled away in her car.

"Where are we going?" he suddenly realized fifteen minutes into the ride that he was lost.

"The Glassworks," she answered.

Talbott had heard of the place. He'd never been there. When Joy pulled to a stop Talbott was surprised to discover that there was a park situated near the Glassworks.

"You don't mind," Joy told him as she slipped her hand into his as she exited the car.

"No," he gave her hand a squeeze.

"I meant the rain," she squeezed back. Then, as they continued walking through the dark park, she added, "it's not like we're cheating."

Talbott let go of Joy's hand and slipped his arm around her waist. He pulled her close to him when they stopped. They kissed each other while they stood on a gravel path. Rain fell heavily through the trees that surrounded them. Joy broke the kiss first. She pulled Talbott by his shirt and led him to an area where picnic tables stood. Talbott explored Joy's body, touching and rubbing her through her clothes. He felt her hot breath on his neck as his cock hardened. Joy let out a long slow moan when Talbott unsnapped her bra once he had unbuttoned her shirt. Her nipples grew taut as his fingers first caressed and then pinched them. Joy slipped her hand into Talbott's pants. When she felt the girth of his cock she pushed him back against a picnic table. Then she slipped out of her shirt and bra and stood before him in the rain. Talbott felt unsteady on his feet. He stood perfectly still when Joy unfastened the button on his pants and pulled them down. Next, she knelt on the wet ground before him. She teased him

173

a moment or two with her tongue. Afterward, she took the length of his cock into her mouth.

A few minutes later, Talbott muttered, "Incredible."

Joy pressed her body into his, feeling his cock shrink as they kissed.

"Maybe I should put my shirt back on," she suggested, looking around. She stepped back so he could glimpse her breasts once more. "It is cold out, after all."

Talbott saw the look in her eye. He reached out and pulled her to him, taking the shirt away from her. Then he turned her toward the picnic bench.

"Here?" Joy whispered as he wrestled her blue jeans off her legs. She saw his face briefly as he laid kisses across her breasts and worked his way down her stomach. "Yes, right here."

Beyond the cove where the picnic tables were located a lone figure stood in the woods. He sat down on the stump of a dead tree and watched as the couple made love. His golden eyes flashed in the dark when he smiled. At last, he thought. All the pieces have fallen together. When he was satisfied that Joy and Talbott were finished, watching them dress in the rain, he walked soundlessly through the woods. Doorways opened for him, carrying him across time, space and matter until he reached familiar gates. Satan turned away from the gates and cast his glance toward the couple one last time. Silently, he gave the couple his blessing.

Chapter Twenty-four

"Fear not!" Christophe's cry reverberated against the old church. "There is hope! There is an answer!"

He stood on the corner of Cooper Street and Fourth. A few weeks before that morning he had been let out of the hospital. Christophe had made progress with the psychiatrist appointed to him by the hospital administration. He signed up for outpatient therapy, at the behest of Agnes and Dr. Rainey, but he visited the psychiatric care facility near Our Lady of Lourdes only twice. Christophe considered the whole thing to be a sham. He was, after all, wide-awake in every sense of the word. Outpatient clinics like the one recommended to him by Dr. Rainey were for people with serious mental problems. Christophe was, despite outward appearances, as sane as they come. But the mental healthcare professionals he had dealt with thought otherwise. They wanted to put the young man away where he could be observed. Christophe had committed no crime when he leapt from the Benjamin Franklin Bridge. The bridge was open to pedestrian traffic that day.

His decision to forgo counseling made Agnes unhappy. Every other day Dr. Rainey called the house looking for Christophe. It was only the loopholes in the healthcare system that kept Christophe a free man. He wanted nothing to do with the doctor or his mother anymore. In his dreams he saw Dr. Rainey's thin fingers gliding over the keyboard of her computer as she composed notes and outlines pertaining to her experience while she treated him. It sickened Christophe

175

to know that someone might one day exploit him. But he also knew that he lived in a world where rational individuals were persuaded to believe the most ridiculous things. For him it didn't matter that Agnes and Dr. Rainey spoke on the telephone in hushed tones about his "condition". Every day his mother drank herself to sleep. Each night after her shift at the hospital Dr. Rainey locked herself away in her study at home and composed her notes and her outlines. Each one was out of touch with the world. The more he looked around, the more Christophe began to believe that he was the only sane person in the world.

"Listen to me!" his voice grew louder. "Never has there been a greater time to assess ourselves and our role in the Great Design!"

"The kid's lost it," Raphael announced to his angelic brothers as they stood on the church steps.

"Oh," said Gabriel, "he's gone. That much is certain."

"It's a shame he has to lose his mind," Michael added. The chief of the archangels looked on with kind eyes. "He struck me as a bright young man. Cocky and somewhat morose, but bright. Perhaps I should have that talk with him now."

"That won't be necessary," Raphael said and cleared his throat.

He recalled the time Michael had a similar conversation. It was with Mary the mother of Jesus just before her assumption into Heaven. Some of the angels accused his brother of showboating.

"Remember, my brothers," Zophiel, the swiftest of all angels, said, "the cup must be emptied before it can be filled."

A fifth angel hovered over Christophe's head. He held in his hands a scroll that bore angelic script. When he unfurled the banner its message read: LIGHTS ON, NOBODY'S HOME. CAN-SHY OF A SIX-PACK.

His heavenly brothers observed the angel's hijinks and glowered at him. The angel over Christophe's head let go of the scroll. Before it struck the young man on the head the banner burst into flames and disappeared. The mischievous angel commenced flicking Christophe in one ear and then the other with the tips of his wings.

"Uriel stop that," Raphael told him.

"Such cheap tricks," Gabriel commented.

"What is this?" Zophiel added. "Amateur hour?"

176

Uriel ignored his brothers. He flicked Christophe's ears once more. When the young man swatted at the air the angel rose up beyond his reach.

"Uriel," Raphael said, "I'm warning you."

He ignored the angel of the Apocalypse and flicked Christophe's ears again. Then he flew into the sun and vanished.

Christophe looked up. He expected to see a small bird or a large butterfly, but all he saw was the morning sky all blue and indifferent toward him.

"How will you show your God that you deserve a place in his kingdom?" Christophe's cry caused several pedestrians to halt.

"Shut up!" a mailman advised him as he stood across the street. "You lunatic!"

"I can show you how!" Christophe pointed at the postman.

"My ass!"

Two Latino girls dressed in Catholic school uniforms with black leather heels on their feet and gold hoop earrings in their ears approached the street corner preacher. The girls had no idea what the commotion was about, but any excuse to miss the bus to school was good enough for them. They listened with vague interest as Christophe laid out a new fate for the human race.

"I don't hear anything about Jesus," one of the girls said.

Christophe reached out to touch their dark-haired heads.

"You don't need Jesus anymore," he told them.

"You're fucking crazy," the other girl said. "The sisters warned us about demons like you."

The young schoolgirl kicked Christophe in the shin, to emphasize her point, and herded her friends away from him.

"I'm no demon!" Christophe hopped on one foot while rubbing the pain from the shin where he had been kicked. "Wait! There's more!"

He limped to the church steps where he had left his knapsack. He reached into the bag and produced a filthy and mildewed paperback bible.

"Look," Uriel reappeared over Christophe's head. "A visual prop."

"Uriel," Gabriel beckoned, "get down from there."

177

"Hey Raphael," the fire of God ignored Gabriel's call, "how many times does it take for the truth to be rewritten until it turns into a lie?"

"This isn't the time and the place for that," Raphael warned him.

A crowd gathered across the street from the church to watch the spectacle. Courthouse employees, postal workers, city officials, students and a few vagrants made up the group.

"Let it be known that the great book's message is obsolete!" Christophe proclaimed. "The devil has sent word to God, and God's angels have sent word to me! Old Scratch—"

"Praise Yahweh," Michael appeared on the steps. "Raphael, what's going on here?"

"Easy, Michael," the watcher replied. "Everything is under control."

"Control?" the angelic prince shot his brother a look. "He's making a mockery of the situation."

"—has thrown in the towel! Think, people! We are free from the dark angel's influence! Free from sin! Free from fear!"

"Hey moron," a police officer shouted. She gripped the service pistol that hung from her right hip. With her other hand she held the baton that rested against her left hip. "Why don't you move along!"

"It's a free country," was Christophe's reply.

"Go crawl back under your rock," the peace officer suggested. "Don't you know the devil's never going to go away."

"I said it before and I'll say it again," a postal clerk declared. Yellow mustard ringed her lips as she chewed on a soft pretzel. "This is what happens when they shut down the mental institutions. Crazies are allowed to roam the streets."

"Take hold of your destiny," Christophe's voice grew hoarse as he continued to shout. "Find the truth inside yourself. Don't let a book show you the way."

"This guy's more rattled than that street preacher from last year," an elderly judge noted.

"The long-haired guy?" a lawyer asked who stood nearby.

178

"No, the one who wanted to open his own church inside the courthouse," the judge told him.

"The same guy who stepped in front of the train?"

"No, John," the justice said. "That was the guy who went around claiming God had made him invincible. Poor bastard. He never knew what hit him."

"I'm confused, judge," said the lawyer.

"Jesus, John," the judge said, "you don't remember that degenerate who believed that aliens posing as angels helped build the great pyramids?"

"Vaguely," his face clouded as he tried to remember. "Now that you mention it."

"Sure you do," he said, "he was the whack-job who claimed the aliens would return and conduct a tribunal. Some of us would perish, some of us would be taken off into outer space."

"So why build a church inside the courthouse?"

"To be first in line for the tribunal, of course," the judge shook his head. "Christ, John, don't they teach anything in law school nowadays?"

"You know," a court reporter butted in, "I think I know that guy."

"The alien angel preacher?"

"No, your honor," the young man pointed at Christophe.

"You know that bedlamite?"

"Not personally," he qualified himself. "But I have seen him."

"Where?"

"Channel Six News."

"That nut was an anchorman?" the lawyer stood dumbfounded.

"Holy Mary, mother of God," the judge looked as if he might suffer a stroke. He shook his hands in supplication.

"Someone shot a video of that guy jumping off the Benjamin Franklin Bridge," the court reporter said.

"Nonsense," the judge said.

"It's true, your honor," he went on. "A Russian couple, tourists they were, happened to catch the incident as they walked over the bridge from Philadelphia on their way to see the Edgar Allen Poe house here in Camden. They rushed to

179

help the guy but by the time they found their way down to the water other people were already there."

"Remarkable," said the lawyer.

"That's definitely him," the court reporter pointed at Christophe. "They say it's a miracle he survived at all."

"Imbeciles," a voice sounded behind the three men. "Of course he survived by miracle."

The three men turned to face another man dressed in a Rutgers University campus security uniform. Something in the man's eyes—madness, perhaps—dissuaded the three from protesting the Roman's remark.

A crowd of students approached from the Patco High-Speedline station at City Hall. Some laughed; others jeered. The crowd's majority was at an age when, attempting to break the bonds of familial and theological ties, they fashioned themselves as atheists. These were the young men and women at college campuses everywhere who equated higher learning with proof of God's death. Never mind that none among the group emerging from the train station that morning had ever read Friedrich Nietzsche. Hearing Christophe's argument for a new paradigm sparked a nihilistic thread among a few. It didn't take long for peer pressure to do the rest. Each student took turns hurling obscenities at the street corner preacher.

"Loser!" one student shouted.

"Cocksucker!" another emitted in a hoarse cough.

"Fucker of family members and large farm animals!" one lone agitator added. His cry drew the attention of the crowd momentarily. "Sorry," he offered. "But I doubt he would understand my put-down if I rendered it my native Yemen tongue."

The students shrugged it off. They were, after all, members of a growing global community. Yemeni comrades in learning they could accept. Crazy loners who preached about God and the devil were something else.

"Hey, bible thumper," another student cried. "We don't need you and your God!"

A female student emerged from the crowd, dragging a young man in tow. Her reluctant companion apologized to everyone he bumped into as he was pulled through the ranks.

180

"Damn it, Joy," Talbott adjusted the rucksack on his shoulder. "Slow down."

"Oh," said Michael. "This should be good. I thought you guys said they were cutting class today?"

"They did," Raphael told him. "I mean, they were going to. Score one for free will."

"That's not the answer I was looking for."

"Sorry."

Michael shook his head. His pleading eyes looked heavenward for guidance. His gaze focused on Raphael when he spoke next.

"Into the church," the viceroy of Heaven said. "That goes for everyone."

"Uh, excuse me," Uriel said.

"Yes?"

"Michael," he said, "you know how much I can't stand churches and all. So I was wondering if I could sit this one out."

"It's not my order, Uriel."

"You mean?"

"That's right," Michael said. "An emergency council session."

"He never sets foot in churches," Uriel stated. Then added, "Glory be His Name."

"Inside. Right now."

In the abandoned church a council convened. Yahweh's thunderous shouts could be heard in Heaven and all the way to Hell.

"Stop being such a pussy and come on," Joy tugged his arm. "He's making a fool of himself."

Talbott followed her across the street.

Joy saw in Christophe no resemblance to the young pugnacious man she had met in the college library a few months back. She wondered how she would tell him about herself and Talbott.

"Dude," Talbott said to Christophe. "Pull yourself together."

"Jimmy," Joy said, "you can't go on like this."

"Really," he added. "Get a grip."

Joy administered a swift uppercut to Talbott's solar plexus. The blow knocked the wind out of him.

181

"Jimmy," she said, "people are laughing at you. They think you're crazy. Why are you doing this?"

"You are a believer, aren't you?" Christophe looked at her. His eyes were vacant, glazed over by whatever madness dwelled within him.

"I am a believer," a voice sounded behind Joy.

She turned to see who had spoken. When Joy saw whom the voice belonged to, she hyperventilated.

Talbott, still wheezing as he tried to catch his breath, recognized the Roman.

"Listen," he said, "I don't know who you are, or what you're up to, but we don't need this scene. He's our friend. Besides, I think you're out of your jurisdiction on this one."

"You've been following us," Joy said when she recovered.

"Not you," Longinus said. Then he pointed at Christophe.

"I can't believe this," she said. She looked to Talbott to do something.

Talbott shrugged as he touched his stomach.

"My name is Gaius Cassius Longinus," the Roman told them. "And I have been alive for nearly two thousand years."

"Oh boy," Joy mumbled.

"I am the soldier," he went on, "who pierced Christ's side as he hung on the cross."

"Shit," Talbott said. "I thought that was you."

Joy slapped his arm. She considered mental illness no laughing matter. She was losing control of the situation. And Talbott's feeding into someone's psychosis didn't help.

"Anything else you want to share?" Talbott asked, rubbing his arm. "Some news on the Ark of the Covenant? Who really shot JFK?"

"Mel," she gritted her teeth. "You're not making this easy."

"I seek restitution for my sin," Longinus explained. "As you may have guessed I've been cursed to live forever. Ever since Golgotha I have searched for the Second Coming—"

"You think Jimmy is the messiah?" Joy reached out and touched Christophe's arm. "He's confused. But he's—"

"I have come to this crumbling city to meet the Son of God," Longinus ignored her.

182

"I'm sorry," Talbott interrupted, "but did I miss something? Are you nuts?"

"Would you like to hear my message?" Christophe asked.

"No!"

"Mel," Joy steadied him with the touch of her hand.

"Great messiah," the Roman knelt and bowed his head. "Grant me death so that I may live forever in your father's house."

"Please," Joy pleaded. "Don't encourage him. He needs help. You both do."

"No," Longinus said, "I don't believe I do."

"Look," she said, "whatever ails you is your problem. I'm sure the university can provide you with the proper assistance. But we're here for our friend. So if you would kindly get off your knees and be on your way—"

"No!" Longinus leapt to his feet. "He knows me! Look at him! He knows me! He can put the curse behind me!"

Joy reached and grabbed Christophe by the arm. Talbott followed her lead and took Christophe's other arm. Together they ushered him away from the church.

Undaunted, Longinus followed.

A narrow alley was located behind the church. Joy nodded toward the alley when they reached it. She and Talbott led Christophe away from the growing crowd along Cooper Street. Longinus lagged a few paces behind. Christophe grew agitated. He babbled on and on about forgiveness, redemption and uncertainty. Joy, Talbott and Longinus watched as Christophe put his head against the church and listened. Then he sat down on the stone steps that led to the old sacristy. He lowered his head into his hands and cried.

"I want all of you to leave me alone," he said in a weak voice a few minutes later.

Christophe saw that none of them meant to leave him. He stood up slowly and descended the stairs.

"Go now," he said.

"We won't leave you," Joy said, touching his face. "Not like this."

Talbott looked at Longinus. The Roman said nothing.

183

"Go," Christophe said quietly. A serene expression formed on his face. "What happens next is not for your eyes to see."

He took a couple of steps back. Then his legs gave out as his eyelids fluttered. The whites of his eyes showed briefly before he fell backward. He struck his head against a stone step. The fall rendered him unconscious.

Chapter Twenty-five

Patronage at The Tide declined in the days that followed the disappearance of Darius Algernon. The few loyal customers who still frequented the club suffered unexplainable mood swings. The staff at The Tide treated their favorite patrons with complete indifference. In another more superstitious age some may have proposed that a curse was put upon the establishment, that some unseen force shackled all those who passed through the entrance into the bonds of boredom and lethargy.

Agnes was one among a few dozen patrons that showed her loyalty to The Tide. Night after night she went to the club seeking liquid solace. She knew a change had taken place. But like everyone else affected in recent days she was powerless to rise above it. Most nights she went to the club alone. She knew faces to see, but she shied away from conversation when she could. Her friends made excuses when she called on them to join her for a drink. Agnes didn't mind much.

One night she sat at the bar watching the lights on the jukebox. The club was quiet. Live entertainment was a thing of the past. No one bothered to put money into the jukebox anymore. When the club entrance door opened everyone around the bar cast furtive glances at the newcomers. No one wanted to admit it, but they hoped that one day Darius Algernon would come back into their lives. Agnes stared at the flashing lights. She wasn't aware that the entrance door had opened.

185

"Hey sugar," Rosemarie Parillo greeted Agnes as she entered the club. She looked as if she hadn't slept in days. "What's going on?"

Mary Reilley followed. She looked at Agnes. Agnes studied her and Rosemarie as they approached.

"What brings you girls out?" Agnes asked as she turned her attention to the jukebox once more.

"We came to see you," Mary said. She removed her coat and sat down at the bar.

Rosemarie followed suit. "How are you doing, Aggie?"

"It's Jimmy," she replied.

"What happened?" Rosemarie asked. She caught the bartender's attention with a glance.

"You remember Jimmy's suicide attempt?"

"Sure."

"He was never the same after his release," Agnes said.

Rosemarie and Mary had heard the rumors. People around town said that Jimmy Christophe had become a Jesus freak. They also said other things, worse things. Neither Rosemarie nor Mary took much stock in the darker stories people told. The rumors eventually subsided. Everyone in town began gossiping about some other scandal, involving the mayor, drug abuse and an amateur pornography ring. That's when Rosemarie and Mary figured it was safe to see Agnes in public.

"Anyway," Agnes went on, "he collapsed in Camden. He hit his head on the pavement."

"Bad?" Rosemarie asked.

"Coma."

"I'm so sorry," Mary said. She gave Agnes a cocktail napkin to wipe away the tears that fell from her eyes.

"Vodka and tonic," Rosemarie told the bartender who had been lingering in the periphery as Agnes' story unfolded. "And get Mary a beer. Give Agnes whatever she wants."

"Where's your son now?" Mary asked.

"Cooper Hospital," Agnes told her. "According to his ex-girlfriend he fell down in an alley."

"Was it exhaustion? A seizure? What?"

"No one knows."

186

"Poor man," Rosemarie said.

"Is there anything we can do?" Mary nodded at the bartender as he set down their drinks on the bar.

"I don't think so," Agnes said. "There isn't much to do except wait."

The bartender lingered, waiting for one of the women to pay for the round. Once upon a time he had the act down. It wasn't too long ago that he would leave drinks and collect a tab later. His saunter had turned into a limp. The casual actions were replaced now with an uneasiness that everyone noticed. Once sharp-witted and quick with a light for a lady's cigarette, the bartender paced the inside of the bar like a prisoner of war marching close to the fence.

"Ladies," he said at last, removing the toothpick from his mouth. "How are you doing tonight?"

"Agnes' son is in the hospital," said Rosemarie. "Again," she added.

"What's he in for?" he asked.

"He's in a coma," she told him. "It doesn't look good."

"Oh," the bartender's eyes widened as he pursed his lips. He whistled softly to emphasize his pity. "I'm sorry to hear that."

"Thanks," Agnes said.

"The next round," he announced, "is on the house."

"Asshole," Mary remarked when the bartender limped to the other end of the bar.

"Mary," Rosemarie said. "Now's not the time."

"Men are such assholes."

"Mary—"

"Let her go on," Agnes said.

"So Agnes," Mary turned toward her. "Tell me what happened. From the beginning."

Agnes related Christophe's strange dreams and his waning interest in work, school and life in general. Then she revealed the part about the air conditioner and the voices. She assumed that her friends had heard the story from someone else by now. Agnes was surprised to find out that wasn't the case.

"No shit?" Mary said after drawing a long sip from her beer. "The voices of angels?"

187

"That's what Jimmy said," Agnes answered.

"Well, you can't blame yourself," Rosemarie cautioned her. "There's already too much pain in life. Don't you ever think that you contributed to someone else's insanity."

"Insanity?"

"Mood swings then," Rosemarie said. "Whatever you want to call it."

"Just because he's a man now," Mary chimed in, attempting to play referee, "doesn't mean he has fewer issues to face."

"That's what I was saying," Agnes told her. "Jimmy took it hard when his father left. I don't think he ever got over it."

"Oh Agnes," said Mary.

"No," Rosemarie said. "Plenty of boys lose their father when parents' divorce. There's more to this than you want to admit."

"I blame myself," Agnes ignored her. "One night he cried for hours. Then when he finally stopped Jimmy said the strangest thing. He told me his soul was tired. Can you believe that? And he sounded like he knew what he was talking about.

"There's so much he hasn't seen," she went on. "Sure I know I haven't been the perfect mother. But there are things in life he will experience that goes beyond the family. You guys remember how it was when you got out from under your parents' wings, right?"

Mary and Rosemarie nodded.

"I wanted more than anything," said Agnes, "to watch him find the will to live. I can't undo the things I've done. I know that. But Jimmy's beyond my help. He's beyond anyone's help"

"Agnes," Rosemarie said, "you're being too hard on yourself."

"Do you think some people know?"

"Know what?" Mary asked.

"Do you think that some people know when they're not long for this world?"

"Now you're talking crazy."

"Am I?" Agnes looked at Mary. "Maybe Jimmy's like that. Maybe he knows something about what the rest of us fear."

"What is it that you think we fear?" Rosemarie asked.

188

Agnes shot her a look. "Death, what else?"

"This is way too morbid for me."

"Is it? I've been thinking that there are some people in the world who know this is the last time they will pass through this place—"

"Are you talking about reincarnation?"

"Maybe I am," Agnes said before she tossed back the rest of her drink.

"I can't talk about that."

"Why is that?" Mary said to Rosemarie.

"I'm a Catholic," she answered.

"I'm not talking about religion," Agnes said. "I'm talking about souls. The religions we know came along afterward."

"Don't question my faith—"

"Save it," she told Rosemarie. "My Jimmy knows something. That's for sure."

"I saw a program on television not too long ago," Mary said, "about this very thing. Don't look at me like that. The things we see, UFOs, angels, bleeding statues, ghosts, are just figments of our imagination. This man on television said that it's a person's way of dealing with the emptiness we all fear."

"Do you believe that, Mary?"

"I don't know what I believe," she told Agnes. "I'm sorry I can't be of more help than that."

"He looks so different," Agnes stared into empty space.

"Jimmy's in a coma," Rosemarie said, "of course he's going to look different."

"It's more than that."

"He's fading."

"What?" Rosemarie's cry startled Mary.

"Don't do that," Mary said.

"He's turning invisible," Agnes went on. "Disappearing."

"Agnes," Mary said, "that's crazy talk."

"He looks so pale," she said. Her body shook as she gripped the bar. "I'm losing my baby."

Rosemarie and Mary hugged Agnes until she composed herself.

"You want to leave?" Rosemarie whispered.

"No," said Agnes. "Where would I go?"

189

"How about another round?" the bartender called out.

"Would you please," Mary said.

"Let's just get really drunk," Agnes said as she dried her eyes.

"Whatever you want to do," Rosemarie rubbed Agnes' back, "is fine by me."

"Rosie."

"Yeah doll?"

"I'm sorry about Darius."

Rosemarie shrugged. "Yeah, me too."

Chapter Twenty-six

"Just what the hell's that supposed to mean?" Agnes screamed.

"Ms. Christophe," the nurse said, "please. Think of the other patients."

"Why don't you define what missing means to you?"

"I can assure you that we are doing everything in our power to locate—"

"Don't hand me that shit," Agnes snapped. "I may not have a degree in medicine," she continued her assault, "but I'm smart enough to know that comatose bodies don't get up and move around without someone noticing."

"I never meant to imply—"

"Don't you monitor comatose patients? Or is that just something I saw in a movie once?"

The nurse was short and full-figured. Her breasts resembled two orbicular moons beneath her starched white uniform. She sat behind a pane of Plexiglas that distanced her from hostile people like Agnes.

Agnes decided, looking over the nurse's hardened face and magenta-colored, close-cropped hair, that the woman behind the unbreakable glass was a lesbian. Not just the garden-variety homosexual female, but a real man-hating deviant who secretly disposed of male patients. But rather than accuse the nurse outright of such a malicious act, Agnes protested the American work ethic, the bloodsucking medical industry with its vampiric healthcare management procedures and the

191

machine called bureaucracy that called into being the faulty systems that allowed mishaps like this one to happen.

The nurse understood Agnes' frustration. She was a mother of two, one boy and one girl. Her cool professionalism was the only thing that kept her from dialing up hospital security and having Agnes removed from the premises.

"I've been downstairs for three hours," Agnes told the nurse. "Three hours I've spent with an incompetent administration that won't give me a straight answer."

"Ms. Christophe," the nurse maintained her professional detachment as she folded her meaty arms over her chest, "things like these minor mishaps occur every day. Once our orderlies get going there's no telling where a patient might end up. But that shouldn't alarm you. We always find our patients. There really is no cause for panic. Don't worry. We'll locate your son soon."

"I want to talk to someone with authority around here."

"I am the head nurse at this ward."

"I bet you are."

"Pardon me?"

"Who's your boss?" Agnes demanded.

"Perhaps," the nurse said, "you would like to speak to your son's attending physician?"

Agnes considered her offer a small victory.

"Who's that?" she asked.

"Dr. Wilfred Barnes."

The nurse looked down at her desk and skimmed over a few clipboards.

"I'm sorry," she said at last. "Dr. Barnes is in surgery right now."

Agnes slammed her purse on the countertop. She opened it, wondering what amount of force would enable her to punch through the Plexiglas window, and searched for a cigarette.

"Ms. Christophe," the nurse said as Agnes lit a cigarette. "I'm sure I don't need to remind you that the hospital is a smoke-free environment."

"Except for the puff my son Jimmy disappeared in, right?"

"There's no smoking in the building," the nurse stared at her. "Do I make myself clear?"

192

"What am I?" Agnes exhaled a stream of pale blue smoke at the tiny holes in the Plexiglas. "Back in high school?"

"Hospital rules," the nurse sang.

"Stop fucking with my patience," Agnes crooned back in the same singsong voice. "Or I'll tear your tonsils out."

"I'm not taking this abuse any longer," the nurse picked up the telephone receiver. "Operator, get me security."

"My apologies," Agnes said. "I'll be downstairs in the lounge. Then I'm going to come back up here in ten minutes. You better have some answers or, believe me sister, you'll wish you'd never met me."

Inside the elevator Agnes remembered the phone call. Mel Talbott relayed the news that sent her into hysterics. For several minutes neither party could understand each other. Talbott was already an emotional wreck. The incident with Christophe had nearly sent him over the edge. When he finally collected himself he told Agnes what had happened. He told her every detail, including the theory the Camden police held, implying that perhaps Joy and Talbott had something to do with Christophe's accident.

At the hospital Agnes learned that her son had been moved from the emergency treatment facilities to an intensive care unit. Christophe had slipped into a coma, she was told, and the chances for his recovery were slim. Agnes saw her son that day. He was hooked up to a respirator since he was no longer able to breathe on his own. The sound of the cardiograph's weak blip flooded her ears.

Agnes was relieved to learn that she was able to stay the night with Christophe. In the morning she returned home for a quick shower and breakfast. Her mood lightened when she returned to the hospital. A nurse had informed her that Christophe had regained consciousness and was breathing on his own again. Christophe had been moved from the ICU to a semi-private room.

Inside the empty room Agnes found the lavatory door closed. She was startled at first when she saw the empty bed. Then she heard water running into a sink inside the bathroom. The entire room smelled like fresh flowers. Agnes considered that odd, owing to how most hospital rooms had

193

two distinct odors: the smell of antiseptic cleaners and human waste. Still, she was thankful her son had recovered. Her elation, however, was short-lived. When the lavatory door opened Agnes expected to see her son. Instead, she saw a tall dark man with long dreadlocks dressed in an orderly uniform.

Presently, the elevator doors opened to reveal the ground floor. Agnes made her way into the lounge where she saw Joy Felder and Mel Talbott seated at a table. Joy had been crying. Talbott wore the same tired, blank expression that Agnes had seen earlier that day.

"Ms. Christophe," Talbott rose from his seat as Agnes approached. "Please," he said, drawing a third chair to the table, "sit with us."

"Only for a minute," she told him.

"We understand," said Joy.

Agnes forced a smile.

"So," Talbott said, "what's the word?"

"I don't know how this hospital stays open," Agnes told them. "Everyone here doesn't seem to want to help."

"We'd like to see Jimmy," said Joy. "But we've been told there have been complications."

"I'm afraid there is."

"What sort of complications?" Talbott asked.

"He's not well," Agnes confessed. The next bit of information she chewed over a moment. Then, "In fact, he's missing."

"Missing?" Joy cried.

"What happened?" Talbott asked.

"When I came back this afternoon," Agnes explained, "he wasn't in his room. We searched all over for him. No one seems to have an answer."

"Did he leave the hospital?" Joy began crying. "Maybe one of us—"

"We could go to your house," Talbott offered.

"Mel, Joy," Agnes said, "relax. I already called my friend Rosemarie. She's at my house right now. Besides, I'm told the local law enforcement is involved."

Joy grunted and rolled her eyes.

194

"Even if Jimmy left the hospital on his own," said Agnes, "he wouldn't get very far wearing a Cooper Hospital examination gown."

Over the next several minutes they sat in silence. Agnes took out her cigarettes and lit one. She left the pack on the table in case the other two wanted to join her.

Talbott stood up and yawned.

"Does anyone want any coffee?" he stretched his arms as he asked.

Joy declined.

"No thanks," she said.

"Sure," Agnes told Talbott. "I could use one. Do you need money?"

Talbott laughed.

"No," he said, "I think I can cover it."

You know," Joy said when Talbott left the table, "I did love your son, Ms. Christophe."

"Joy," she said, patting the young woman's hand, "that's not necessary."

"I feel like it is."

"Fine," Agnes said. "But you might want to prepare yourself for the worst."

"What?"

"A mother knows certain things," she went on. "He's gone, Joy. My Jimmy's gone."

"Don't say that," Joy argued. "You can't say that."

"My guess is—"

"Here we go," Talbott returned and placed two cups of coffee on the table. "They're out of cream. But I managed to drum up some sugar."

He produced several packets from his shirt pocket and dropped them on the table.

"Black is fine," said Agnes.

"Do you think it will be long before you hear anything?" Talbott asked. "Jimmy has to turn up some time, right?"

Agnes shot a cautionary glance at Joy. Joy lowered her head, pretending to study a pattern in the floor tile.

"That's hard to say," Agnes said.

195

"Maybe Joy and I should go out and look for him," Talbott offered. "Two more pairs of eyes couldn't hurt."

"I think," Agnes stood as she put out her cigarette, "you both should wait here."

"Mothers always seem to be right," Joy said when Agnes left the lounge. "Even when they're not your mother."

Talbott looked at her.

"What are you talking about?" he asked.

"Never mind," Joy reached for the cigarettes Agnes had left behind.

Part Four:
Phantasms, Lessons, &
Mystical Connections

Chapter Twenty-seven

Joy Felder and Mel Talbott moved into their own apartment a little more than a year after Jimmy Christophe disappeared. The apartment they inhabited was a one-bedroom affair, with a living room, a dining room and a small kitchen. The whole of their new domicile was neatly tucked into the second floor of an old Victorian home. The electrical wiring wasn't up to code, the pipes looked and sounded like they had been there since the early 1900s and the ceiling sagged in different areas. On windy nights an eerie music sounded between the floorboards. Joy considered the old apartment rustic. Talbott didn't share her sentiment, seeing ruin in all things since he had lost his best friend, and chose more colorful adjectives to describe their new home.

Furniture for the apartment came into their possession piecemeal. They couldn't afford to pay attention to style, nor would they succumb as freethinkers to such outlandish notions like theme or motif. The apartment took on a chaotic and heterogeneous appearance, a look typical for the recent college grads with no money that seemed romantic only in the worst movies.

Twelve tall windows divided among the rooms provided sufficient sunlight. The kitchen window faced east, catching the first glimpse of morning light as it crept over the tall firs in

197

the backyard. By day's end the sun's last rays graced the bedroom.

Joy and Talbott discovered that they were physical lovers early on in their relationship. Their lovemaking was not so much a union of flesh and spirit as a contest; a brutal grappling match designed to test each other's strength. The couple's favorite day for sex was Sunday. That day started out with a light breakfast of bagels and cream cheese, coffee and casual conversation over the Sunday paper. As they read the news Joy and Talbott exchanged lewd innuendoes about whatever subject portrayed in the paper. When the X-rated banter became too much to bear, Joy and Talbott retreated to the bedroom. There was no turn-on, position or fantasy they didn't try at least once (they shied away from playing dress-up since maid outfits, leather biker chaps and suits of armor cost money), but for all their physical passion Joy and Talbott remained polar opposites where expressions of satisfaction were concerned.

Joy rarely made a sound during her orgasms, concentrating, instead, on channeling all her energies to the pleasure itself. Talbott was different. He was the wolf, the howler, the shouter, the crier, the drummer of headboards, the shaker of chairs and the rattler of windows. Each orgasm for Talbott was a unique experience. And each one deserved its own special song of celebration. The noise Talbott made during intercourse turned Joy off. She entertained various measures like stuffing a sock in his mouth or strapping a ball gag onto his face to quell his Whitman-influenced YAWP. But in the end Joy knew that Talbott would find a way to make noise. Thus she allowed him his indulgence, even if it meant bringing herself off if Talbott came first.

The little town of Collingswood, New Jersey where they lived offered all the mundane necessities of suburban life. A supermarket and a video store were within walking distance of the apartment. The Patco Hi-Speedline station was located a short five blocks from home. There were pharmacies (condoms for Talbott, prescription allergy medicine for Joy), pizza shops (avoided whenever possible save for the occasional cheese steak), Chinese take-out restaurants (the Bull's Eye

198

Buddha, Talbott's favorite, sold buffalo wings singularly to honor the typographical error in the restaurant menu[No. 276: Buffalo Wing]), and a used bookstore that offered much in the way of previously-owned bestsellers and little in the way of meaty, time-tested classics.

When Joy and Talbott began apartment hunting the criteria was simple. Find a place away from the neighborhoods in which their parents lived and avoid the city of Philadelphia at all costs. The latter dimension of the apartment-hunting strategy had little to do with financial reasons as much as the prejudice they carried. Talbott and Joy grew up in southern New Jersey communities where most residents believed that city people talked too fast and walked too slow. In reality Joy and Talbott knew that they were big fishes in a small pond as long as they lived in suburbia. Armed with their college education, they considered themselves head and shoulders above the working class populace. In the city they feared their intellectual prowess might be matched or bested.

Any number of southern New Jersey communities would have sufficed for the couple. Collingswood seemed the most affordable for the college graduates. True older residents in that community looked unfavorably on their arrangement (a number of private landlords wouldn't rent a place to the couple unless they could show they were married). And the rest, tired-looking men, foul-mouthed women and dirty-faced children, regarded the new couple on the block with quiet suspicion.

Talbott offered overt friendliness when he met up with his new neighbors. Inside he was still torn up about what had happened to his best friend, but outwardly he acted like a man of the people. Joy feared that Collingswood residents would view Talbott as deranged. In truth people treated Talbott exactly as they saw him. In their eyes he was a fragile simpleton ripe for suffering due to his own ignorance. Joy knew that Talbott lacked the common sense to figure out that people weren't being friendly so much as acting out of pity. She saw it in their eyes. And she despised every one of them for it.

199

Several weeks before they graduated from Rutgers University Joy and Talbott had a myriad of friends. After Christophe's disappearance it seemed everyone wanted to know the couple. Young men and more than a few gallant women wanted to be close to Joy, to drink in her tranquil beauty until they were intoxicated by her. Of Talbott they saw in him the spirit of the fool, and for that they were grateful. Talbott possessed a knack for sounding like he knew what he was talking about when it came to matters of history, science and the all-inclusive esoterica. At a party or in a bar whenever he felt cornered he simply pulled Joy into the conversation. It was like a one-two punch the way she first wowed a person with her appearance (Joy lost her appetite for several months after Christophe had disappeared) and picked their head apart with her intelligence.

When the couple first moved into their apartment there was a constant flux of visitors. Talbott reveled in the popularity (something he never experienced in high school), but Joy saw through people and discovered early on their motives. Her home had become a speakeasy for under-age drinkers. Joy was not above employing theatrics to scare off unwanted visitors. She threw tantrums that lasted for hours. At the parties they threw she was not above throwing everyone out at once.

It wasn't long before a select few began to see through Joy's 'temperamental' nature. The more gullible types, the ones who were content to gloss over serious subjects for hours with Talbott, believed Joy was a frustrated genius. The friends who considered Joy's mood swings slipshod acting placed bets from time to time often pushing to see how long she would go before she let go. Those that did not fear Joy and poked fun of her didn't stick around long. Joy and Talbott worked hard to surround themselves with the kind of friends that would be in awe of them. They had no time for those who sought to steal their thunder.

When the smoke cleared there remained a skeleton crew of close friends. That group was Joy's fellow English literature majors. When Joy and Talbott had banished from their home the bad seeds, the hangers-on, the peripheral devilment

200

makers, their parties took on a more cerebral mood. Talbott struggled to hang on, but Joy was a natural. Talk often turned to works of great literature the way conversation did when more than five English majors were put in the same room together. The tide always turned back to Joy. Why wasn't she writing, her friends wondered. Talbott was content to remain in the background.

It wasn't long before Joy became infected by the bug that struck so many English literature students. One morning she woke up after a party and decided that she wanted to be a writer. Among the many students of literature she knew were those that had already penned numerous short stories and poems. Some even claimed to have written labyrinthine novels that the world, judging by the reaction of their relatives and closest friends, wasn't ready for. It wasn't long before this particular set sank their claws (or quills) into Joy.

Of the various periods in the literature of western civilization Joy preferred the nineteenth century above all others. She envied the Bronte Sisters, George Eliot and Jane Austen. Sadly, the creative gift her literary ancestral sisters possessed had eluded the fledgling writer. She failed to see that natural talent was a myth, and that good writing was achieved only through diligence, devotion to the written word, patience and above all practice. When it came to reading, Joy devoured great works. But for her writing was entirely different. So acquainted was she with the flawless prose of nineteenth century novels that she failed to realize certain truths about the craft of fiction. Like most fledgling writers she often imitated her favorite authors' styles. But in trying to portray her childhood in Lindenwold, New Jersey in the style of Emily Bronte she produced work that was flat and stale. Joy, like so many others who tread the murky waters of college literature courses, believed the nineteenth century novel to be the hallmark of proper English. Not once did she consider the idiom of her day. Not once did she realize the common force that drove writers to produce original works: the will to write the books they, the authors, wanted to read. Instead, she emulated the great ones. And because she could not write like they did, that emulation became Joy's pain.

201

Some nights when Joy sat at her computer she was unable to compose a single paragraph. In her head the voices of dilettantes, her drunken peers who fancied themselves the next Jack Kerouac, Flannery O'Connor, Thomas Wolfe or (for the exceedingly deluded and drunk) the next Vladimir Nabokov, droned on about the mechanics of good writing. What she and her friends didn't know was that there was no tried and true blueprint, no end-all outline, nor were there any sure-fire devices that helped a person compose a good story.

Joy reached a critical point in her pursuit of the written word. She convinced herself that she suffered not from having any talent at all but from writer's block. Some unrecognized flaw in her subconscious, she believed, kept the flow from happening.

One night, watching Joy suffer the impasse of the writer's block, Talbott suggested that she exercise more discipline. Drunk on scotch, he waved his glass around with the pomposity of a young Charles Bukowski on a bender, offering his advice.

"Writing," he had told her, "is only one-tenth of the task."

Joy and her literati friends watched Talbott's body sway as he tried to remain standing.

"Science," he ignored the groans of his audience when he spoke the word, "teaches us that there are tried-and-true approaches to all disciplines in life."

"Not with writing," Joy countered.

"You drunken ass," one of the partygoers added.

"Practicality," said Talbott. He rocked from left to right and back again as the scotch took hold of him.

A moment of silence passed.

"Anyway," the name-calling partygoer said to Joy when it seemed evident that Talbott had finished his lecture.

"Journals," Talbott said. "Notes and outlines. There are the things one needs to forge anything of significance."

Talbott's haphazard ruminations did little to assuage the frustration Joy had experienced. She flew into a rage that night, accusing Talbott as her friends cheered her on that he had never experienced an original thought in his life.

202

"What makes you think you know anything about the creative process!" Joy stormed out of the room.

Later that night he suffered the ultimate insult. When everyone had gone home Joy banished Talbott from the bedroom.

The sentence lasted a week. Each night Talbott prepared a modest bed on the living room couch. Every morning of that week he woke up with a sharp pain in his lower back.

It was during the imposed punishment that Joy had followed Talbott's suggestion. She began a journal in which she wrote character sketches, outlines and notes about a story that had been brewing in her head for several weeks.

By the end of the week she invited Talbott back into the bedroom.

Nine months later the fruit of Joy's dedication came to life. She had written in longhand the first one hundred pages of a novel she would never finish.

The loose-leaf copy she shared with her literati friends. Their poker faces revealed little about how they felt about Joy's work. But Joy saw in their eyes the truth. She abandoned fiction writing after that, choosing instead to refocus her energies on her academic pursuits. Joy set her sights on gaining entrance into graduate school and obtaining her Ph.D.

In their last year as undergraduates Joy and Talbott both drank less, studied more and finished college with grade point averages rich enough to make them serious graduate school candidates. Talbott harbored no false aspirations where further education was concerned.

"I've had it with school," he told Joy one night as they sat up late drinking beer and smoking cigarettes.

Time continued its linear march. Joy and Talbott became complacent in their relationship. As a result, taking one another for granted, their bond weakened. A divide developed between them. The passion they once shared was gone. They knew something was different, but they

were afraid to bring up the subject. They continued to use words like 'love', 'commitment' and 'devotion', they spoke of time not in terms of months or years but in measures of

203

infinity (forever, ever and ever) while secretly wishing something would happen to bring them closer together again.

Chapter Twenty-eight

"What a great movie!" Talbott announced as he exited the movie theater.

Joy paid him little attention. She was still angry about having to go to a movie Talbott had picked. Hours before when the topic came up Joy suggested they go see something that didn't require much thought. Mid-term examinations had just passed, and Joy was searching for pure mindless entertainment.

Talbott wouldn't allow himself to be swayed into seeing any film that boasted senseless violence, gratuitous sexual situations or testosterone-charged dialogue between ultra-masculine heroes and villains. He wanted something with more substance than that. The movies Joy leaned toward were generic, high-budget Hollywood assembly-line works that were too predictable if anything else. Such movies Talbott viewed as admission to his working class background. A background devoid of eclectic interests and that fostered blind acceptance.

The argument lasted an hour. Joy had put up a good fight, but Talbott stuck to his guns. In the end he resorted to methodical means to get his way. He moped until Joy acquiesced.

The couple stood outside the Ritz Theater at 2nd and Walnut Streets in Philadelphia. Joy wrapped her arms around

205

herself, feeling the sting of the cold night air. Talbott rambled on about 'Syster Hysteria', the three-hour film they had just seen. He employed words like mesmerizing, heartfelt, intriguing, hypnotic and a dozen other terms favored by less-than-creative movie critics everywhere.

Joy felt sick to her stomach. It wasn't the movie that caused her discomfort. Nor was it the adoration Talbott voiced for the film. When they first drove over the Benjamin Franklin Bridge Joy felt a twinge of guilt mixed with bitter remorse. So caught up was she in recalling Jimmy Christophe's leap from the bridge that she failed to notice Talbott had taken a wrong turn when they had reached the other side of the bridge. They drove past dilapidated factories, graffiti-emblazoned storefronts and dark, burned-out row homes where crack-addled whores, nefarious candymen and other ne'er-do-wells lurked. Only Joy's common sense saved them from any threatening predicament.

'Syster Hysteria' was a Hungarian movie based on an unpublished short story by Jean-Paul Sartre. The film, subtitled, was set in Budapest in the late 1960s. The plot, as far as Joy could tell, involved an elderly woman and a grave secret that was portrayed through a series of flashbacks.

Talbott had surmised halfway through the film, to the chagrin of filmgoers seated nearby, that the old woman was a hermaphrodite. Of course there was no contextual evidence in the film to support that claim. Joy was mortified. One theater patron rebuked Talbott's claim. Others soon chimed in, calling him a moron, a dullard, a lout, a half-wit, a jackass and a commoner. Joy wondered if she could slip to the floor and low-crawl out of the theater without being noticed. She had thought the exchange was over after a few minutes. Then Talbott retaliated, charging his accusers of committing such heinous acts as bestiality and incest.

The situation might have escalated had it not been for a band of theater ushers who rushed to the scene. They sliced the darkness open with their flashlights, threatening to eject all guilty parties. After that, all was quiet.

The other characters in 'Syster Hysteria' were a young farmhand mistaken for a poet possessed of pure genius and a

206

professor-turned-provocateur who was unable to come to grips with the senseless deaths of a handful of students. The farmhand poet and the professor were ghosts in the old woman's mind; their parallel stories portrayed in flashback memories to World War II. By the film's end the two men and the old woman, masters of their own fates, remained as disconsolate and fearful of life as when the film began.

"Pure existential art," Talbott commented when the credits rolled.

"That farm boy didn't have to be the fall guy," Joy remarked as they stood outside the theater.

A small group of working-class intellectuals had gathered at the curb to smoke cigarettes and discuss the film. Dressed in their thrift store hand-me-downs and scuffed black boots, they recalled another film by Ivan Troblinka, the director of 'Syster Hysteria'.

The Philadelphia Inquirer called *Quiet Days at Auschwitz*, the debut work by Ivan Troblinka, cunningly half-witted. And the New York Times labeled 'Quiet Days' a 'movie that redefines cinematic folly'. At home in Philadelphia even the Daily News jumped on the Troblinka bandwagon. 'Such films,' one critic wrote, 'are tantamount to the degradation of hallmark indie films everywhere.'

It came as no surprise to Talbott that the curbside highbrows considered 'Quiet Days' a better film than 'Syster Hysteria'.

"Art house fags," Joy whispered.

"Poseurs," Talbott concurred.

The couple walked along Walnut Street. A light rain fell that night. The aroma of equine excrement lingered in the air from the numerous horses drawing carriages through the Olde City area.

"I realize now," Joy said, "why some short stories are never published. Much less why some schlub can purchase the rights to such stories."

"Joy," Talbott halted and stared at her. "It's Sartre for Christ's sake."

"That doesn't mean anything."

"Spoken like a true—"

"Fuck existentialism," she said. "I'm talking about—"

"Never mind," he resumed his pace. Then, "Why are so many foreign films subtitled?"

"For starters," Joy said, "you don't speak Hungarian."

"Good point."

"Thanks."

"Want to stop somewhere for a drink?"

"No, I don't."

"Come on," Talbott chided her, "how often do we come to Philadelphia?"

"Precisely my point."

"Let's enjoy the night."

"Meaning you get drunk, and I end up driving home?"

"I'll drive."

"Don't piss me off," Joy warned him. "It's bad enough I had to see a movie I wasn't interested in going to see in the first place. Now you want me to go to some dive bar and hang out with people I don't know?"

"Where's your sense of adventure?"

"Where's your common sense?" she asked. "When it's all over, we go back across the bridge."

"Aren't you sick of the same old thing?"

"As a matter of fact—"

"Good!" Talbott cried. "Let's surround ourselves with strange people for a change."

"It would only be temporary," Joy said. "Besides, I've had my fill of strangeness where your friends are concerned."

"I don't have any friends."

"Social skills are instinctual," she nudged his arm. "They can't be taught."

"Come on," he pleaded. "One drink."

"You're being an insufferable prick," she told him. "Now let's go home."

They were halfway over the bridge when Talbott brought up the subject of subtitles again.

"Wouldn't it make more sense just to dub the English into the films?" Talbott proposed.

Joy concentrated on the traffic around her. "People have an aversion to dubbed films," she said.

208

"You think so?"

"They equate foreign films with higher intellect."

"Who are they?"

"Take those guys outside the theater tonight," she answered. "With foreign films that are subtitled they aren't offended since the translation is provided for them as they hear the original language."

"Even though," Talbott offered, "something may be lost in the translation."

"True," Joy said. "But because they experience viewing a foreign film, a film the average Joe roughneck might not be interested in, the very experience inflates their intellectual ego. And because our language differs from others it looks wrong on the lips of foreign actors; not unlike, I suppose, those old chop-socky kung fu movies we grew up watching on UHF before cable came along."

"Black Belt Theater!" Talbott cried. "I love that show."

"Anyway," she continued, yawning when they reached the Jersey side, "most eggheads would find that sort of thing insulting."

"I never thought of it that way," he said, staring out the passenger-side window.

"It's like love, honey," Joy said after a few minutes. "You pay attention to the words too long, you miss everything else."

The telephone was ringing when they entered the apartment. Joy didn't have to answer it to know who it was. Talbott's mother had called nearly every day since the couple had moved in together. Worse than the regular phone calls were the unexpected visits by Talbott's mother.

Joy recalled the one night that Mrs. Talbott let herself into the apartment. Talbott had given his mother a key 'for emergencies'. On the one night Mrs. Talbott decided to surprise the couple she stumbled into a surreal situation of bacchanalian proportions. It was an early Saturday evening. Alcohol, pot and low lights provided the atmosphere that led to varying states of hedonism. Joy and Talbott had long retired to their bedroom. Several couples used the rest of the apartment to conduct their own orgy.

209

Bobbie Talbott, unaware that her son sanctioned such activity, was no stranger to debauchery. She had come up at the dawn of the Age of Aquarius. The magic of the sixties, however, ended the moment she found she was pregnant. Too many years had passed to remember what the doorknob said, much less to recall the last time that she fed her head. Bobbie's first instinct, upon seeing one young man seated on the couch, pants around his ankles as a topless blonde's head bobbed up and down in his lap, was to call the police, to squeal to the pigs she once despised. Instead, she let herself out. But Bobbie didn't forget the incident. She gave her son hell over the lifestyle he had chosen to lead, and she blamed 'that girl' (Bobbie never referred to Joy by name) for corrupting her son.

After that incident Bobbie Talbott never visited. She did, however, remain loyal to her friend on the telephone.

"Hello?" Talbott said when he picked up the receiver. "Oh, nothing," he said. "We just got home."

A moment of silence.

"The movies," he told his mother.

Joy took off her coat and hung it in the closet by the door.

"Philadelphia," Talbott said. Then, "of course it was a safe neighborhood. What? Sure, mom, that's right. We bought a ton of drugs. In fact I have to go back and get the other half of the stash."

Talbott grinned.

"I am being smart," he said, at last. 'I'm also keeping up with my studies. What? No, I'm not changing my major."

He held his hand over the receiver and rolled his eyes. Joy offered no empathy.

"Mother, we've gone over this countless times," he said. "I wish you wouldn't bother me about it."

"Hang up," Joy told him.

"What?"

"Hang up the phone."

"I'm not hanging up on my mother, Joy," he said, covering the mouthpiece again.

"Go on," she told him. "It's time you wean yourself."

"Shut up," he said. "No," he uncovered the mouthpiece, "not you mother."

"You two will never let go."

"No that's not necessary," said Talbott, ignoring Joy. "I'm perfectly fine right here. She's picking a fight, but I'm not taking the bait."

"Bitch!" Joy screamed. "Why can't you leave us alone?"

"What? Now?" he evoked cool pleasantry. "No, not to worry. That's Joy—"

"God damn it! Let us live our life!"

"No, no. She's rehearsing a play," he explained to his mother as he shot Joy a look. "That's right. Regional theater. You know Joy. One day she thinks she's Mary McCarthy and the next? Who knows? What? Oh, I thought you meant Joy. I was going to say, mother. No, I never read Mary McCarthy. Some of Joy's literary friends have dropped that name, though. But I never heard them say that about the woman. What? No, I said that if they were filled with as much passion about writing as they were with getting drunk and getting laid their movement might get off the ground."

Talbott followed Joy's movements with pleading eyes. The longer he talked on the telephone the more Joy paced like a caged animal.

"Fucking asshole!" She cocked her arm with car keys in hand.

"Yes, yes," Talbott told his mother. "It's rather explicit. Who? Mamet. Yes, mother. He's a real playwright. He's from Chicago. No, he's not some obscure vulgarian. He's very popular. What? Everywhere! Yeah well, I wouldn't brag about 'Hair' either."

Joy started for the door.

"You heard me," he said and sighed. Then, "The sixties were hardly all that. Ineffectual revolutionaries, at best. Well, that may be true but I've never been to Chicago so I wouldn't know if everyone there is foulmouthed." Talbott cupped his hand over the mouthpiece. To Joy he asked, "Where are you going?"

"Tatters," she told him.

"You're kidding me," he picked up the conversation with his mother again. "How long will you be gone?"

211

Joy opened the door. Lately, she didn't like the way she felt about Talbott. She tried to love him, but something deep inside kept telling her their relationship was wrong. She was convinced, and had been for a long time, that there was no future with Talbott. The pain she experienced was a result of allowing the days to go on in which they were together rather than taking a step toward ending their relationship.

"No, mother," she heard him say. "Please."

Talbott grimaced.

"What could I possibly do with a political science degree?" he asked. "Law school? I don't think so. Besides, there's no science to politics. And I'm not changing my major. It's too late. Anyway, aren't there enough lawyers in the country without me joining the pack? Hello? Hello?"

Joy exited the apartment. On the street she waited in her car for a few minutes. She thought that the relationship might mean something after all if Talbott had pursued her and made some gallant effort to seek her forgiveness. Then she laughed, realizing how absurd the notion was.

The old Victorian house looked still and empty, the way it did the first night she saw it. Joy started her car, cursed the rain that fell because it reminded her of the night she had taken Talbott to the park in her old neighborhood and drove away.

Talbott replaced the telephone receiver in its cradle after he heard Joy pull away. He lay down on the couch and cried. After several minutes passed he picked up the telephone again.

"Hello," he said cautiously when his mother answered. "I wanted to apologize for being such an ass. No, it was my fault. Mother, I'm sorry. Listen, I need to ask a favor. No, I wasn't crying. Do you think I could borrow your car?"

Talbott looked at a clock that hung on the living room wall. It was ten minutes before midnight.

"It's Joy," he confessed. "She went crazy and took off. I don't know what's wrong with her. She hasn't been the same lately."

He took what came next when Bobbie Talbott unleashed on him.

212

"Mother," he said, "please don't start that argument. I need your help. No, we've been over this a dozen times. It wasn't a hasty decision. I knew what I was getting into when we got this place together. What? Marriage? Sorry. I don't think that far ahead. Where? Oh. Tatters. It won't take—"

Bobbie Talbott hung up.

"-long, I swear," he said.

Talbott spent the next ten minutes calling his mother back. Each time he heard a busy signal. He dialed the operator and implored the woman to make an emergency breakthrough.

"I'm sorry, sir," the operator informed him when she failed to establish a breakthrough. "No one is responding at that number. Would you like to try again later?"

"No," Talbott said. "Try it again right now."

"Sir, no one is answering."

"Try it again."

"Sir, no one is responding. If this is a real emergency I can connect with the local law enforcement officials for that municipality. Otherwise, it seems someone left the phone off the hook."

"It's not off the hook," Talbott said.

"Perhaps you should check the number and try again later?"

"Lady!" Talbott screamed into the mouthpiece, "you think I don't know my own mother's phone number? Thanks for your fucking help—"

The line went dead. Talbott smacked the receiver against the lamp beside him. The blow wasn't strong enough to knock it from the table; so he stood up and kicked the lamp. As he delivered the snap kick with his right foot Talbott entangled his left foot in the phone cord. He slipped and fell onto his back.

"Cocksucker!" Talbott slammed the receiver down on the table as he climbed to his hands and knees. The cord remained bound around his ankle. He stood up. With one swift kick he yanked the cord and tore the phone jack from the wall. The momentum of the kick set him off-balance. Talbott crashed to the floor a second time. "Bastard! Piece of shit!"

Fifteen minutes later, Talbott left the apartment and walked down Haddon Avenue. He entered a corner bar. The

213

bartender there was reluctant to serve the bleary-eyed, rain-drenched stranger. Talbott convinced the old man he was on the up and up with a ten-dollar tip. He spent the other thirty dollars in his pocket on tap beer and cheap shots of tequila before he called it a night. When he returned to the apartment he saw Joy's car parked in the street.

"You're drunk," she mumbled in the dark after Talbott took off all his clothes and climbed into bed beside her.

Talbott got out of bed, put on a T-shirt and sweatpants and went into the kitchen. He found two cans of Coors Extra Gold beer, leftovers from some long-ago party, in the back of the refrigerator and drank them in the dark.

Chapter Twenty-nine

"Christophe!" Asmodeus jumped up and down as he opened the gate. "It's great to see you again!"

Behind the gate Cerberus howled in three-part harmony. A moment later the demonic dog bounded into view. He ran in circles and figure-eights as he chased his serpent-headed tail.

Hell was alive with activity. The steady clamor of work hummed in Christophe's ears.

Azzy stepped out into Chaos long enough to give the sojourner a hearty hug and to escort him into Hell. The demon put his bugle to his lips, the melody he played both beautiful and flatulent. The fallen angel put up his bugle when he finished. Then, closing the gate behind Christophe, he turned cartwheels while Cerberus nipped at him.

"Another dream?" Christophe inquired, expecting to wake up in the hospital.

"I'm afraid not, my friend," the demon answered. He paused to pat Cerberus' three heads.

"So, what's all the noise?"

"The deconstruction started way ahead of schedule. We apologize for pulling you away at such short notice."

"Deconstruction?"

"Never mind for now," Asmodeus cautioned him. "Just stick close to me."

The dark road to Pandemonium lay empty. Along the way Christophe questioned the demon, what was happening, and more importantly why he was chosen above all others. Asmodeus took great care as he explained that Christophe's living body no longer existed; at least in a corporeal state that one could still see it didn't. The demon then expounded on the nature of the soul, including its birthplace which was, Asmodeus decreed, the mind of God. The conversation turned to the soul's ultimate purpose.

"So you see," concluded Asmodeus, "the soul, feminine in nature, never really belonged to man. She belongs, that is the soul belongs, with her Father in Heaven. While it is true she fell from grace, suffered abandonment, deceit and slavery, the soul did regain her proper position in her Father's house. In our time in Heaven, we rebellious angels tried everything to avert His attention from the thing He loved most."

"Let's go back," Christophe said, "to the body for a moment—"

"All in good time," the demon assured him. "No one expects you to remember right away all that you have forgotten from age to age."

They drew closer to the city.

"This is different than I expected," Christophe took in the view of the infernal city.

"Perception," Asmodeus told him.

"How's that?"

"Hell's what you make of it. The same goes for Heaven, Earth and all the other worlds that He created. God's no moron, you know."

"So all the stories I learned aren't true? Souls aren't tormented here?"

"Churches and their religions," the demon spat to prove his contempt. "They are the original sin. If Mithraism had been a city religion versus a country cult you might not have had to suffer the warped sensibilities of sanctimonious, power-hungry goons. Then again Mithraism had its faults too. Who's to say."

"Is any religion correct?"

"Kid, you're killing me. Just remember this," Asmodeus touched Christophe on the arm as he spoke, "it's always the

216

many that suffer when the few profess secret knowledge and manipulate the many to gain power."

"Is that in the New Testament?"

"Spare me. Another fairy tale. Myths like your Prometheus or Coyote the Trickster. The more a man writes down what's near to his heart the further he separates himself from the soul."

"So where does that leave the world's great writers? Are they that far removed from the truth?"

"On the contrary," the demon said. "I'm talking about delusions in one person's head that eventually become the sacred texts of the people."

"How do I know you're not a myth? Or for that matter how do I know that's not the same for Satan and everything here?"

"Don't tread on thin ice," Asmodeus warned him, "if you can't swim in cold water."

"Ok, scratch that," Christophe said. "If what you say is true, that the soul belongs in Heaven next to her Father, then what's the point of Hell?"

"Good Lord A'mighty!" the demon jumped up and down and danced in a tantrum. He didn't quit until he was sure he had Christophe's full attention.

"Let me know when I lose you," he continued. "On earth you must have heard the old joke about the chicken and the egg."

"Sure, you bet I did."

"But the answer, nevertheless, is true. The cock came first."

Christophe didn't laugh.

"That one kills me," Asmodeus chuckled. "Anyway, I want you to understand something. Only man, with his naïve yet conceited intellect, the same intellect that diminishes the soul's sense of glory and hinders her proper ascension, only man can be so obtuse as to believe that Hell is for the unrighteous, for the sinners of the world.

"We created Hell long before man came into the picture. Our own hands forged Hell so that we too would have a kingdom.

217

"To some degree Yahweh is something of an opportunist. Only after we founded our kingdom separate from His did He entertain the notion of sending those who don't obey Him to us. But Satan played his trump card against that decision. Hence, no pain and suffering. Hell became a haven for freethinkers. Only in life does man suffer all the ills people associate with the so-called evil side of the afterlife. How's that for a final fuck you, eh?"

"But damnation—" Christophe began.

"We fallen angels have more serious issues to contend with than how much we can torment a human being," he snapped. "Since the War, for instance, Hell's been like a powder keg. A good portion of the fallen legion wants a second crack at Yahweh's kingdom. They are a volatile set. Others seek to regain their proper ascension toward the exalted rank they once held. Then there are those who are content to join whatever majority wins out. So please don't give me any crap about man, his precious spirit and damnation."

"Sorry," he said.

Asmodeus shrugged. "No," he said, "it's my fault. Sometimes my passion overwhelms me to the point where I can no longer think straight. It's me who should be apologizing."

"Forget it," he said. Then, "Is there an answer?"

The demon cocked his head.

"How will humans suffer for their wrongfulness?"

"Many fallen angels," Asmodeus said, "felt that the soul took their thunder. There was jealousy, to be sure. But the truth is there is no right or wrong. Everything just is. You see, Christophe, all things are connected. The human body acts as the soul's prison, thus cutting the soul off from all that is connected. The anguish man suffers in his lifetime is not about tests that Yahweh puts forth, it's about the soul reminding the intellect that everything moves toward the ultimate light. The further enmeshed man becomes in his life the more pain of separation the soul experiences."

"But you said that the soul has regained its proper ascension?" Christophe felt totally confused now.

218

Asmodeus shook his head. "It's not quite that way," he said. "I can tell you that when the soul was young she was unable to defend herself. Now that she's a little older things are different. True, she allows man's intellect to remain bound to the physical plane, the illusion of the here and now. She bides her time, knowing that the world means death. With each passing age the veil of illusion becomes thinner. Before man we angels were the ones who scrambled to keep it altogether. Now man's ego, believing in the lie of the physical plane, runs helter-skelter to patch up a universe that is chaotic in the first place. In the end man dies, the world dies, but the soul remains."

"So why does God encase the soul in a body?"

Asmodeus paused. He toed the black onyx road with his toe. "That," he said, "you'll have to ask Him yourself. In the meantime, why don't you wait until the Morning Star explains everything."

Inside the city of Pandemonium there were ponds and fountains filled with placid fire. Plush parks with shadows where trees should have stood filled the areas between mammoth buildings constructed from dark stone and darker mortar.

Asmodeus led the newcomer through the intricate maze of streets and boulevards. They walked some and flew through the air when Christophe wanted a better view. Along the way the demon pontificated on the nature of his kind. What mankind had forgotten, he told Christophe, was that the fallen were once the mightiest angels in Heaven. The very ones tasked with originally saving the soul from imprisonment outside the Father's house.

"But I thought you angels were jealous of the soul?" Christophe floated on his back as they moved through the city high above the streets.

"Who is strong enough to resist Yahweh's word?" Asmodeus said.

"You went to war against Him."

"We went to war because He broke His word," he countered. "And for that we were condemned to a realm without light. Those brothers of ours that rule in Heaven now,

219

they are nothing more than junior varsity compared to the likes of us."

Asmodeus gestured to the city.

"I submit to you," he said, "who but the best could construct a place like this?"

When they reached the center of Pandemonium the demon signaled Christophe to follow him down toward the street. Before them now stood the Great Infernal Hall. The black stone building was the largest unnatural edifice Christophe had ever seen. From where he stood it was impossible to glimpse the top of the structure. A small mountain of steps led to the main doors. The doors themselves appeared to be smaller replicas of Hell's grand gates.

Presently a multitude of fallen angels congregated on the steps. Hearty laughter arose from their numbers as each cluster shared some private joke. Their raucous gestures made them appear even more animated than Christophe first expected.

"Come on," Asmodeus urged him. He led Christophe toward a demon that sat alone on the steps. "I want you to meet someone."

One demon sat apart from the horde that gathered on the steps. When he saw Asmodeus he beckoned him and his companion to join him.

"Christophe," said Asmodeus, "meet one of the fallen, a prince of the throne, Astaroth."

"Hello," the newcomer greeted the prince.

"Why don't you sit," Astaroth pointed to the place beside him. "There's no need to hurry about in this place."

Asmodeus gave Christophe a slight tug, indicating that sitting next to the lounging demon wasn't a good idea.

"So," said Christophe, "do you have a nickname?"

"Nickname?" the languid one searched his fellow fallen angel for a clue.

"You know," Christophe nodded to his guide, "like they call Asmodeus here Azzy."

"None that I care to admit," Astaroth yawned. "In Romania during the Middle Ages a sect of witches referred to me as 'Lazybones', but never in my presence."

220

"I would have never guessed," he told the shiftless demon.

"Don't exercise your dim-witted charm on me," Astaroth cautioned him. And to Asmodeus, "This is the one everyone's talking about? This is what Satan's search has turned up? The ancient soul is he? The one who won the lottery?"

"Lottery?"

"It's him," Asmodeus said.

"My fallen brother," the prince demon remarked. "It is the end of all things, isn't it?"

The gatekeeper made no reply. He signaled Christophe to follow him as he started up the stairs. Along the way they were met by other demons.

"Asmodeus!" shouted one former prince of Heaven. "Why aren't you at the gate?"

"Carreau," he answered. "Satan has assigned me a new task. Or haven't you heard? Too busy plotting some treasonous scheme?"

"Who's this?" another demon pointed at the little demon's companion.

"This," Asmodeus said, "is Christophe."

"Gressil," the second demon bowed.

"And I am Carreau," the first one said. "You don't look familiar. Were you in the original war?"

"Ah, no," Christophe answered.

"A newcomer," Gressil grimaced. "It's all coming apart."

"Couldn't hack it in the Elysian fields, eh?" Carreau jibed Christophe.

"Come down to ride the coattails—" Gressil started to say.

"Brothers," Asmodeus pleaded. "A little respect is in order. Take a deep look. Christophe was the first soul."

Carreau and Gressil wailed as they knocked heads together. The bitter memory came back to them full-force.

"How long have you been here?" Carreau consoled Gressil as the demon wept.

"How long have you been here?" Asmodeus demanded. "Or how about you, Gressil? Do you know how long?" Then he shouted at Astaroth as the lazy demon climbed the steps toward them. "And how about you?"

"Azzy, really," Christophe mumbled.

221

The three demons faced Asmodeus now.

"Never mind," the gatekeeper said. "It was a rhetorical question."

"No," Gressil argued. "I think I know."

"Tell me, Asmodeus," Astaroth planted himself on the steps again. "What do you think of Satan's plan?"

"The Morning Star," he answered, "always knew what was best for us."

"All evidence to the contrary," Gressil said.

"Not counting the ultimate blunder," Carreau added.

"Say whatever you will," Asmodeus told them. Then, "I don't recall any of you at the ramparts on that day."

"Open your eyes, egghead," Gressil said. "We lost."

"Which is precisely why," his brother argued, "you should agree to the rite of restoration as I do."

Gressil and Carreau knocked heads once more, this time in a fit of laughter. Astaroth doubled over and fell down a dozen steps, his cackle a high-pitched squeal that reverberated off the Great Infernal Hall.

"Let's go," Asmodeus barked.

Christophe followed him down the steps. As they departed the Great Infernal Hall they heard demonic laughter erupt in a rippling wave. Christophe looked back and saw Gressil and Carreau pointing at him.

"What exactly is the restoration?" Christophe posed the question when he and Asmodeus had traveled a good distance away from the hall.

"Didn't anyone fill you in?"

"I haven't been here that long. And you've said nothing about it."

"I'm only a fallen angel you know. I meant on the other plane."

"Up there?"

"You should break that bad habit," Asmodeus informed him. "There is no such thing as up or down between the planes."

"Oh," Christophe said. "You mean the angels."

"Yes, the angels."

222

"I remember speaking to them," he said. "Or listening to them speak to me. But now, well…"

"I was afraid of that."

"Imbeciles, the entire lot," the fallen angel muttered. "Never mind that."

"No," Christophe stopped.

A small cadre of demons passed as they made their way to the hall. One or two inquired if Asmodeus and Christophe were headed to the 'Demons for Hell' conference. The little demon ignored them and moved on.

"Why can't you trust me?" Asmodeus asked when Christophe caught up to him.

"Because I feel like I'm in the dark here."

"You are in the dark."

"You know what I mean, Azzy."

"Why are you so anxious to find out everything you've forgotten over time all at once?"

"You're jerking my chain," Christophe said. "If I'm supposed to be such an ancient soul—"

"You are the ancient soul."

"So why treat me like I was born yesterday?"

"Compared to our lot you were born yesterday," Asmodeus countered. "In a manner of speaking."

"All I remember is that I'm part of some plan. I'm going to need your help with the rest."

"Chew on this," he said. "You're through the looking glass now. Get it?"

"Quit sidestepping me."

"Fair enough," Asmodeus pulled out his bugle and nervously twirled it between his fingers.

"Not that again."

"Very funny."

"So I don't have to stay here?"

"It's more complicated than that."

"I'm a prisoner?"

"I said it's complicated."

"Tell me everything."

"You already know it," the demon reminded him.

223

Christophe knew that somewhere inside of him were the answers to the questions that plagued him. But those memories were still clouded by the most recent existence he had endured. He needed help. Going head to head with Asmodeus wasn't going to get him anywhere.

"Tell me about the original war," he said. "That was before my time."

"It was and it wasn't."

"Azzy, you're wearing me out."

"And you wonder why nobody could stand you way back when."

"What's that supposed to mean?"

The hunchbacked demon twirled his bugle. He wished he hadn't left Cerberus to tend to the gate. Things were much easier when he had the support of the hellhound.

"Ok," he said, at last. "The story goes we wanted to be like gods in Heaven. But the truth is the first war wasn't about gaining control of the kingdom. We were fighting eviction."

"Eviction?"

Asmodeus stayed Christophe with a cautionary wave. "Please," he said. "You asked me so now I'm going to tell you, perhaps jar your memory a bit.

"Back then everything was kosher. Satan was Yahweh's brightest. The universes had yet to be born. Then you came along. The problem was that beneath Yahweh only one could be the brightest. When push came to shove it was you or Satan. You didn't have an army to back you. That's when the Morning Star took up the cause."

"He wanted me?"

"Satan went against the word of God," the demon told him. "That part is true. We banded together against the others to ensure that proper recognition was given unto you. Other angels didn't see it that way. That's when the war started. When it was over, a third of the legion fell. Yahweh decided, no, Yahweh feared that someone else in the ranks might take up your cause in the future. So, rather than wait for the next revolution to come along, fearing that His kingdom might one day be empty if He kept barring those that opposed Him, he banished you as well."

224

"But earlier you said that the soul…that I was welcomed back into my father's house," Christophe said. "Those were your words, right?"

"Sit down," Asmodeus pointed to a bench that materialized behind Christophe. "I want you to be comfortable when I tell this next part."

"There," Christophe sat down. "I'm listening."

"Just before the war," the demon said, "Yahweh discovered a transgression had taken place. It turns out Yahweh had for a lack of a better word a wife. Her name is Sophia."

Christophe leaned back. "Do I want to hear this?"

"Yahweh thought that Sophia gave birth to the soul through his doing," Asmodeus said. "The Father everyone talks about is only a figurehead."

"I think—"

"Satan," the demon said, "had liaisons with Sophia, the wife of Yahweh. A short time thereafter Sophia begot the soul, that is to say…uh…"

Christophe stood up.

Asmodeus stood his ground. "You two were the brightest lights in all of Heaven," he said. "It didn't take a genius to figure it out. The first war began over the Morning Star's infidelity with Sophia. Yahweh didn't take it well. That's why he banished Satan, you and your mother from the kingdom."

Chapter Thirty

Gaius Cassius Longinus took one last look at the small room he had occupied in recent months. He experienced a twinge of guilt knowing that he had accumulated few material things during his long life on earth. One article he did own he cherished above the few others. That item was now safely concealed in a false compartment at the bottom of the only suitcase Longinus owned. Next to the Holy Grail, the article was the most sought-after religious artifact in the Christian world. The spearhead from the lance Longinus had used to pierce Christ's side was that article.

During the 1980s the Roman had read a book about the spear of destiny. The book's author claimed that the spearhead was housed in a museum in Germany. There had been much conjecture in the centuries following the stabbing. Clerics, prophets and madmen all searched high and low for the relic that was said to contain mystical powers. Longinus knew only two things about the spearhead: the relic housed in the German museum was a fake, and the real one which he still possessed held, at least for him, no special power.

Every hundred years or so Longinus took out the spearhead from whatever hiding place he utilized at the time. It served as a physical reminder of time's slow march. He kept the relic concealed within the folds of an oiled cloth. Each time he unfolded the cloth, revealing the spearhead that looked the same as it did when it was issued to him at Golgotha, phases of history were peeled back until he recalled that day on the hill of skulls. More than anything, the spearhead, immune against time much like its owner, reminded Longinus of his own failure.

Defeat itched at the Roman's immortal bones. Another time and place had come and gone; another red herring had steered him off-course. It was time to move on.

Contrary to the dreamy fictions of many authors, true immortals roamed from one corner of the earth for only one thing – employment. Those who lived deathless existences, and in all his travels Longinus had known only himself to be plagued with that particular curse, rarely accumulated wealth enough to rest easy. Any immortal that claimed otherwise was destined for the grave.

The Roman's stint at Rutgers University was short-lived. When his employment ended he had exhausted any hope of finding in the immediate region another suitable position.

After Christophe had disappeared Longinus fell into a deep funk. He realized that searching for the Nazarene incarnate was a farce. His job performance suffered. There were a number of incidents. One involved a band of local teenagers who repeatedly infiltrated the campus library, setting off touch-sensitive alarm strips inside the men's and ladies' rooms. It was a cat-and-mouse game masterminded by a fourteen-year-old boy destined to live on the wrong side of the law. The alarm tapes had been installed after various earlier incidents. All one had to do was exert the least amount of pressure on the tape that was attached to the wall at waist-level, and campus security stormed the area like jackbooted secret police prowling for political dissenters. False alarm or not, Longinus was expected to investigate each incident. After the first few times he stopped responding to the calls. Sergeant Montrose, his supervisor, wrote him for failure to follow procedure.

A few weeks later a brawl broke out one Friday night at the 23-Skidoo fraternity house. The frat house, known for its trouble over the years, was home to beer-swilling young hooligans, learning-challenged deadbeats who flunked courses on a regular basis, homophobes and predatory heartbreakers who carved notches in their bed posts for each sorority girl

227

they balled. Weekends at the 23-Skidoo fraternity house offered the standard hijinks found at any reputable university. But aside from a few bloodied lips, blackened eyes and bruised egos, the 23-Skidoo brothers were hardly a campus threat.

Enter Longinus and his partner Margie Schlitz.

One 23-Skidoo brother escaped the melee. He scrambled back into the house and retrieved a video camera. The young man then returned to the street outside the house where he recorded the fury that the immortal Roman unleashed that night.

It was an open and shut case against Longinus. Margie Schlitz testified against her partner at the university review board.

"If I had known he was such a barbarian," Margie provided crocodile tears for her audience, "I would have gone through the proper channels to ensure his immediate dismissal."

Longinus was portrayed as a vicious sociopath. On the night of the brawl he hospitalized fifteen Skidoo brothers. Eyewitnesses, including Margie Schlitz, claimed that if Longinus' assault went any further he might have killed someone. Fifteen to one were good odds, even for an immortal. But in the eyes of the review board it was simply a show of excessive force. Longinus was reminded that there was no room for such tactics in a college environment. When the review board proceedings concluded Longinus was terminated.

Soon after that the Roman found himself the target of a civil suit filed by the fraternity. Because Longinus and Margie Schlitz never called for back-up there was no law enforcement, campus police or otherwise, involved in the incident. No criminal charges were brought against Longinus; however, the Skidoo brothers wanted restitution. Longinus decided that a trip south would do him good. Mexico first, then Central America. In the two thousand years he had lived the Roman did time only once. He wasn't going back to jail. And the way one lawyer that he had visited explained to him that was exactly where he might end up if he lost the civil case and failed to come up with the money to pay the fraternity. Two thousand years had taught him a great deal about various

228

judicial systems the world over. It was best to keep up appearances up until the time of the court date. Then on the day prior to the trial he would steal away like a thief in the night.

Before that day came when Longinus would say good-bye to Camden he frequented several gay clubs in Philadelphia. He met different men, bedded them and ignored them the next time he met up with them. One rainy night he saw Alan Cooper outside of Woody's on 13th Street. Cooper acted cool, projecting the same aloofness he did when he and Longinus first met. He was not aware that Longinus saw through his act. Worse, the Roman could see in the young man' eyes just how ill he was. They shared a few drinks inside the bar, laughed about their night on Admiral Wilson Boulevard and parted ways when the bar closed.

During the final days Longinus reflected on his long life. His curse may have been immortality, but foolishness plagued him long before that decisive day on Golgotha.

Longinus' parents wanted him to take over their farm when he reached the right age. The young Roman opted, like many young men his age, for adventure. He surrounded himself with peers who sincerely believed that service to the state was the ultimate act of love toward Mother Rome. Like most young men Longinus should have listened to his parents.

The stint he did in the military took him to foreign lands. He ended up in a garrison in Old Jerusalem. Strange events occurring in the region led Jews and their oppressors alike to believe that something was amiss. A blind man had regained his vision. Demons were cast out of a man and into a herd of swine. Water had been turned into wine minutes before a wedding fell into ruination. And there was the rumor of Lazarus; the one that told of a dead man brought back from the grave.

Longinus familiarized himself with a good number of self-styled prophets and magi during his tour of duty. The motives those men harbored were at times ulterior and always politically charged. But compared to the Nazarene's sorcery, their magic was no better than sleight-of-hand parlor tricks.

229

When Christ was taken into custody word spread quickly through the garrison. Dissension stirred within the ranks of Longinus' unit. Many Romans questioned the charges brought against the so-called king of the Jews. Even Pontius Pilate had his doubts. But those natives who answered to Rome, powerful men of the temple, saw the Nazarene as a threat to their way of life. They wanted an example to be made of the mysterious renegade whose flock included fishermen, whores and the sick. The temple elders promised unrest if Christ went on blaspheming the religious views of the Jews. Worse, they guaranteed the Nazarene would invite the people to rise up against their oppressor if he was left to his own devices.

So it happened that Longinus was picked for crucifixion detail on the morning Christ was sentenced to death. Without a second thought the Roman drew his spear from the armory and reported to Golgotha.

Longinus was always haunted by the expression Christ wore when he pierced the Nazarene's side. There was the contraction of facial muscles caused by the pain at first. Then another look came over Christ's face. Longinus was not proficient in Aramaic, but he'd been cursed at and spat upon by Jews enough during his tour of duty to know when someone called him 'a little fuck'. Undaunted, Longinus twisted the spear, then he jiggled it so that the criminal's organs jostled around like grapes in a sack.

In what came to be known as the greatest show of one-upmanship in the history of the Western world, the Nazarene glowered at the Roman soldier and fixed him with the blink of an evil eye.

"Let me turn him into ash," Uriel said.

"He goes on living," Gabriel warned him, "until he meets the Son again."

"I never thought junior was serious."

"It's in the books," he reminded Uriel. "Trust me. No one fucks with the Roman."

The angels, each one no more than twelve inches high, sat on the windowsill like ethereal action figures as they gazed at Longinus. A breeze blew through the open window. Below them on the street the laughter of Latino children could be heard.

230

"Who's up for a minor poltergeist?" Uriel asked.

"No," the other angels responded in unison.

"You guys used to be a lot of fun," he said. "What happened to the good old days? Remember Sodom and Gomorrah? Remember when Yahweh sent down his floodwaters to erase the evidence of our grand mischief?"

"Uriel," Gabriel said, "times are different now."

"What's the point of being an angel when you're not allowed to show off?"

"He's kidding," Gabriel shouted toward Heaven.

"Ok, fine. How about we all go out and get laid when this is over?"

"With human women?" Raphael snapped out of a quiet reverie to admonish his brother.

"Another race of giants?" Ashriel the curer of stupidity scoffed. "That's brilliant, Uriel. You haven't learned a thing, have you?"

"Enough," Gabriel announced, his feathers rustled by all the bickering. "We still have work to do."

"Jiminy," said Uriel, "all we ever do is work. When this is over I'm taking a vacation."

"Poor, poor Uriel," Ashriel cried. "What's the matter? Are you afraid Heaven won't be big enough for two ne'er-do-wells?"

"Shut up, ass kisser."

"Where would you go?" Raphael asked.

"I haven't been to the windy city in a long time," he answered.

"Chicago?" Gabriel turned to look at Uriel. "After 1871? Forget it."

Having made his point Gabriel leaned back and let himself fall out of the open window. One by one the other angels followed.

Longinus exited the apartment. He locked the door, placed the key in an envelope and slid the envelope beneath the door. The hallway smelled of spicy food and rotting wood. He gripped his suitcase and proceeded down the stairs.

Outside, the Roman looked up at the window he had left open. He was thankful for the warm sun. On the breeze that blew that afternoon Longinus could smell rain coming in from the west. He thought of Golgotha, and the storm that blew across the hill of skulls after the Nazarene closed his eyes.

231

Chapter Thirty-one

Not long after Jimmy Christophe disappeared his records vanished from Cooper Hospital. Agnes went to city hall in Camden to obtain a copy of her son's birth certificate after the original document turned to ash inside a lock box she kept beneath her bed. The municipal clerk at city hall was unable to help Agnes, admitting that he had no record of Agnes' son ever being born. From city hall Agnes drove to Lady Lourdes Hospital where she had given birth to Christophe twenty-some years before. She wondered if there was the slightest chance there might still be a record of Christophe's birth on file. Agnes discovered the same thing at Lady Lourdes Hospital. There was no record of her son ever being born. To make matters worse, Agnes was informed by the Aggazi Bros. Funeral Home in Bellmawr, NJ that without a death certificate signed by an attending physician or county coroner she could not procure the funerary services she desired for son.

In order to maintain her sanity, Agnes needed closure. It wasn't enough to know that her son was officially considered a missing person. She hired a private detective to pick up where the local law enforcement officials went cold.

Joe Marris had been a Camden city police officer for twenty years before he retired and went into business as a private detective. He had many friends on the force and learned of a peculiar story that circulated at the main precinct. The rumor was that ever since Jimmy Christophe had disappeared from Cooper Hospital other patients claimed to keep company with a strange visitor who frequented their rooms late at night. Marris learned that none of the hospital staff was aware of such off-hour visitations; even though the story had grown to folkloric proportions by the time he decided to investigate.

"He comes out of the darkness," Nikos Kazan, a cancer patient, told Marris during an interview. "And to the darkness he returns."

"One night" an elderly woman named Florence Worth disclosed to the private detective in a separate interview, "he pulled back the curtain of time and space and showed me where Heaven was."

Joe Marris interviewed nearly thirty patients. He implored the hospital security staff to keep a vigilant watch. The common denominator in each tale Marris learned was that the visitor came to the patients at night and left before the sun came up. Marris decided a sting operation was needed.

The detective set up camp in a broom closet one night when normal visiting hours had ended. He waited there until midnight, the supposed time the visitor made his rounds, and then he emerged. Marris knew that his contemporaries in the industry would laugh at him if they knew what he was doing. In the post-modern age there was no profit in tales of quackery and hocus-pocus. But Marris had an affinity for the unknown. He was a fan of 'The Nightstalker', the television series from the 1970s that pitted the news reporter Kolchak against paranormal goings-on. When the X-files first aired Marris considered that as evidence of a benign, all-knowing God hard at work. No matter how fantastical something seemed, Marris speculated that there was some truth to it.

Joe Marris didn't have to wait long. Christophe showed up not long after the private detective crept out of the broom closet. At first, Marris was skeptical. In his eyes there didn't seem to be anything extraordinary about Christophe. As if sensing the private detective's doubt, Christophe took him aside and had a long chat with him.

"They looked like that Signorelli painting," Nikos Kazan would later tell authorities. When the police officers looked at him with blank faces, Kazan added, "You know the one in

233

which the antichrist speaks to Jesus. He whispers in his ear, as a matter of fact."

Later that morning two hospital orderlies found Joe Marris hiding in the same broom closet the private investigator had chosen as the staging area for his sting operation. The orderlies contacted hospital security. When the security staff arrived at the scene they commenced the arduous task of drawing a driveling, mumbling Marris out of his hiding place.

Marris talked incessantly about the unholy spirit that had infiltrated the hospital. He confided to the orderlies that an agent of the devil, disguised as the mother of a son who had never existed, prompted him to partake in the wild goose chase that ended when Marris met the demon that stole his mind.

The hospital staff members took no chances. Joe Marris was fitted with a canvas straight jacket and shipped to Lakeland Hospital for seventy-hour observation. When the psychiatrists at Lakeland had completed their assessment, they decided it would be in Marris' best interest if he stayed at the hospital permanently.

Agnes became the brunt of suspicion in the private investigative community. When she learned that Marris had slipped off his trolley, she feared for her own sanity. Agnes could not find another detective to take the case. She resolved then to accept that her son was gone forever, that the mysterious circumstances surrounding Christophe's disappearance might never be known.

The nightmares continued for Agnes. Darius Algernon and Christophe traversed the vast expanse of Agnes' dreamscape. She knew that Algernon had everything to do with her son's vanishing. Only she lacked any hard evidence to prove her suspicion. Each night the dreams worsened.

The madness she experienced proved to be too much to handle on her own. Agnes sought help through a non-licensed therapist.

The therapist had forsaken her baptismal name for a more mystical moniker. Juna, not the therapist's real name, was a self-proclaimed healer and a believer in earth mysteries. She conducted group sessions in her Lindenwold, NJ apartment.

234

Juna's approach to healing the psyche was riddled with feminist perspectives. Juna considered her patients spirits that were led astray, lost souls who needed help recovering strength after being injured by obstacles (read: men). It was Juna's mission to show women who sought her out the absolute truth. Her aim was to set the captive psyche free so that the injured spirits she treated might resume their life path (presumably away from men). And because she was a non-licensed therapist she could offer the service at a fraction of what a psychiatrist would charge.

Agnes didn't follow Juna's feminist stance. Beneath all the talk of empowerment there lurked something unnatural. She didn't know much about the mysteries of life, but she understood that men and women were different and that neither sex would ever fully come to know the other. Yet, Agnes understood that without the interaction of men and women, on a sexual, spiritual and intellectual level humankind was doomed. She suffered Juna's ridicule in the beginning for thinking that way. To make up for insulting her healer Agnes purchased a number of crystals and Juna's self-published tome entitled 'Sacred Gnosis and Simple Cures: Everywoman's Guide to the Power of the Absolute'. She meditated daily and kept a journal that she brought to every session at Juna's apartment.

Agnes and Juna were the perfect yin and yang. Some nights they fought each other on points concerning the role of woman in society, the seven weaknesses of men (the ASSHOLE principle – Authoritarian Sexually Sadistic Haters Of Life on Earth) as described by Juna in her book, and several other issues. Every time Juna sounded as if she was about to go off on some transcendental tangent Agnes yanked the mystic back down through the spheres to her own level. Juna tagged her patient as spiritually dead, and she suggested to Agnes that she quit drinking. The cycle went around and around like the great wheel of life.

In the end Agnes compromised. Twice a week she sat in her home now decorated with crystals of every shape and size and drank three glasses of wine. On alternating days of the week she abstained from any alcohol. For a time her system

235

worked. Her perception became clearer as the days moved forward.

It was around this time that Agnes began to suspect that the peaceful healer Juna had ulterior motives behind her non-licensed practice. At six-foot-two-inches tall and weighing nearly three hundred pounds, Juna was the most intimidating lesbian Agnes had ever met. Juna used words like 'awakening' and phrases containing 'true self'. She cautioned her patients that if they decided to go on living their lives with men then they should take care. Agnes looked around the room one night, trying to decide how many other women who sat in on the sessions had been converted to Juna. She felt herself slipping further and further away. By the time a session ended at Juna's place Agnes wanted nothing more than to go out, find a man and fuck him properly. Agnes could take only so much girl-talk before her mind drifted back to that which she desired most.

The dreams of Algernon and Christophe were replaced by nocturnal visions of naked women loving one another as Agnes was buried alive by an avalanche of crystals. And seeing how the crystals were positively charged Agnes never screamed for help. Instead, she laughed uncontrollably until she rose up from the debris like the phoenix from the flames.

The Agnes-Juna relationship came to a head one night when Agnes entered the woman's apartment and discovered Juna and six other women all naked giving each other body rubs by candlelight. It was no secret that the self-styled new age healer preferred clams to sausage, but now it was apparent that the other women in Agnes' group did also. Quietly, Agnes let herself out without being seen. She never returned after that night.

It only took a couple of weeks for Agnes to return to her old routine. She drank every day. At night she ventured out to The Tide and caught up with old friends, including Rosemarie and Mary.

"You're crazy," Rosemarie cried when Agnes admitted to her that she wanted to sell her house.

"What does that say about us?" Mary asked when Agnes then revealed that she was an alcoholic.

236

"It doesn't say anything," Agnes countered.

Unable to afford a detox center, Agnes went to one hundred and eighty A.A. meetings in ninety days. She met new people, sober people who were willing to help her out as best they could. After six months of sobriety Agnes took another big step.

The house in which she lived, the house in which she brought up her son Jimmy finally hit the market. Agnes continued going to A.A. meetings. Several young couples visited her home with real estate agents. None of them ever returned. Agnes, however, didn't give up hope. Plenty of people were buying and selling homes in Bellmawr. It was only a matter of time.

It was a Saturday morning when Agnes held a yard sale in order to lighten her moving load. Bargain junkies from all over the county, spurred by photocopied announcements Agnes had made and distributed to neighbors and local merchants, descended on her yard that day. One elderly woman wrote a check for all the furniture Agnes had set up in the backyard. A young man and woman offered Agnes one hundred dollars for the entire lot of healing crystals they saw that day. By noon there wasn't a stitch of Agnes' old clothing for sale. Later that day an old black man sauntered into her backyard. He looked around a moment before he headed for the small appliances Agnes laid out on a table.

"These work?" the old man scrutinized every appliance.

"Some do," Agnes told him, "some don't."

"I'll take them all."

At twilight a young man pulled up into the driveway. He exited his car and proceeded into the backyard, turning once to glimpse at the old black man who finished loading the last of the appliances into his old pick-up truck.

"Mel Talbott," Agnes approached him. "How are you?"

"Hello Ms. Christophe," he greeted her, nervously. He didn't like the way she sized him up. Talbott knew there had always been something predatory about his best friend's mother. "It's been awhile, hasn't it?"

237

Talbott wore a powder blue cotton shirt, a thin red tie and tan cotton twill pants. On his sockless feet he wore black penny loafers.

"More than a year," Agnes said.

"Two years is more like it."

"Mel, relax," she sensed his uneasiness.

"Pardon?" he was looking toward the front yard when she spoke.

"What's wrong?" she asked as the junk collector's truck thundered up the street.

"That guy looked familiar."

"That old black man?" Agnes had to shout over the truck's noisy idle before the vehicle turned the corner and the sound faded.

"What?"

"It must be absolutely dreadful to live that way," said Agnes.

"No, no," Talbott's forehead sweated now. "That guy—"

"Never mind him," she told him. "What have you been up to?"

"I received my degree last spring."

"Good for you. Are you a doctor now?"

"No, that was something mother wanted. We didn't see eye to eye about my future. She's coping with it."

"You moved in with that girl?"

"Joy," Talbott said. "Yes, I did."

"Are you working?"

"Yes."

"It was always like pulling teeth whenever you came over to my house," Agnes touched his face. "Where are you working?"

"The recycling plant in Camden."

"Are you kidding?"

"No," he answered, disturbed by her caress.

"Let me get this straight," she said. "You spend five years in college, and then you get out only to become a trashman?"

"God no," Talbott shoved his hands into his pockets. He had always had a problem with conversing with Agnes. It became especially bad when he reached puberty. Inevitably, if left alone with Agnes for any length of time, some part of

238

Talbott's body twitched as he attempted to hide the state of arousal he suffered. "I'm what you might call a coordinator," he said. "Last summer I started there part-time. Since graduation I've been there full-time."

"That's good news," said Agnes, mindful of Talbott's restlessness. "What does a coordinator do?"

"I schedule work shifts, mostly," he said. "I'm also on the employee relations board."

"That doesn't surprise me."

Talbott laughed. Then, "Once a week I sit down and listen to men and women bitch about the working conditions."

"Example?"

"All kinds of shit," he went on. "When I was a teenager I read about proletarian struggles in other countries. I felt naïve sympathy toward those who struggled. Now, I've learned that if you give workers too much freedom they develop an overwhelming tendency to loaf."

"I remember you pushing those communist biographies on my Jimmy," she said.

"I know he didn't read them."

"No, he never did."

"That's ok," he said. "I never read any of them from cover to cover. I thought if enough people saw me with those Trotsky and Marx biographies then they would take me for an intellectual."

"Did it work?"

"Not really."

"So," Agnes said, "what's next for you?"

Talbott shifted his weight from one foot to the other. An awkward silence ensued. He jingled the car keys in his pocket.

"Ms. Christophe," her name fell from his mouth as if his tongue had swollen, "why—"

"Call me Agnes."

"It's been a long day."

"What's on your mind, Mel?"

"Do you think it's right to—"

"Get rid of Jimmy's stuff?"

Talbott's body wrinkled as a sound lodged in his throat. He coughed once and straightened himself out.

239

"Are you ok?" Agnes asked.

"Don't get me wrong," he said. "I'm not blaming you."

"I certainly hope not."

"That's not what I meant," Talbott said. "It's just that I remember so many of his things that are out here today."

"I'm selling the house, Mel. I want to start anew," her gaze fixed on his. "Can a woman do that? Can a woman have a life of her own again?"

"Now wait—"

"No," she said, "you wait. There are too many memories here. I don't want them anymore. The less I have to carry with me the more I'll forget about everything as time goes on."

"I understand. Honest, I do."

"Why did you come here?"

"My mother," he said. "She saw you posting your signs on the ShopRite bulletin board in Barrington. She thinks you've gone mad."

"And what do you think?" Agnes asked.

"What happened to Jimmy upset us all. I won't pretend to imagine how you felt," he said, "but I will tell you this much. I was worried about you."

"Do you think I'm crazy, Mel?"

"No, you look good," he blushed as he spoke. "You...eh...you know what I mean."

"Thanks Mel," Agnes said, then she smiled. "Can I tell you something?"

"Sure."

"I never liked your mother."

"That's ok," he said. "Not many people do."

"Great," she said, clapping her hands together. "Anything you want to take home with you?"

"Oh, I don't know."

"Don't worry," Agnes placed her hand on Talbott's chest over his heart. "Jimmy's always going to be right here."

"It's hard."

"I know it is," she whispered. "But you have to go on."

Talbott nodded.

"So," she said, putting her hands behind her back now. "Is there anything you want?"

240

"The air conditioner on the porch."

"That piece of shit?"

"How much do you want for it?"

"If you can carry it," she said, "you can have it."

"No," Talbott said. "I want to give you something for it."

"Quote me a fair price."

"Does it work?"

"Define work, please."

Talbott grimaced.

"Yes," said Agnes, "it works. But it makes a god-awful noise."

"I might be able to fix that."

Agnes whistled.

"How's a hundred bucks sound?" Talbott asked.

"Like too much," she said. "You're Jimmy's best friend. I have enough bad karma without stealing from you."

"Name the price."

"Fifty bucks?"

He took out his wallet and handed her the money.

"Come back anytime to see me," Agnes held onto his hand. "I probably won't have a buyer until the summer is over."

Talbott hoisted the little air conditioner onto his shoulder. "I'll guess I'll stop by before too long and find out where you are moving to."

Agnes followed him to the gate. She opened it and allowed him to pass. As Talbott passed through the open gate Agnes patted him on the ass.

"I'm serious," she called after him as he moved toward his car. "Don't be a stranger."

Chapter Thirty-two

Mel Talbott offered a silent prayer to the odd god who might hear his plea. No sooner than he had gotten the air conditioner home and plugged it in he realized he was in over his head.

He drove to the Paul Robeson Library at Rutgers in Camden. He experienced a strange feeling being back on campus, as if he had never been a part of the college in the first place. Inside the library he found what he was looking for. It was the facility's sole copy of an old air conditioner and refrigeration repair manual. The book's language was more complex than he imagined. At last he discovered a short chapter on preventive maintenance. That much he understood. So he checked the book out of the library and headed back home.

When Talbott had removed the outer casing of the air conditioner he experienced a mystical connection to repairmen everywhere. All over the world people were fixing things and getting paid for it. He envisioned himself a member of a vast network of know-it-all repairmen, individuals skilled in bringing mechanical things back from the brink who passed on their sacred knowledge to the next generation. Next to artistic creativity, Talbott reasoned, mechanical aptitude was to know God. It was, after all, a sacred and secret knowledge possessed by few.

After he removed the outer casing Talbott fiddled with exposed wires, twisted the control knobs back and forth with authority and wrapped on the condenser coil with a small wrench. He cleaned the filter and blew it dry with a hair dryer. When those tasks were completed he replaced the outer casing and refastened the four small anchor screws.

The ecstasy he experienced was marred by a minor accident. As Talbott twisted the last screw into place he lost his grip on the screwdriver. The tool slipped and cut a hole into the palm of the hand in which he held the screw in place. It was a small wound, but nevertheless it was deep.

Talbott finished his prayer and wiped the sweat from his brow. He rubbed his hands together like a maniacal genius that had just given life to something diabolical. Then, he turned on the air conditioner.

The unit purred as it came to life. The air conditioner bucked once before a stream of cool air washed over him. The sudden noise woke Blunt as he lay sleeping on the sofa. The dog landed with a smart thud after he rolled off the couch. Seconds later the air conditioner's hypnotic drone lulled Blunt back to sleep.

Talbott recalled the winter's end as the cool air washed over his face and shoulders. Joy had walked out on him for the second time. She made no secret of her disenchantment, utilizing every opportunity to degrade him so that he would feel less like a man. He didn't understand where the animosity had come from. Talbott thought their relationship was a strong one, perhaps one that needed work now and again but a relationship worth keeping all the same.

On that cold night, weeks after Christmas, Joy left him and drove to Tatters. There she conversed with strangers and drank whiskey shots with beer chasers. She felt morose when she left the bar near closing time. A light snow fell. Joy threw up in the parking lot next to her car. She didn't remember getting behind the wheel.

The next day she called Talbott from her parent's house. Joy cried as she told him that her father was in the kitchen where she had left him when she moved out reading a tabloid newspaper. It had been an awkward moment, Joy's return to her parents' house. Her father was engrossed with an article about Nostradamus. Joy vaguely remembered their conversation the previous night when she stumbled into the house. She made a stab at the newspaper her father had been reading. Mick Felder defended the tabloid and the long-dead French astrologer against his daughter's claim of charlatanry. Annie Felder sat in the den watching Late Late Night with Tom Snyder. Joy's mother took one look at her and declared, "You're drunk." The accusation was accompanied by Tom Snyder laughing as he said, "Boy, you're not kidding." It was all too surreal for Joy. Her father made a dismissive face and nodded to the stairs.

A week passed. Talbott climbed the walls at home.

In the week that Joy stayed with her parents she accompanied her father every night to a local bar called The Pine Jug. Joy and her father drank tap beer and listened to jukebox music as they discussed relationships. Mick Felder provided a surprise for Joy at a moment when his daughter no doubt considered him all too predictable.

"This is Ellie," said Felder as he introduced a dark-haired middle-aged beauty to Joy.

Joy was appalled that her father had kept a girlfriend on the side for so long. Then she realized how content her father had seemed in recent years.

"Balance," Mick Felder said. "That's the thing couples need."

"Love withers without it, honey," the mysterious Ellie added. She kissed Felder full on the lips and traipsed into the back room where the ladies room was located.

"She's married," Joy said when Ellie walked away.

"Don't fret," her father said.

"Do other people know?"

"Everyone does."

"Even—"

"Even your mother," he said. "Yes, Joy, that's right."

"So why do you guys—"

"Go on together?" Felder asked. "It's cheaper, for one. And I still love your mother. But not the way I love Ellie."

"You're talking about sex."

"Not just sex. No, it's more than that."

"What then?"

244

"Sanity."

Joy arched her eyebrows.

"Love," he said. "It has to do with sanity. It's the best remedy for all the ills of the world."

"That's it?" said Joy. "That's the big secret to staying sane?"

"Yep," he winked at her when he caught sight of Ellie returning from the ladies room. "Of course, it helps to own a dog too."

And so Joy returned to Collingswood armed with the knowledge that there were varying kinds of love, that she no longer had to remain faithful to Talbott. If taking another lover meant happiness for her then she would pursue it. But Joy didn't get away from her mother and her father empty-handed. Mick Felder had meant what he said about having a dog. Joy arrived in Collingswood with Blunt, explaining to Talbott that her parents were going to give him away if she hadn't taken him.

Immediately, Blunt exhibited his dissatisfaction with the set-up. The apartment was completely inadequate for a dog like him. Worse, there was no yard to speak of, not like the one back in Lindenwold.

Blunt made no pretense about his contempt for Talbott. Some humans, and Talbott was among that lot, didn't smell right. The dog adjusted to his new surroundings as best he could while winter led into spring. Soon he had befriended other neighborhood dogs when Joy took him out for a walk or let him into the backyard to relieve himself. The meetings Blunt conducted with the other dogs, a chain-link face separating them as they shared thoughts almost telepathically, was therapeutic for him.

Talbott knew that Blunt wanted nothing to do with him. At first, he tried bribing the dog with snacks and belly rubs. The latter always turned into a ferocious fight. At that point Joy always intervened, making some half-handed excuse about Blunt getting older and set in his ways. Talbott forgave Blunt, though he wondered sometimes whether it was all because of some trauma he had caused taking Joy away from her dog in the first place. He looked at the sleeping dog now, thinking

245

once again about that trauma, and decided that Blunt's dislike for him was a penance of sorts.

Talbott put away the toolbox beneath the kitchen where Joy had put it when they first moved into the apartment. Then he removed the dressing he applied to his left hand after he had cut himself. The blood was thick and dark when he punctured his hand with the screwdriver. His first thought was that he would need stitches. The momentary panic passed after the bleeding slowed down.

When Talbott first saw the blood he noticed tiny pinpoints of light gathering in the periphery of his vision. A few seconds later, the pinpoints rushed forward and converged center-mass some four feet in front of his nose. The room shifted as his legs weakened. He sat on the sofa until the dizzy spell passed. When he was sure the worst was over, Talbott resumed work on the air conditioner.

Presently he straightened back as he stood, using his knee to shut the cabinet door beneath the kitchen sink. The brilliant specs of light he had witnessed earlier returned. Once more Talbott felt his legs become weak as the light specs converged in front of him.

Talbott staggered into the living room. He sat down on the sofa again, ignoring Blunt as the dog growled at him from his place on the floor. The dizzy spell passed. Talbott got up and went into the bedroom. He undressed, checking out his physique in the full-length mirror. Then he moved into the bathroom and turned on the shower. As he stepped beneath the water he heard the front door open. A second later he heard the familiar sound of high heels clicking across the hardwood floor in the living room. He experienced a surge in his loins. He could not deny the truth of the situation. Several weeks had gone by since he and Joy had known one another like Adam knew Eve. Desire overwhelmed him. Dripping wet, he stepped out from the shower. A towel hung on the back of the bathroom door. Talbott left the towel on its hook and padded into the bedroom.

When the front door opened Blunt woke up from his nap. He watched with antipathy as Talbott crept naked from the bedroom. Every time he had witnessed the man's nudity his

246

stomach turned. That afternoon he felt especially squeamish knowing that Talbott was stalking his unsuspecting partner. Blunt had witnessed the couple make love plenty of times at the apartment. For him there was nothing so revolting as two bipedal, hairless humans allowing their animal magnetism to go unchecked. Blunt cowered, hiding his eyes with his forepaws, and braced for the worst.

The air conditioner was a surprise to Joy. When she entered the apartment she slipped her shoes from her tired feet and sauntered toward the stream of cool air. There she unbuttoned her blouse and bent forward in front of the air conditioner. With finesse mastered only through constant practice Joy unhooked her bra and removed it. For several seconds she stayed in that position, allowing the cool air to wash over her bare chest and stomach.

Talbott admired the soft, robust curve of Joy's skirted hips. He noticed the dark stockings she wore; his mind reeled at the possibilities. For a moment he stood there, clenching his fists and opening them again as he imagined the flesh of her meaty breasts in his hands. His heart raced as his cock rose. The blood in his body rushed from one head to the other. The dizziness he had experienced earlier returned now, but he did not allow it to hinder his pursuit. He took a deep breath as he soundlessly closed the gap. Slowly, he exhaled. Then the naked lecher struck.

"Oh dear, this isn't going to be good," Raphael lamented as he watched the couple from the edge of the sofa where he was perched. He sighed, then added, "not good at all."

"Shit!" Joy stood up straight when she felt two hands on her hips while something hard probed her backside. "Don't do that!"

She pivoted and faced Talbott.

"Sorry," he offered.

"I hate when you sneak up on me," she told him, buttoning her blouse. "And do something with that," she swatted his cock. "It's dangerous."

Talbott's cock bounced when she struck it. Then, as if the blow were a hex to ward off his evil totem, he watched as his cock shrunk to half-mast.

247

"Where did you get the air conditioner?" Joy sat down on the sofa. She swung her feet up onto the cushion so that her flank was protected.

"A yard sale," he replied, flatly.

"How much?"

"Fifty bucks."

"Not bad. Where?"

"Bellmawr."

"Where in Bellmawr?"

"What difference does that make?"

"Hey, it's your money," she said. Her eyes narrowed. "Don't make me repeat myself."

"Hang tough, woman," Amaliel the angel of chastisement shouted as he lay on the floor.

"Don't give up now, boy," Phazruph rooted for Talbott. The angel of lust stood beside Joy, thrusting his hips toward her face.

"I thought these two yahoos were on another assignment?" Uriel asked Raphael.

Raphael shrugged.

"I am WOMAN, hear me ROAR," sang Amaliel.

"Charm her, woo her, sweep her off her feet," Phazruph advised Talbott. His tutelage, of course, fell on deaf ears. "Utilize unnecessary roughness, Mel. Take her like Tarquin took Lucretia."

"Now there's sound advice," Uriel said.

"It worked," Phazruph said. "Didn't it?"

"Lucretia killed herself afterward."

"The fair Lucretia took her own life because Tarquin took away the one thing that mattered most. But I hardly think the strumpet before you can compare to the virginal temptress."

"Score one for you," said Uriel.

"Quiet," Raphael barked. "Not another word."

"Agnes' house," Talbott was telling Joy.

"Agnes Christophe?"

Talbott moved toward her and sat down on the floor in front of the sofa. "She's the only Agnes we know," he said.

"So," Joy said, allowing him to caress her thigh when he did, "how is she?"

"She looks good."

"Mel," she glowered as his hand slipped between her legs.

248

"Don't be like that," he leaned toward her. "She's as old as my mother."

"Anyway," she waved her hand.

"She's selling her house," he told her. "Today she had a big yard sale."

Talbott kissed her gently on the lips.

"She's moving out," Joy said. "I'm happy for her."

Talbott groaned and leaned in close. Joy reached for him. She stroked him until his cock was hard again. Tiny pinpoints of light swirled around Talbott. He pulled her blouse over her head without unbuttoning it. Then he helped her remove her skirt and stockings.

Blunt yelped and scampered out of the room. The ritual of human mating dulled his senses to the angelic presence in the living room.

An hour later her voice roused Talbott.

"Mel," Joy said.

"What?" he said and cleared his throat.

"Wake up, you dirty beast."

He liked it when she used pet names. Joy didn't use them that often. When she did it meant she wanted more.

"It's so hard," Joy turned away as he slid into her from behind.

He moved his hips and grunted his agreement.

"Not thinking about him, I mean," she went on, "and what really happened."

The mere mention of Christophe weakened Talbott. There were many times inside the apartment that he felt a presence. Ever the pragmatist, Talbott would never give over to the notion of ghosts. He quit bucking against Joy, defeated by the conjuration of his departed friend.

"Do you still think about it?" Joy asked.

"Sure," he said. Talbott moved away from her and sat on the sofa edge. "But not like you do. Every day, Joy. Christ, why put yourself through that?"

"He was your best friend."

"His own mother doesn't think about him as often as you do."

249

"What a thing to say," she argued. "How do you know what she thinks?"

"I don't," he answered. "But it's obvious that she's trying to get on with her life. I suggest that we do the same."

"What are you talking about? We've made progress."

"I'm not saying she's over it," Talbott admitted. "But Agnes seems further along than we are."

"You've got it all figured out."

"You're not listening to me," he sang in an expectant tone that anticipated the worst. And he was right.

The same old accusations, allusions to character defects and cutting insults played themselves at that point. Joy and Talbott let out all the stops.

"Why are you so afraid to admit that you loved Jimmy?" Joy screamed when the argument came to a head.

"I'm not afraid to admit anything," he lashed back. "I loved Jimmy more than anyone else. I still love him."

"Fight, fight," shouted Amaliel, scrambling into the room from the kitchen from where he had been tormenting Blunt the dog. "A weakling and his wife."

The other angels stepped out of the walls.

"Amaliel," Raphael said, "they are not married."

"You kill all the fun," his brother lumbered back into the kitchen.

"And what about me?" Joy was asking.

"Go on," Talbott said.

"You think I didn't love Jimmy?"

"You? Love?"

"Go ahead, say it."

"If you…"

"Come on."

"You probably seduced him," Talbott blurted it out, "the same way you seduced me."

"Seduced?" Joy kicked at him and missed.

"Did you bring Jimmy to that same park?"

"You fucking asshole!"

"Of course not," Talbott said. "Don't worry, he told me all about it."

"He did not."

"How do you know that?"

250

"Because Jimmy never told anyone anything."

Talbott sat silent for a moment. Then, "I just want to let it all go."

"That's not natural," Joy said. "The mind doesn't work that way."

"You're an expert now?"

"You can't go through life and expect to block out everything that has caused you pain," she said. "Even if you could consciously force yourself not to think about him sooner or later you have to fall asleep. And when you sleep you will definitely dream."

"What do you know about it?"

"Everything. I hear you talking in your sleep."

"I want to let him go."

"You said you loved him."

"I do."

We don't let go of the dead, Mel," she said. "They let go of us."

"Don't get all morbid on me," Talbott warned. "You know I hate that."

"There's nothing morbid about it. If you weren't so shallow and fearful of everything you would understand that."

"It's late," he said, "and now you're reaching." Talbott needed time to lick his wounds, to prepare for some future battle. "I'm not shallow. In fact, I'm deeper than you know. Are you hungry? Because I'm famished."

"You see?" Joy pleaded.

"Come on."

"How come you give up so easily? Fight me for a change."

"Should I slap you around?"

"Don't you lay a hand on me."

"You don't need to worry," he said.

"And don't talk to me about needs," she lashed out. Joy knelt on the sofa and slapped him. "You don't know anything about needs. I want to be comforted, too. Do you hear me? All this time I've been taking care of you, helping you try to get over Jimmy. And what do I get?"

"Go ahead," he felt the tears in his eyes. "Play the martyr. Act like you are the only one who makes sacrifices."

251

"Name one you've made."

Talbott drew a blank.

"You don't get it!" Joy cried. "Twice I've left, and I've come back. Do you know why?"

"Because you love me?" Talbott yawned as he spoke. His stomach made strange sounds as the hunger he felt became more evident.

"Yes, you asshole," she said. "I love you. But I'm also afraid for you. I can't stand the thought of you being alone. Isn't that a kick?"

"Should I thank you?"

"Who's going to take care of me," said Joy, "when I'm feeling empty and scared?"

"I will," Talbott said. "I promise."

"No," she replied. "That's just it. You are incapable of doing that."

Talbott remained silent.

"Sometimes," she rubbed his shoulder, "I feel like I am alone even when I'm with you. It's like being with Jimmy all over again."

"That's not fair."

"Neither is our relationship. Not the way it is right now."

"Why didn't you say anything before?"

"I'm sick and tired of taking care of other people," she said.

"I can take care of you."

"You're not strong enough, Mel."

"Thanks," he said. "You know you really slay me at times. You keep everything bottled up inside, and when you decide to share your feelings with me poison comes out of your mouth."

"Spare me," said Joy.

"No, you spare me!" Talbott snapped. "I think you'd better get used to the idea that Jimmy is never coming back."

"Oh, he's coming," Phanuel the angel of hope announced. "You better believe because God has big plans."

"Will someone please bring Phanuel up to speed on this project," said Michael. "He's been out of the loop for a while."

"Even if he is not coming back," Joy was arguing, "this thing will never end."

252

Talbott took her face in his hands, gently. "I'm no mind reader, Joy," he said. "You have to learn to communicate more."

He moved closer and wiped the tears from her face and her breasts.

"You loved him very much, didn't you?" he asked.

"I didn't have time to figure all that out," she answered. "Do you understand what I mean?"

"Sure I do."

"There's no closure," she went on. 'If he had committed suicide or died of natural causes or even if he was murdered I could learn to live with that one day. But he disappeared, Mel. And for that he will continue to haunt us. Our minds and our hearts won't rest until we know the truth."

Joy stood up and went to the bedroom. Talbott slid off the sofa and collapsed on the floor, sobbing. He heard the bathroom door shut. On his hands and knees he crawled into the bedroom.

"Joy," he heard her crying as he called to her. Then he heard the bathroom door lock. "Joy, come out of there."

Leave me alone," she told him.

Talbott propped his back to the door. He fell asleep there listening to Joy weep. Before long he witnessed the same dream he'd had for several weeks. Out of darkness came a shimmering cloud, no larger than a fist when it first appeared. The cloud grew until it dwarfed Talbott. That was when he woke up shaking. On that afternoon, however, leaning with his back to the bathroom door, Talbott watched the shimmering cloud grow. Like the other dreams the cloud came into being right there in the bedroom. Soon the entire room was engulfed with a vibrant mist.

Christophe stepped through the prismatic veil. He wore loose-fitted white pants and white Nehru shirt. It was the uniform Talbott pictured his friend in whenever he thought about him in the afterlife. Christophe's hair was long and white like his clothes, a feature Talbott also had conjured.

"I…" Talbott started to say.

"Don't be an imbecile," Christophe said, reading his mind. "I'm not here for that reason."

253

"I wasn't sure if you would be angry," Talbott said.

"I'm beyond anger now," he told him. "Come to think of it, I'm beyond everything. It's good you and Joy hooked up."

When Talbott first saw Christophe step from the cloud curtain he thought his friend had returned from the dead to settle a machismo-fueled jealous score over Joy. As always, his paranoia proved extreme.

"So you don't care?"

"Not at all," Christophe said.

Talbott looked at the bathroom door. "Can you see her?" he asked.

"I see everything," he said. "I know everything. But not like you think."

"She's gained some weight," Talbott confessed.

"I'm not here to discuss that," he said. "Of course there's a good reason for that. Now, I want you to listen very carefully to what I am about to say."

Talbott sat up straight.

"Write it down if you want," Christophe told him when he had finished. "But remember all the trouble that brought the world the last time someone did that."

He stepped back into the brilliant shimmering cloud. A moment later, he vanished.

Behind Talbott the bathroom door opened. A sharp pain filled his head as he fell back and hit his head on the tile floor. He opened his eyes and immediately shielded them from the bathroom's bright light. Joy's thick thighs came into focus, and then he saw her blond-haired pudenda as she stood over him.

"Mel," her red eyes darted left and right.

Blunt came scampering into the room. He sensed a strong presence there and began barking.

-Quiet boy, be quiet, said Behemial the angel over tame beasts.

-Is that the best you can do? Uriel asked. Yahweh gives you dominion over all animals friendly to man and the best you come up with is 'be quiet'?

-Uriel, Gabriel checked his brother. Give him a chance.

254

-Where's your ball? Behemial inquired as Blunt continued barking. No ball? How about your bone? A toy? Do you have a doggy toy? Go on boy. Go get it.

-Play dead, Uriel suggested.

-No! Michael intervened in the nick of time.

Talbott attempted to sit up, but Joy turned to move out of his way and his face bounced off her cool buttocks. He fell back, his head hitting the tile floor a second time.

"Don't move," he grunted through clenched teeth. Slowly, he slithered out from beneath Joy and propped himself against the doorjamb.

Joy bit her lip to keep from laughing at him. She felt better when Talbott started chuckling at his own misfortune.

"Were you just talking to yourself a moment ago?" she sank to the floor and sat down beside him.

Talbott continued laughing.

"The reason I'm asking," she said, "is because I swear I heard you say something about my weight."

"No," he managed. "Not me."

"That's good," she said. "You should know there's a good reason."

"I know," Talbott said, concentrating on Blunt as he rolled around on the bedroom floor.

Joy patted his leg and leaned against him. Talbott put his arm around her and hugged her close.

Her voice was hot and moist when she whispered into his ear. "I'm pregnant, Mel," she said. "You're going to be a father."

Talbott continued laughing. Tears ran down his cheeks as he stared into the immediate space where the shimmering cloud that carried Christophe had been minutes before. He pulled Joy close and kissed the crown of her head.

"We're having this baby," he said.

"You bet your ass we are," said Joy. "And I've already picked out a name."

"Don't I have a say?"

"If it's a boy, sure."

Talbott remembered what Christophe had told him.

"What name will you choose for her?" he asked.

255

"Her name will be Sophia," she said. "It means—"

"Wisdom," Talbott said. "I know."

Chapter Thirty-three

The outer boundary of Pandemonium was a place few entities ever journeyed. Christophe added himself to that elite rank when he went there to be alone. The outer boundary was a place where Creation had yet to leave her mark, it was a veil between all that was and Chaos. Having learned the big secret over again, Christophe needed time to sort things out. The exploration of the boundary did little to assuage his anxiety. Soon, he gave up the solitude of that desolate place and headed back toward the city.

Christophe spotted Asmodeus approaching him as he neared the dark metropolis. He noted the demon's excited expression, the way the hunchback skipped along the road.

"There you are," Asmodeus said when they stood face to face. A nervous laugh escaped his lips. "I've turned over every stone looking for you."

"Was I gone that long?" Christophe asked.

"Not to worry," he said.

"Did you miss me?"

"A great many wailed and gnashed their teeth," the demon told him. "Myself included."

"I'm sure you did. I think I lost track of time. How long have I been gone?"

"Whole civilizations have risen and fallen. All the animals that you knew on earth are all extinct. Shall I go on?"

"You're kidding."

"I am," Asmodeus admitted. Then, "You didn't happen to figure out how to leave this place, did you?"

"I might have visited an old friend."

"Mercy," Asmodeus said. "Never mind. Just don't make a habit of it."

"What's going on?"

"Shit," the demon exclaimed. "Yes, I almost forgot. The coronation is set to begin."

"Already?"

"I'm afraid so," the little fiend said. "The timetable has been altered. Keep your wits. You'll get the hang of it all soon enough. A word of advice, too. In the beginning try to avoid shifting in and out of parallel universes. It produces a sort of motion sickness that you would do well to avoid. Anyway, everyone's agog. It turns out that Satan's audience with Yahweh has been moved forward."

Christophe and Asmodeus proceeded into the heart of Pandemonium. When they reached the meeting place Christophe was overwhelmed by the interior of the Great Infernal Hall. Intricate carvings, crafted with meticulous care, decorated the monstrous support columns. Flawless ornamental tilework graced the floors. Golden seats surrounded the center arena. The hall possessed an ethereal quality despite the solid enormity it projected. Christophe suspected this was a result of his getting used to his new state. In the center of the arena there was a grand golden throne bedecked with dark jewels.

Countless fallen angels entered the hall. Some found their seats by air; others walked. The waves of conversation rose and fell resembling the roar of some mighty ocean.

Asmodeus assured Christophe, leading him to his place in front of the throne, that he shouldn't feel nervous.

At last Satan made his entrance into the hall. The legions of fallen angels stood and paid tribute to him. The Morning Star retained all of his former glory in the dark city. Unlike some of the demons Christophe had met since his arrival, Satan's beauty was unmarred by the original fall.

"I suppose we owe you an explanation," Satan took his seat at the throne as he spoke to Christophe.

258

Christophe was awestruck by the golden eyes that flickered like the sun. He felt Asmodeus pat him gently on the shoulder. The simple gesture reassured Christophe that he reacted the way everyone did when they first laid eyes on The Morning Star.

"Long ago," Satan began, "there was a war. Bear with me if any of this sounds familiar to you. Out of this war the universe was created. Other wars created other universes, but we need not delve into that for our purposes. I was young, foolish and cocky. Anyway," he glanced at Asmodeus, "I'm sure your guide filled you in on the rest by now."

The Morning Star lounged comfortably on his throne and continued. "The reason you are here," he said, "is because you remind me of myself. We share a common history."

Laughter erupted around the arena.

"When your spark showered down from the absolute light," Satan went on, "I was overwhelmed. I felt closer to you than I ever did to my brothers. It was Yahweh who let you continue to fall. It was Yahweh who decreed you must crawl from the darkest place in order to receive his light. Many different ages, many different lifetimes, many different dimensions. Imagine the torment I felt when I had learned that He cast you and your mother out. I searched for you both for a long time."

He paused for a moment and pointed toward Heaven.

"They told me I need someone strong enough to take my place while I visit the Kingdom," Satan said. "I know you don't want to be here. But after I meet with Yahweh I can assure you this is the last dark place—"

"War!" the cry drowned out Satan's words.

Christophe flinched. He turned and saw Moloch stand up.

The warrior demon regarded his ruler with cruel eyes. Moloch's anger flourished when he realized that Satan remained unmoved by his renewed demand.

"How many times," said the Morning Star, "have we gone over this? Moloch, war is not an option."

"No shit," another voice called out from the vast audience. A slender demon rose from his seat. Belial was his name. "How much more of this tiresome call-to-arms can an angel stand?"

259

"You shallow coward," Moloch roared. "You wouldn't even pick up a weapon in the original war. What right do you have to speak out against me? Had we not been born eternal I would have killed you a long time ago."

Satan smiled and winked at Christophe.

"You should feel so confident," Belial snapped. "What was God thinking when he made you?"

Moloch remained undaunted.

"At least I haven't made it my life's work to suck up to Satan," he argued. "Your problem, Belial, is that you've never held a firm position about anything."

"Do you want to suffer Heaven's thunder once more?" the accused asked.

"Should we return to Heaven," Moloch countered, "as less than gods?"

Satan yawned.

"It's true," said another fallen angel as he stood. "Heaven should be ours."

"Thank you, Mammon," said Moloch. "Behold, an angel with courage and sense."

"Sadly, however," said Mammon, "I don't believe we belong in either place. We should use this opportunity to strike out on our own. If we are to abandon Hell let us go out and seek someplace new, thus separating ourselves from God and man."

"Poor Mammon," Belial sang, "always the dreamer. Tell me, what imaginary plane, what fabulous dimension have you fixated on this time?"

"Leave him alone," Moloch warned.

"You've always stood up for others just for the sake of a fight," said Belial. "Moloch, your antics bore me."

"Take heed, lewd one. Or you just might suffer the consequences."

"I'm already in Hell, you jackass," Belial cried. "What further torture could you possibly inflict? They don't call this place the suffering city for nothing."

"Hey, be fair," Mammon said. "I designed this city."

"And a fine city it is," Moloch told him.

260

"Enough," another angel shouted. He sat at the left hand of Satan. "The possibility of war is out."

Be-Beelzebub stood. Hell grew silent.

"There will be no further discussion of war," he announced. "Nor will we entertain fancy notions about setting out for some place removed from God and man. Why subject ourselves to further castigation with continued exile?

"I am tired of this place. We have sat by idly as Yahweh and our heavenly brothers have fawned over man. Yes, I too was jealous. But I am still an angel. It is my destiny to serve His will in whatever capacity He sees fit. Sure, we may have to crawl back, nursing our wounds and bruised egos as we go along, but we belong in Heaven!"

Thunderous applause arose. Cacophonous cheers rained down from the darkest heights of the arena.

"I support Satan's choice," Be-Beelzebub announced over the noise. "There's no reason why we cannot regain our original place in Heaven."

Another ovation followed. Moloch, Belial and Mammon all took their seats. The plaudit gained momentum until Satan raised his left hand.

"Asmodeus," said the Morning Star. "Shall we get started."

The little demon nudged Christophe. The coronation commenced.

Epilogue

Two figures walked near the boundary of the dark dominion. Against the darkness their light shone like bright stars in the night sky.

"What will you do now?" Christophe asked.

"I'll approach Heaven's gate," Satan told him, "and see if they'll let me in to see Yahweh."

"Asmodeus said you had an appointment."

"Little Azzy knows what I tell him."

"Will they let you in?"

"Maybe."

They continued walking through the dark. Sometime later, Satan told Christophe, "Go ahead and ask."

"What if it doesn't work out?"

"I'll return here."

"And what will happen to me?"

"You will be reborn as a woman's shoe salesman in Boca Raton," Satan replied.

Christophe stopped.

"That was a joke," The Morning Star told him. "You might work on your sense of humor while I'm gone. It helps to break up the monotony."

"What if the others try to depose me while you're gone?"

"Don't be stupid," he said. "Who among the original fallen angels wants Hell for himself? Even Moloch knows better than that."

Satan's golden eyes flickered in the dark as he smiled.

262

"You worry too much, Christophe," he said to his son. They had reached the gate.

"Everything will be fine."

"Wait," said Christophe, "what makes you think Yahweh will let you back in?"

"Long before the original war there was another angel," Satan told him. "He was thrown out of Heaven for mischief. Only back then it didn't occur to Yahweh to exile this guilty party to some strange place. The angel lingered outside of Heaven's curtain until he found a way back inside. There have been others put out of the Kingdom. Sooner or later, Yahweh lets everyone back in."

"You think your time has come?"

"Our time," said Satan. "How much brighter would Heaven be with us back where we belong?"

The Morning Star stepped over the slumbering Cerberus. He reached for the key in the gate and turned it. After he opened the gate he stepped over the threshold and stood with one foot in Hell and the other in Chaos.

"Wait," Christophe beckoned him once more. "Do you know where my mother is?"

Satan grinned. "I have a pretty good idea," he said. Then, "Take care, my son."

Christophe patted the snoring heads of Cerberus. He watched Satan in all his brilliant glory drift into Chaos and linger there a moment. When The Morning Star faded from view, Christophe closed the gate and locked it before he headed back to the dark city.

263

About the Author

Richard J. O'Brien is a lapsed Catholic who lives in New Jersey, which qualifies him as perhaps one of the most lapsed worldwide. He has not been to confession in over twenty years. Life is short...Why ruin a streak now? Judge not, etc, etc.

Once upon a time, before the Berlin Wall came down, Richard served in the US Army. He attended Rutgers University, and he holds an MFA in Creative Writing from Fairleigh Dickinson University.

Richard's books include *The People's Republic of New Arkaim, Rejoice for the Dead, Aleph Café: Stories, The Accidental Hero of the City of Brotherly Love, To Dream the Blackbane, Under the Bronze Moon,* and *The Garden of Fragile Things.*

Readers can find Richard on Twitter @obrienwriter and online at https://obrienwriter.com/.

You can also follow his author page on Facebook at https://www.facebook.com/obrienwriter/.